# Good Housekeeping

## My Unexpected Adventures in Domesticity

PATRICIA J. PARSONS

MOONLIGHT PRESS | TORONTO

For information or permissions:

Visit www.moonlightpresstoronto.com
Or email moonlightpressinfo@gmail.com

*For Art*

*…the one who knows the real Erica and the real Betty better than anyone else!*

# Some other books by Patricia J. Parsons

**The "almost-but-not-quite-true" stories**
*The Year I Made Twelve Dresses* (Book 1)
*Kat's Kosmic Blues* (Book 2)
*The Inscrutable Life of Frannie Phillips* (Book 3)
*Something I'm Supposed to Do* (Book 4)
*This is the Way the Story Ends* (Book 5)
*It All Begins with Goodbye* (Book 6)

*Plan B* (lit-for-intelligent-chicks)
*Confessions of a Failed Yuppie* (lit-for-intelligent-chicks)
*Something More Than Love* (historical fiction)
*Grace Note: In Hildegard's Shadow* (historical fiction)

1

# When You Make That One Wrong Move

*Take your life in your own hands, and what happens? A terrible thing: no one to blame.*
~ Erica Jong

IT DOESN'T SEEM TO MATTER WHAT YOU SAY THESE DAYS: someone is going to choose to be offended. It's a given. Taking offence is something of a national (no, scratch that: international) pastime. Sometimes, what sparks that righteous indignation is something you had the bad luck to say decades earlier at, oh, say, a frat party after maybe three or six beers. But that doesn't matter to the perpetually offended. Someone will take present-day offence. Sometimes, though, the spark that starts the offence happens one sunny afternoon while sipping coffee. And if you have a massive platform—let's say you're the co-host of a wildly popular daytime talk show with zillions of Instagram followers—there are even more people to take offence at your ever-so-slight bitchiness. The truth about me is that I've pretty much built my reputation on bitchy, but one thing I never intend to do is to offend. Not anyone. Oh, maybe once in a while, but I'm only human.

My name is Erica Flanagan. Welcome to my life. Come with me today to the television studio where I make my living, and I'll introduce you to my colleagues: my producer, my floor director, my co-hosts and my makeup consultant. These are the most important colleagues, anyway. And then I'll tell you how I got myself into so much shit. You can decide if I deserved it.

~

Trevor was already sitting in his usual spot at the head of the table when I pushed open the door to the bullpen. I had always thought it interesting that a bullpen can be where the pitchers warm up for a baseball game or the lockup behind a courtroom where the prisoners are held. In my early days on the job, I thought the glass-walled room with the massive boardroom table surrounded by a dozen or more swivel chairs was named for the baseball analogy—here, we warmed up before taping every show. Lately, however, it was beginning to feel more analogous to the courtroom scenario. In any case, there was an actual sign on the door that said, "Bullpen." I sighed, sat down three seats away from Trevor, and awaited his pep talk.

Trevor Goulet, our esteemed producer, is a seasoned television man. Way back in his early career, he had planned on becoming a serious journalist—as I had been in a former life—but he had taken a turn along the career journey and waded into the swamp of daily afternoon television. Trevor and my husband, Andrew Taylor, former national news anchor extraordinaire, had graduated from journalism school—J-school, as people in the know are wont to say—together a few years before I did. That made Trevor about sixty years old, a good six or seven years older than I was. I liked to think I was aging better than he was, but that's only one of the open questions I must explore as we go along.

Trevor traded on his gnarly old journalist personality, the crusty, on-the-ground reporter I always figured he missed becoming. Instead, for the past dozen years, he'd had the dubious privilege of producing this bit of afternoon television fluff called *The Exchange*, a rather overly ambitious name for a show that could have more accurately been described as The Yak, The Natter, The Gab or even The Gossip in recent years. And I'd been one of the four co-hosts for all of those years.

I looked around at the rest of the assembling masses, but before I had a chance to wax nostalgic about how the years had flown, Jennifer Katsaros, my young millennial co-host, shook her mass of dark curly hair and lifted the script in front of her on the table. "Guys, I'm, like, so pumped about today's line-up. I just wanted to say that before we got started. I feel you've been listening to me." She stopped for a moment to make meaningful eye contact with Trevor. *Dear god*, I thought, *please don't tell me she's sleeping with the boss.* That would open up a world of awkwardness for everyone. She continued. "I see we've started taking, like, the influencers seriously."

Influencers? My eyes shot down to my copy of the script, really more of what I'd call a rundown of the topics and guests for today's show with a small pile of cue cards next to it for each of us on-air types. Anyway, the very thought of social media influencers beginning to take over guest spots made my neck go all funny and clenched. I seemed to have fully embraced my role as the senior citizen among the on-air people. But since I was only fifty-three, I wasn't sure how this could be a thing.

I reached for my reading glasses and placed them daintily on the bridge of my nose as I peered at the words now coming into focus. I wasn't sure what I was reading. I looked across the table at my other millennial co-host, Veronica Lumley, who was a slightly older millennial, to see if she could illuminate Jen's absurd proclamation about influencers infiltrating our afternoon talk show. Veronica was still grappling with turning forty and was peeking through her own new reading glasses as if she didn't need them (which she did) and looked at me. She shrugged. I looked over toward my other co-host, Sylvie, for support.

*"Tu ne peux pas être sérieux."* Sylvie said as she peered down at her notes. "Trevor, you cannot be serious." Sylvie Boisonne, my third co-host (and only five years my junior, making her forty-eight years old and counting), was now holding her notes out in front of her, waving them like a flag. "This suggests we are interviewing one of those internet wife persons." She stopped waving for a moment and looked at the top page. "And this. What is this?" She said, pointing halfway down the page. "It is one of those hashtags. What does this #tradwife mean?"

"Ladies, ladies," Trevor said, waving his arm as if to swat away any concerns from his minions, "you are misinterpreting this whole thing. Yes, one of our guests this afternoon is an influencer," he pronounced the word carefully as if no one at the table understood its meaning, "but she is so much more than that. She's an author. You know Wednesdays are for our author spot."

"And if you haven't read her book," Jennifer said, "you really must. I think it's especially important for the older among us," (was she emphasizing the word older as she looked at me?), "to embrace the new thinking."

I was slightly perplexed by this turn of events. A new way of thinking? I was looking at the media release for the guest's new book, improbably titled *From Good to Better to Best: Becoming the Wife You Always Dreamed of Being* by someone called Laura-Lee Cox. And suddenly, I realized that the hashtag Sylvie saw meant one thing and one thing only—this thing people were calling the "trad wife" movement. Traditional wife. *New* thinking? I couldn't help myself. I started snorting.

The moment I started, Sylvie looked at me and burst out laughing.

"Trevor, you got us this time. This is quite a joke," I said, tapping my pen on the page in front of me.

Trevor looked confused—or more confused than usual. I had never understood why someone with such a weak grasp of women's minds had ever been appointed to produce an afternoon talk show directed squarely at a demographic he so deeply misunderstood. Then I remembered he'd had ambitions to produce serious news programming, but there had been some kind of scandal—no, nothing about sexual harassment. That would have been too much for even Ted Thomas, the television station owner, to cope with when searching for a producer for his brainchild of an afternoon show for women. No, I'd heard something about the misappropriation of travel budgets or something like that. Anyway, here he was, making daily decisions about what kind of programming went into living rooms and kitchens across North America.

"Erica," Trevor said, looking at me as he cleaned his glasses with a questionably clean handkerchief (who even owned handkerchiefs in the twenty-first century?), "please control yourself. This is not a joke. You should have at least skimmed the book by now." He turned to Miriam, his mousey intern, who was sitting beside him with a laptop, a phone and a tablet all blinking in front of her. "Miriam, you distributed the copies of this week's book to all the hosts, didn't you?"

Miriam's eyes opened wide behind her round, black-framed glasses, and she began wildfire tapping on her tablet. "Yes, Mr. Goulet, sir. I have it right here on my schedule. I distributed the books to each of the co-hosts precisely between 2:07 and 2:21 last Friday afternoon."

I rolled my eyes. Was it utterly impossible for anyone under the age of twenty-five to simply remember doing a task? Couldn't she just say yes? And what was all that about precise timing? A tad obsessive, don't you think? Miriam was a second-year journalism student doing a four-month internship with us. Since Trevor's PA had gone on maternity leave—inconveniently, as I believe Trevor put it when he announced the year-long sabbatical—he had decided to give Miriam her position. I tapped my pen on the desk, thinking about how nice a year-long sabbatical sounded, although, at age fifty-three, a maternity-related one was certainly not in the cards. Who was I kidding? Working was how I stayed sane.

Trevor put his glasses back on and ran his hand through his unruly salt-and-pepper hair. "Well, Erica, did you at least take it home over the weekend and take a quick look? I don't expect you to read every word of every book we feature, but you know you're all at least supposed to skim the books we feature on Wednesdays."

Again, I turned to Veronica, who had said nothing up to this point. As I mentioned, Veronica had just turned forty, making her the older of our two millennials. "Veronica, what do you think?"

Veronica never had much to say unless there was a camera trained on her. Maybe it was because she was the newest co-host, having recently replaced a long-time colleague who had been fired for posting something salacious on her Instagram feed. Again, Veronica just shrugged.

Jen slid her copy of the book over so I couldn't possibly miss it. I looked at the colourful cover featuring a smiling woman decked out in a housedress (Dear god! Who wears housedresses in the twenty-first century?), gazing lovingly at a perfectly roasted turkey with a man (presumably her husband) and a young boy (presumably her son) gazing over her shoulder, sniffing contentedly. It could have been right out of a 1960s ad campaign for kitchen appliances, except for the gleaming Thermador Professional Series wall oven strategically placed behind them. We had done a spot on the newest and best major appliances only a month or so earlier, and I recognized it as a brand-new model that sells for north of thirteen thousand dollars. I wondered how much the company had paid for that placement. Anyway, I stared at the cover, my eyes riveted to the book's subtitle: *Becoming the Wife You Always Dreamed of Being*.

"You really shouldn't be so dismissive, Erica," Jen was saying as I tried to come to grips with the reality of what I might be expected to do with this. "There's a whole new world out there, in case you hadn't noticed."

I wasn't sure exactly what Jennifer was getting at. A new world? Women retreating to domestic drudgery was a whole new world? And, was she suggesting that since I was (horror!) over fifty, I was now a dinosaur? As I contemplated the sentiment that the book so clearly demonstrated, I wondered if Jennifer, all of twenty-eight years old, even realized she was promoting a *return* to the dinosaurs. I shook my head to try to clear the confusion. I turned to Trevor.

"Okay, Trevor, let me get this straight," I said. "We are interviewing the author of this new book, who is what?" I peered at the woman on the cover. "Under thirty years old? I'm presuming this is this Laura-Lee person on the cover." I tapped my pen on her face.

Jen said, "Yes, that's her, and she's only twenty-eight—the same age I am." Jen seemed to be inordinately proud of this factoid.

Oh, that was so much better. "Thank you, Jennifer, for the clarification," I said as I watched my sarcasm fly swiftly over her head and into the ether. I turned back to Trevor. "So, we're interviewing the young author of a book that seems to be propelling women back to the 1960s."

"Erica, Erica," Trevor said, shaking his head, "you've got this all wrong. No one is suggesting women move back into those old roles. I would be the last person to suggest that." *Yeah, sure,* I thought. "But we have a growing millennial demographic, and they're embracing these new ideas."

There was that word again: new.

Sylvie reached for the book and slid it over in front of her. "Trevor, I think Erica has a point. These are hardly *new* ideas. This seems reminiscent of that interview we did last month. You remember that young woman who started all that social media chatter about the stay-at-home girlfriend. Remember the one who described herself as the same as a stay-at-home mom without the marriage or children?"

Oh, I'd almost forgotten that one. I think I'd blotted it out. Just thinking about it made me want to hurl a bit and worry for the future of my daughter, Maddie, who had just turned thirteen. I remembered the interview clearly now because it had been all I could do to keep from slapping that stay-at-home girlfriend up the side of the head. But I was a professional journalist—perhaps not the professional journalist I'd once been, but a professional, nonetheless—and professional journalists did not literally slap people. However, a figurative slap often did the trick.

"That was an interesting perspective on changing societal conventions," Jen said, sliding the book back in front of her.

I wondered how long she'd been practicing saying "societal conventions." If there was one thing Jennifer Katsaros wanted more than anything else, it was to be taken seriously. But if she kept up this haranguing about influencers and moving women back into the dark ages, I seriously doubted that could happen in our field. Then again, as I listened to Trevor as he began spouting on about demographics, market share and younger audiences, I realized I might be wrong. Maybe I *was* a dinosaur.

Our floor director, Samantha, was sitting beside me. She leaned over and whispered, "Just be sure to breathe when you're interviewing her, okay?"

I knew why she was saying this. I had been close to exploding the day we'd interviewed Katie Kessler (I finally remembered her name), that internet TikTok person who was the queen of the stay-at-home girlfriends. When she said the role had been "super natural," I had to bite my tongue to keep from pointing out that I could think of other words for her "supernatural" experience—synonyms like bizarre, eery, and unnatural came immediately to mind. That day, I had heard Samantha's voice in my head—well, it was really in my earpiece, but still—saying, "Breathe, Erica, just breathe."

Sam and I had been working together on *The Exchange* since the beginning. Thirteen years earlier, when the show was in development, I had recently finished a three-month maternity leave, and Samantha Gordon was fresh off the evening news where she'd been an assistant director. She had just been promoted, becoming the floor director for this new show, so we grew up together on afternoon television. For all of those thirteen years, at least once a month, unless one of us was on vacation or was otherwise occupied with family obligations, we had dinner or cocktails together when we would bitch about Trevor (or his very short-lived predecessor who had lasted two months—the less said about him, the better), so, Sam knew me well. She could see and feel when I was about to blow. More than once, she had kept me from erupting on camera. She was a godsend. I nodded, and she sat back.

I sighed and took a deep breath. "So, I guess this young woman is another feminist with a message about doing what she wants to do regardless of how it looks to those who came before her and gave her the opportunity to live up to her potential, and yet she chooses to do the very things that kept women immobile in society."

Jennifer looked puzzled while Sylvie and Veronica nodded.

"I'm not following that train of thought precisely," Trevor said, "but I believe I get the gist of it. I suppose that may be the case."

I tapped my pen on the table. "You know," I said as a thought began to form, "perhaps we could have that Dan Ho person on the show next week for a bit of counterpoint."

Jennifer cocked her head slightly as if she might be trying to figure out who I was talking about. Whenever Jen tried to think, she looked ever so slightly constipated. You know the look—vaguely pursed lips, slight squint. "I'm not sure I know him," she said, reaching for her phone, no doubt to search for him.

Sylvie smiled. "*Bien sûr*! Of course! I do remember him. Did he not write a book?"

I nodded. "He certainly did. In fact, he wrote two—the ever-relevant *Rescue from House Gorgeous* and my personal favourite, *Rescue from Domestic Perfection.*"

"But I believe it may be rather old at this point, is it not, Erica?" Sylvie said.

"Maybe, " I said, "but anyone who's been dubbed the anti-Martha Stewart is still relevant in my books." I turned to Trevor. "What do you think?"

"I'll take it under advisement," he said. "Miriam, make a note." He looked around at the rest of the people at the table. "I presume we've finished our discussion of that spot. May we move on? We have many more to cover."

No one said anything.

"Okay, then. Jennifer," he said, "you're up today for our kitchen segment. Chef Simon is here."

Jen practically clapped with glee. I noticed she seemed to have quite a crush on our regular guest chef, who owned two restaurants in the city and one in cottage country up north. "What's on the menu today?" she said.

Trevor checked his notes and turned to Miriam, who tapped quickly on her laptop this time. She whispered something.

"Speak up, Miriam," Trevor said.

"It's Chicken à la Simon."

Of course, it was. Simon named most of his dishes after himself or one of his cats. I knew this because he told us every time he came to do a guest spot. We completed the rundown, and I headed to makeup. It was two hours to airtime, and I had notes to review.

~

*The Exchange* was live on the air every weekday afternoon at three pm Eastern Time in front of a studio audience. I had worked in television before this, but I'd been an on-air reporter, reporting from the field. It was a job I'd adored. Andrew and I both travelled the world doing live reporting from places like London, Paris, China, Chile, and the list goes on. Andrew, however, gave all that up several years before I did when the station offered him the evening national news anchor position. He had been in his late forties, and the timing was right for him to move into the studio. My time came when I realized we were expecting a baby. Given my passion for live news reporting from the front lines of any story, you might think it had been a difficult decision. However, once Andrew and I decided we would be parents, I knew that would come first for me. But that didn't mean I wasn't looking for a more appropriate opportunity. After Maddie was born, *The Exchange* opportunity came up, and I was ready to move from being a journalist to being a television personality. One of the reasons I'd said yes to the opportunity was because of the live audience format.

I'd always enjoyed the live reporting from the front lines of news, and I realized I needed to find something that might come close to replacing that exhilaration while permitting me some level of family life. Live television came close. There's a kind of energy and excitement that comes from performing (because we were certainly performing every day) in front of the audience rather than just a camera operator and various director types. As I got used to the format, I found the immediate feedback from the audience in the studio incredibly energizing. I fed off their laughter, their applause (despite knowing they were being told when to applaud), and their reactions. Sometimes, I could hear a gasp or a chuckle, a deep in-breath, a wow! I always felt there was a measure of authenticity that emanates from the live audience format because, unlike other shows that used a live-to-tape format (a throwback term to the days before digital, but the name stuck), where the live taping was aired the next hour or the next day, ours was truly live. The live-to-tape format allowed for fixing bloopers. We didn't have that luxury. What the at-home audience saw was what really happened in the studio in real-time. Once the cameras started rolling each afternoon, the atmosphere was charged and dynamic in a way I hadn't experienced before. But after thirteen years, I had begun to notice the dynamism starting to dull.

I was thinking about this as I reviewed my notes while Angela, my favourite makeup artist, made me look like the best version of my fifty-three-year-old self. I was constantly amazed at how good this woman could make me look. She was a true artist with her little paint pots and brushes of every imaginable size and shape. Over the years, I'd often asked her for make-up tips, but I never could quite get the hang of it, tending toward minimalism when off-camera. Of course, on-camera makeup is a whole different kettle of fish because we need so much more in these days of high-definition, where even the tiniest of pores becomes visible for all to see (and comment on later).

Angela flicked the last of her magic highlighter in the exact parts of my face that needed it, then picked up her coffee and stood back to admire her handiwork. "You know the old saying, Erica, all things are possible with coffee and highlighter."

"Who said that?"

"I have no idea," Angela said, laughing. "Probably me, but it's true, isn't it?"

I could not disagree.

"Break a leg, bitch!" Angela said as she did every day.

Now I was ready. I returned to my dressing room to retrieve my cue cards for the day. Finally, the ten-minute call came. The studio audience had been warmed up by Samantha's assistant, who had a much better sense of humour than any of the rest of us, and we were getting our lapel microphones settled while we stood behind the set pieces. Once we were ready, the cameras would roll, and we would make our entrance to much applause—cued by the flashing lights that told the audience when to clap. I looked at my co-hosts. I was always fascinated at how our stylist managed to find outfits that reflected who we were as individuals (or at least what our producer wanted us to project), yet we never clashed.

I was decked out in a tweed suit that resembled something by Chanel with its collarless jacket over a silk blouse and jeans. I was always in a suit jacket. Sylvie's jeans were topped by a flowing peasant blouse, while Veronica looked more subdued in a sweater and jeans. Jennifer always wore a dress with a boho vibe. I suppose the audience thought we dressed ourselves, but they couldn't have been more wrong. And the audience got to see that three of us wore jeans under the table. The at-home audience probably thought I wore a suit every day.

"Why the twitching?" Sam said as she came by to see if we were ready.

"This jacket is a bit itchy," I said.

Sam smiled. "Just try not to scratch on camera, Erica. The itchy bitch?"

I shrugged. Sam did know me well. It was time.

The four of us walked out from behind the screen to the sounds of wild clapping over our intro music. We smiled and waved to the audience. As usual, the studio was packed to the rafters. Tickets to our live shows had become coveted commodities in recent years as the show grew in popularity, making its way to the top of the ratings pile for afternoon television. And I have to say I'd noticed the audiences seemed to be getting younger. Maybe Trevor was onto something.

We took our places at the high-top counter, where mugs with the show's logo marked our individual spots with our names emblazoned on the backs facing us so the audience couldn't see. The mugs contained water, although I suspected Sylvie spiked hers occasionally. Recent guests had me considering the same thing. Once we were settled, we began with our quick snappers about the news. Sometimes, it was easy to come up with news stories we wanted to present or skewer. Sometimes, it was more challenging. Today was one of those slow news days, and we seemed to be scraping the bottom of the barrel. Sylvie got only one laugh, and I got a single groan for my bitchy comments on the latest gossip about some celebrity or another. How had I fallen so far from my journalistic roots?

After our first commercial break, we went to Jen's cooking segment. The audience seemed to be as much in love with Chef Simon as Jen was, so they were mesmerized by him while we fanned ourselves with our cue cards and yawned, waiting for it to be over. The author's spot was up next.

As the senior member of the team—in more ways than one— I was the de facto leader of the pack who introduced the guests. "Ladies and gentlemen," I put my hand over my eyes to shade it from the lights and peered out at the audience dramatically, "there are a few gentlemen out there, aren't there?" There was a smattering of laughter as I noticed Jen's pointed stare. I could almost feel her telling me that ladies and gentlemen was an outdated gendered salutation. I didn't care. "This is Wednesday, and you know that means it's time for us to introduce you to a new book and its author."

Although it pained me to do so, I picked up the copy of the book that Miriam, no doubt, had helpfully placed beside my mug, which I now definitely wished had vodka in it. After all, it might only have been just after three o'clock here in Toronto, but it was almost drink time in Newfoundland, and I had little doubt that I'd need a drink after this interview.

I looked at the book whose cover was now on the split screen I could see on the computer monitor under the glass top of our desk. "*From Good to Better to Best: Becoming the Wife You Always Dreamed of Being* is just out this month, and already it's trending to the top of several bestseller lists. We're delighted that its author has found the time in her busy interview and social media schedule to join us for a chat. Please join us in welcoming Laura-Lee Cox," I looked down at the cue card that told me exactly what I was supposed to say by way of introduction, coughed slightly, and continued, "influencer extraordinaire, best-selling author and extraordinary wife." I left off the last bit—I was supposed to say "from which aspirations emerge," but I just couldn't. It was enough that I didn't choke when I read the title of the book out loud.

Laura-Lee Cox walked out from the wings, smiling and waving to the apparently adoring crowd. Or were they simply responding to the flashing light like Pavlov's dogs? I couldn't be sure.

She was petite, perhaps five-foot-two or so, with a mass of blonde hair that bounced on her shoulders as she walked. Her bright-white smile was luminescent, suggesting a recent visit to her cosmetic dentist. Her bright red lipstick seemed to be infused with sparkles. Her eyes were deep green (contact lens green, perhaps?), and she was wearing a skin-tight sheath dress the exact green shade of her eyes. It was a modest knee-length, and she was accessorized with pearls—yes, a two-strand necklace that looked like the one my mother wore with her boat-necked, white lace wedding dress in the 1965 photograph. Laura-Lee bounced onto her stool at the opposite end of the counter from me so that I could watch her directly as we proceeded with our "chat." Oh, joy.

"I'm so excited to meet ya'll," she said before we could say a word. I was taken aback by the soupçon of a southern American accent I could hear. I thought she was from Vancouver. "I've been a fan of *The Exchange* ever since I was in braces!" She flashed her fantastically straight teeth.

Dear god. Now, I did feel old. But that gave me an idea. First, I wanted to be sure she knew all of us, so I began introductions. I needn't have done this since, of course, she knew us all. I was ready to plunge right in.

"Let's talk about what inspired you to write this book, Laura-Lee. Surely, it wasn't our little show?"

"Well, you know, Erica," she said, "it might have been after all. I fell in love with cooking by watching your show with my mama." Oh, it was worse than I thought. I was beginning to think I'd spent the past thirteen years inspiring young women to take a giant leap back into the 1960s. I hoped Maddie wasn't watching.

Jen, who was sitting beside Laura-Lee, cut in and began asking specific questions about various chapters in the book. There were chapters on menu planning, housekeeping, diet and exercise, entertaining, shopping, makeup, and the list of domestic bliss went on.

Sylvie butted in. "All this talk about homemaking, Laura-Lee, surely you cannot imagine that young women these days will focus their considerable energies, talents and education on this when they have so many other opportunities."

"Well, Sylvie, I believe that through my homemaking, I project the kind of person I want to be. If I can approach perfection in my home, then I can approach perfection in the eyes of, well, god."

Oh, this was getting to be too much for me. Once they invoke the god thing, I know I'm going to start to gag, but I still held my tongue.

Laura-Lee continued. "Most people don't realize that cleaning the toilet, for example, is a gift to your family. Wouldn't you agree that it would be wrong to miss an opportunity to give a gift?"

I was about to speak when Jen piped up. "So, what you're saying is that keeping a perfect house is a gift."

Laura-Lee bobbed her head up and down like a bobblehead doll on the dashboard of a pickup truck. "Yes, you have it just right, Jennifer. I mean, any woman who cannot approach perfection in her home surely can't expect to achieve much of anything in her life." She fluttered her lengthy eyelashes and looked up through them directly at me on the opposite end of the counter.

That was a stab to my heart. Housekeeping perfection—cooking, cleaning, and all the rest of it—were not things I excelled in, mostly because I loathed them. Those were fighting words.

"*No woman gets an orgasm from shining the kitchen floor*," I said. Sylvie and I high-fived—something I detested, but it seemed to be appropriate in the moment—and I continued, but not before I heard a whisper in my earpiece. "Careful, Erica." It was Sam's voice. I continued. "It's not original. Betty Friedan wrote that, but it's appropriate, don't you think, Laura-Lee?"

Jen and Laura-Lee both looked at me with wide eyes. I wasn't sure whether it was the sentiment they found astounding or they had never heard of Betty Friedan. Their reaction might even have been because neither of them had ever heard the word orgasm on television or, worse, coming from the lips of a woman my age—their mother's age.

"Ask your mothers who she was," I said, "or maybe even your grandmothers. *The Feminine Mystique*? Perhaps you should read it." Still nothing.

"Being the perfect wife is my form of self-expression," Laura-Lee said. "Women have the talents and capacities to be homemakers, and that's what they should do. It's what they're good at. Taking their energies to the outside world is simply making those energies dissipate. It's no wonder husbands these days are so unhappy. I mean, like, so many women over forty can't even take the time to make their faces up before their husbands come home. What does that say to the husband? It says you don't care."

I wondered what Andrew would think if I started making up my face just for him. First, he'd wonder if he was in an episode of the invasion of the body snatchers. She was still talking.

"For example, you wouldn't serve a frozen dinner to guests, would you?" Laura-Lee looked around the table, where everyone, including Sylvie, nodded in agreement. I was still considering whether I'd actually done this or not. Had I ever served frozen dinners to guests? Probably. Laura-Lee was on a roll. "Well, why would you serve one to your husband if you wouldn't serve one to guests? Doesn't he deserve the best of you?" She smiled sweetly as she came in for the kill. "No offence to all of you here, but it would probably be better for you in your lives if you spent more time perfecting your home fronts than sitting here in the afternoon projecting things to women. Although, I do enjoy what you're doing with your cooking and tidying segments."

I'd had quite enough. "Are you for real? You are a self-righteous little moron." I was just getting warmed up. "Where do you get off telling a group of accomplished women what they should or shouldn't do with their lives? Just because your imbecilic pea-brain doesn't seem to have the capacity to look beyond the oppressive walls of a house and the domestic drudgery that passes for your life, you think every woman should take your fatuous advice. Maybe you should move to some country that makes you wear a burka."

There was a new voice in my ear. And it wasn't soft. "Back off, Erica. Now!" It was Trevor. I pulled my earpiece out of my ear and placed it gently on the table.

I was on a roll, and Trevor was not going to take up real estate in my head. "I am sick to death of you twenty-something half-wits getting in front of your considerable audiences and telling them that you know something about the world. Your pea-brained ideas might influence your fellow cretins but know this. You. Know. Nothing. Not a fucking thing!"

I could hear a commotion in the audience and possibly Sylvie suggesting it was time for a commercial break. Laura-Lee was pulling off her microphone and standing up, her perfect mascara and eye shadow perfect no more. Were those tears? Poor baby. Was she feeling personally abused? Or at least offended. I don't know. All I heard her say over the buzzing in my ears was something about her lawyer.

I slid off my stool and walked calmly off the stage to complete silence, with Sam's assistant director guiding me with her hand in the middle of my back. Was she pushing? I walked with deliberate steps, one foot after the other, to my dressing room, where Miriam was standing outside my door. I at least had the presence of mind to turn off my microphone.

"Ms. Flanagan? Sorry to bother you, but Mr. Goulet wants to see you."

I stood with my hand on the doorknob. "Miriam, I'm tired. Tell Trevor to text me."

Miriam shifted from one foot to another, looking decidedly uncomfortable. "I'm not really sure this is something that can be discussed in a text. Anyway, he said he needs to see you in person."

"Too bad for Trevor. I'm tired, and I'm not in the mood for him. Tell him I'll be in at nine." My usual time was noon. So, this was something—what that something was had yet to be decided.

# 2

# When You Didn't See It Coming...But Should Have

*Fame means millions of people have the wrong idea of who you are.*
~ Erica Jong

WHEN I FINALLY CONVINCED MIRIAM THAT I WAS NOT, under any circumstances, prepared to see Trevor at that moment, I opened the door to my dressing room, walked in, shut the door firmly behind me and fell onto the cream-coloured sofa lining the wall to my right. As I lay there, one hand over my eyes to keep out the glare from the overhead lights, I was puzzling over why it seemed I'd been rushed off the set. I was the resident bitch, after all, and what I'd said to that moronic young woman would most certainly resonate with my fans. Wouldn't it?  I heard a text ding from my phone, which I'd left on my dressing table as I always did when I was on the air. Then there was another and another. It was time to go home.

I sighed, dragged myself to a standing position and walked over to the dressing table. My phone was on top of a stack of file folders, all containing material for possible upcoming guests. I know, I know. Why are we still using so much paper? As much as I loved a digital file, there was still something about the feel of a piece of paper that you could wave around for emphasis at a meeting and feel in your hand as you contemplated.

As expected, the first text was from Trevor, the man himself. **What were you thinking? Were you thinking at all? My office. Tomorrow morning. 9 am. Don't be late. T.**

I sighed and deleted it as if I could erase it from my life as easily. The second one was from Samantha. **Moron? Imbecile? I'm not sure you can say those words to someone in public these days, Ricky. Don't do anything rash. Talk later. S.** I suppose she might have had a point.

I opened the Uber app on my phone and found a ride five minutes away. It should be there by the time I got an elevator and made my way to the front lobby. If I was lucky, I figured I might not run into anyone on the way. I was in no mood to interact in any way with anyone. I checked my watch. The show should just be getting over, and my co-hosts should be chatting amiably with the audience. I wondered briefly how the chatting might be going after today's little drama.

Thankfully, my ride was already there when I pushed through the revolving door out onto the busy street in front of the television studio building. As I sank into the back seat of the car, my phone pinged once again.

**WTF honey?? You going to need my services?? Matt.**

"Oh my god," I said out loud, causing my driver to turn abruptly. "Sorry, that wasn't meant for you."

I turned off the ringer and shoved the phone back into my purse as quickly as I could as if it might be tainted with poison or infected with a lethal virus—and maybe it was. Matt was Matthew Bennett, my best friend since fifth grade and one of the best legal minds in the country if you were a big corporation in need of a litigator who could make even the most plausible lawsuit evaporate before your eyes. And now he was asking me if I needed his services. How in the world had he already heard about my on-air meltdown if that's what it had looked like? He never watched daytime television, although his husband Marcus occasionally did.

Marcus was a choreographer who ran his eponymous dance company (The Marcus Campbell Dance Collective) and often worked in the evenings during the company's performance weeks. If I remembered correctly, this was one of those weeks. Andrew and I were taking Maddie with us to one of their performances next weekend, so that could explain how Matt knew so quickly.

Marcus must have been watching the show (god love him for being a fan) and must have told him. I'd call Matt later.

It was not quite four-thirty when the Uber pulled up in front of my house, and I spilled out onto the sidewalk. I dragged myself up the walkway, and by the time I walked up the five steps to the porch, I seemed to have finally progressed from the dazed and confused phase to the slightly vain and narcissistic phase. As I turned the key in the lock, I squared my shoulders and thought, *What the hell is all this self-flagellation about? I was right to skewer that sanctimonious little shit.* I walked into the foyer feeling much better.

I knew I'd be alone in the house for at least a little while since Andrew was picking Maddie up from her after-school activities today. Despite my crazy work schedule that consisted of five-day-a-week on-air related activities and assorted social and charitable events the television station required us to attend on their behalf, I still prided myself in knowing Maddie's schedule. Today was photography class. Maddie fancied herself a budding fashion photographer. At least that was better than fancying herself a fashion model, in my view.

I considered pouring myself a drink before strategizing about how I'd approach Trevor in the morning. On second thought, I figured it might be better if I waited for Andrew.

Just a year earlier, Andrew had retired from his position anchoring the national news after winning awards as the top news anchor in the country six years in a row. His producer was apoplectic when he made the announcement that he was leaving the show, but Andrew always knew when to go. He subscribed to the song lyrics about knowing when to hold them and when to fold them, followed by knowing when to walk away. He left when he was firmly on top, signed a lucrative publishing deal for his memoir, and started a part-time lecturing position at the journalism school. I think they'd made him the Thomas D'Arcy McGee professor or something like that. He was in love with the new schedule that permitted him to do Maddie's after-school pickup, and, joy of joys, he had learned to cook, and even better for all of us, he loved it. On the other hand, I was the master of spaghetti only when accompanied by bottled sauce. I was staring into the refrigerator, contemplating take-out for dinner, when I heard the front door open and in clattered my little family.

I poked my head out the kitchen door and looked out into the foyer. "Hi all!"

Andrew's eyes widened as he turned from where he was hanging his jacket in the closet. "You're home," he said, sounding surprised. I suppose I couldn't blame him. Andrew and Maddie always arrived home before I did on weekday afternoons.

Maddie dropped her backpack on the floor with a thud. "OMG, Mom! What were you thinking?"

I was perplexed about their reaction to seeing me home before them. And what was Maddie talking about? Surely, my presence didn't warrant such shock. Then I wondered. *Is it possible they've already heard about what happened on live television this afternoon? Surely not.*

Maddie marched over to where I was still standing in the kitchen doorway and firmly thrust her phone toward me so that I was looking squarely at the screen about a foot from my eyes. I pushed it back (after all, I didn't have my reading glasses on).

"What's this?" I said, trying to figure out what I was looking at.

"Do you know what a meme is, Mom?"

"Of course I do. But what is this?" I took the phone from her hand and looked at it closely. Nothing was computing.

"Erica, my dear, you've really done it this time," Andrew said, heading toward the dining room. "Drink?" I nodded.

"Mom, are you getting this? You are an internet meme! All my friends have seen it. Life as I've known it to this point is over!"

I looked again at the little jerking picture in my hand. It was me—I guess. At least it was someone who looked like me. And she seemed to be sitting exactly where I sat every afternoon, wearing exactly what I had been wearing earlier that day, saying "self-righteous little moron" and "imbecilic pea-brain" over and over and over. Yup, it was me.

"And, Mother," Maddie called me Mother only when she was severely pissed at me, "it's gone viral! Viral! And they're saying you should be cancelled! Do you even know what that means?"

"I'm sorry, Maddie, but before you make me the total villain here, I think you should watch the whole interview."

My thirteen-going-on-forty-year-old daughter nodded. There was one thing I knew to be true about Maddie. She always wanted the whole story. I watched her as she thudded up the stairs, no doubt on the way to her bedroom, where she would probably log into our home server, where I had an automatic recording set up for every show so I could easily find them if I needed to see something later. It was probable that the station might already have cut out that offending interview in their online version. Maddie would probably watch it, as I'd suggested. Then we could talk.

I joined Andrew, who was now sitting in the living room, his iPad open on his lap and an open bottle of wine on the coffee table in front of him.

"It seems you've had an eventful day, Erica," he said. "You know, this is rich, even for you." He turned his tablet toward me so that I could see he was watching the interview in its entirety. "I've seen you in full on-air bitch mode more than a few times in recent years, but I must admit, this one tops them all. I suppose Trevor will have no choice but to sack you," he said.

"Sack me? As in, fire me?" I took the glass of wine Andrew offered to me and sat down. "You know he won't do that. I'm his golden girl. The bitch everyone hates to love. Or loves to hate."

Andrew's eyebrows twitched upward. "Are you sure? Everyone has a line, Erica. You might have stepped over his. Or Ted's."

Andrew knew the station owner, Ted Thomas—who had also been in journalism school with Trevor and Andrew years ago— better than I did. To tell you the truth, despite my status as one of the co-hosts of the most popular show the station produced, I hardly knew my boss's boss. Andrew's multi-year, on-air position at the top of the television news food chain (which included all the major television stations in the country) opened many doors for him. I'd met Ted—my big boss way above Trevor—only two or three times and always at Andrew's side at some obligatory social event.

I sipped my wine thoughtfully. "You think so?"

"Erica, my dear, you said some things that have long been on the list of inappropriate ways to address people. You used labels that people find insensitive at best—and politically incorrect, not to mention potentially litigious. And you did it in the most public way possible."

I sighed. "My one consolation in all this is that she truly is everything I said. What's more, I suspect many of my fans feel exactly the same way about these influencers who get out there in front of their audience and use their platform to say any outrageous thing that comes into their minds. What they don't seem to understand is that some of what they're spouting is as toxic as the propaganda from Nazi Germany."

"Whoa, Erica. Maybe slow down on the self-righteous indignation and turn down the volume on the smugness. You might also want to tone down the older-woman rhetoric just a bit if you know what's in your best interests."

"Older-woman rhetoric? I cannot believe you just said that. Is this because I believe my generation has come a long way, opening opportunities and equality to this generation of women who want to take us back to the dark ages? Barefoot and pregnant? What are you saying? That I'm too old to embrace new ideas? Too old to be on the air?" I threw back a large gulp of wine and continued, cutting Andrew off as he opened his mouth to speak. "It was Betty Friedan who wrote, *'Rights' have a dull sound to people who have grown up after they have been won*, about the hard-fought rights women now enjoy. And when I shared her quote about orgasms, that stupid child didn't even know who Betty Friedan was."

"Slow down, my love. I didn't mean anything by it except this. You and I both know that many things have changed as we've moved through our careers. This situation is possibly the most blatant example of one of those things. You have a privileged position in a way, but in another way, it's not *your* position. It belongs to your producer and his boss. That particular soap box you stand on every weekday afternoon doesn't really belong to you."

That took some of the wind out of my sails. "What about all that rhetoric about living my personal truth?"

"Have you been reading that book again?"

Andrew was referring to psychologist Jordan Peterson's book, *12 Rules for Life*. The author had gotten into a lot of hot water recently, but I found his original book insightful. I mean, who could argue with living your personal truth and getting your house in order before criticizing others? At least, I hoped my house was in order.

I was thinking about this when Maddie bounced into the room. "Okay, Mom. I see your point. I just watched you talking to that woman this afternoon, and she really did have it coming. I mean, really. When she started on about toilet cleaning being a gift to her family, I thought I'd puke. I'm starting a new hashtag. How about #notoiletcleanngforme? Then I thought maybe it should be #girlsagainsttolietcleaning? I'll have to give it a bit more thought." She turned to Andrew. "What's for dinner, Dad?"

Didn't kids usually ask their mothers that question? Who was I kidding?

Later that evening, Matt called. He was serious when he asked me if I thought I might need a lawyer. "These things have a way of taking on a life of their own," he said. "The moment someone starts a public conversation about how their mental health has been affected by someone's words—your words—you're about to face a shit show." Matt knew what he was talking about. He'd been front and centre for more than a few corporate clients who had done just that. "Anyway, Ricky, one of my partners is a master of the defamation defence."

"Defamation? I didn't defame anyone. I just told her like it is under the guise of my on-air persona. You know, the bitch? You know she's not really me. She's just a part I play on television."

"You keep saying that over and over until you believe it. It's a brilliant defence strategy. I think we can work with that."

As I crawled into bed later, the only thing on my mind was how I would make Trevor see that this was what he was paying me for. After all, I was Erica Flanagan, television personality extraordinaire, and he needed me. (I only hoped he needed me more than I needed him.)

~

I rarely arrived at the television studio before eleven o'clock in the morning. As I pushed into the revolving door the following day at eight-forty-five, many administrative staff were just arriving for work. In addition, there were gaggles of women on the sidewalk outside waiting to see if there were any rush tickets for the morning taping of the popular *Cityview* show. Today was Thursday, and that meant today's topic was Fashion Focus. And fashions on Thursday meant lots of giveaways like makeup and scarves. I knew this because whenever anyone I knew had friends visiting the city, they would inevitably call me to ask if I had a way to score tickets for them. I always put on my on-air persona (the bitch) and told them I didn't—although to tell you the truth, I'd never asked.

As I swiped my ID card, I could feel the eyes on me. The security guard mumbled something like, "Good morning, Ms. Flanagan," but couldn't meet my gaze. The three young women at the reception desk noticed me and then immediately busied themselves with more interesting things on the desk or a computer screen to avoid engaging, no doubt. But I did see them peeking.

I squashed myself into the elevator with half a dozen other worker bees and pressed twenty-two, the top floor where Ted Thomas held court and where the station had its fanciest boardrooms. Miriam had sent me a text this morning telling me to meet Trevor there rather than in his office so as not to "disturb the cast and crew." *Huh*, I thought, *as if any of them were even there this early*. The only aspect of this that gave me pause was that it was Ted's domain. I sincerely hoped he wasn't going to be there.

"Planning to excoriate any other unsuspecting young women today, Erica?"

I craned my neck toward the back of the elevator where the voice seemed to have originated. I saw a familiar face just past the suit-jacket-clad shoulder of one of the other occupants who was bopping to whatever was playing on his AirPods.

Joel Morgenstern was a reporter at one of the local newspapers. About forty years old, Joel represented those reporters who were always searching for that story that would make their careers.

"Very funny, Joel," I hissed as people began disembarking from the elevator as we made our way up.

Joel and I were now the only two people who hadn't reached their floor.

"Headed to see the boss?" he said.

"Wouldn't you like to know," I said as the doors opened. I walked out into the sumptuous foyer with its blonde wood and Nordic flair. Joel followed me.

"Mr. Morgenstern," the receptionist said to Joel, ignoring me. "He's waiting for you."

Joel thanked her and nodded to me before going down the corridor toward where I knew Ted's office was.

"Ms. Flanagan, please take a seat. Mr. Goulet called to ask me to tell you he was running a bit late."

I was fuming as I sat in one of the round chairs upholstered in what appeared to be cream-coloured shag carpeting. It was so like Trevor to take the passive-aggressive approach and make me wait. The receptionist didn't even offer me a cup of coffee. Trevor had probably given instructions not to offer anything resembling common courtesy. It was a tactic, and I didn't like it one bit.

I sat there for half an hour, my gaze riveted to the elevator doors each time they opened—which wasn't often. Finally, the door opened, and Trevor walked into the lobby. The receptionist looked up and smiled. "Good morning, Mr. Goulet. They're just setting up the boardroom for you."

Trevor smiled and thanked her, then turned to me. "Good morning, Erica. I'll be a moment." And he disappeared into the hall while I continued to bristle.

A full ten minutes had passed when the receptionist answered her intercom and then looked up to tell me I could go in. The board room was down the first hall and to the right.

By the time I reached the open door to the boardroom, any conciliatory thoughts I'd had about this meeting had evaporated. I was angry for being hauled onto the carpet for what I considered part of my job. I was angry at Trevor for treating me with such disdain this morning. And I suppose I was angry at myself—although I couldn't put my finger on why.

It is an immutable law of physics. *For every action in nature, there is an equal and opposite reaction.* So says Newton's third law. If one object—let's call it object X—exerts force on a second object—let's call this second object Y—then it happens as day follows night that object Y will exert an opposite and equal force on the offending first object. At least, that's how I was interpreting the laws of nature as I took my seat in the boardroom to which I had been directed, beginning to feel the forces of nature as they exerted themselves on me.

I had never been in this room before. It was more blonde wood that exuded the feeling of a high-end Ikea store. The light wood table was brushed to a satin sheen, and around it stood more than a dozen chrome and cream-coloured upholstered chairs with smooth, silent wheels, like sentries standing guard.

The table was set as if for a board meeting for two. There were bottles of water, a glass, a blank piece of paper and a pen emblazoned with the station's logo at two places.

Trevor took the seat opposite mine, placed a pile of printed pages on the table in front of him and cleared his throat. "Erica, I hardly know where to begin. Your behaviour yesterday was nothing short of shameful—quite shocking, in fact." He lifted a sheaf of pages that looked like they had just been pulled off a printer. "Do you know what these are?" I considered this a rhetorical question since I couldn't possibly know what they were. He continued. "I'll tell you what they are. These are pages and pages of online reaction to your evisceration of our guest yesterday. Our guest! Need I say more?"

Clearly, in my mind, he did need to say more. I remained silent.

Trevor started reading from the page on top.

#cancelericaflanagan for her flagrant disregard for mental health issues.

Dumb bitch needs to learn some manners.

Take her off the air. Right. This. Minute.

Wait until her mental health issues surface. Then we'll all laugh at her.

Shame on you Erica.

I put my hand up to silence him. "I get the picture, Trevor. Now, tell me, were there any supporters?"

"Oh, yeah. There were the far-left wing feminist wingnuts who said you had a point, but you said it wrong."

"Tsk, tsk, Trevor. Wingnuts? Surely, that will bring on the political correctness police."

If looks could kill, I'd have been keeling over at that point.

"Erica, I don't think you grasp the seriousness of this. And it's not the first time this has happened. I've had to pull you back from the brink on several occasions over the past three years. Is this all because you turned fifty?"

I could feel my ears getting red. It was my tell that I was getting angry. Was this all about ageism?

"And before you get on me about being ageist—god forbid any of us should point out that some older on-air personalities might be becoming a tad out of touch—this isn't about that. It's about how you don't seem able to control your personal vendetta against the world these days. That young woman has feelings and the right to her point of view, Erica. And she was an invited guest, might I point out."

Oh, this was just too much. An invited guest? Her publicist probably bribed someone to get her on the air. And her feelings? Please. "Trevor Goulet, you don't give a damn about any young women's feelings. Do I have to remind you about the Alexandra incident?" I could see him blanche at the mention of that name. Alexandra had been a young intern about ten years ago who had fallen for Trevor, and he hadn't done anything to deflect her admiration. Let's just say she went away without going online with the #metoo hashtag, but it could still happen.

"Okay, then, let's talk ratings," he said, hastily changing the subject.

This was more like it. Ratings were something substantial, unlike the opinions of the nutbars who trolled the online communities looking for something—or someone—to trash.

"Erica, you have been one of our top draws on *The Exchange* for over a decade, but recently, your popularity has been waning." This was news to me. Before I could object, he continued. "You're not testing as well. The bitch persona seems to grate on our younger viewers. They seem to be offended by it."

There it was. Didn't I mention that someone will always choose to be offended no matter what you do or what you say? He still wasn't finished.

"The new numbers suggest our current audience is mainly women under fifty, and you're beginning to..." He didn't (or couldn't) finish his thought.

"I'm beginning to what, Trevor? Age out of the business? Make the viewers feel they're watching grama?" I could feel the anger rising. This wasn't good. "Trevor, is this about what I said yesterday or is it because of something you've wanted to discuss with me for some time?" He shrugged and said nothing. "Well, let's figure out what we're going to do about it."

"*We* are not going to figure this out, Erica. *I* am. It's *my* job. The situation is worse than you could imagine. We've been receiving death threats for you because of your," he looked down at one of the pieces of paper in the pile, "tone-deaf insensitivity, to quote one of the emails I received this morning from a legal firm representing our young author from yesterday. And don't get me started on what our in-house legal team is saying."

I certainly had no intention of getting him started down that road. I sighed. "So, are they suing us?"

"I sincerely hope not, Erica, but that depends on what we do next."

"If you want me to apologize on camera, I'm not sure how sincere I could be. Even Maddie thinks that girl is a moron."

"Erica, just stop. An on-air apology isn't going to be enough."

"What does she want? A pound of flesh?"

"She might not want one, but I'd settle for one right about now. Erica, we need to take a different approach." He cleared his throat again. "I think it's time for you to take a sabbatical."

Had I heard him correctly? At that moment, I remembered that only yesterday, I'd envied Trevor's PA for her year-long maternity leave/sabbatical. I could hear my mother's voice in my head: *Be careful what you wish for.*

My head was buzzing so much that I could hardly hear his next words. "Six months at least." "Half-salary." "Take a vacation." "Write a book."

As he spoke, I could feel object X (Trevor) strengthening its force on object Y. Object Y (me) was only beginning to feel the force and getting up to speed on the opposite and equal force that might be warranted.

Before I could even begin to gather my ammunition, Trevor said, "It's only four weeks to Christmas, and we'll be running reruns as usual starting the week after next. By the time we're back, we'll have sorted out the hosting situation, and you'll be well into your sabbatical. I think it would be best if you just went directly home after this meeting. I'll direct Samantha to touch base with you later today so you can let her know what you'd like to have packed up from your dressing room."

My dressing room? I couldn't even go to get my things? "I suppose you want me to do the perp walk out with security."

Trevor ignored my last remark. He cleared his throat again. "We will need your dressing room for," he hesitated for a moment, "other people. We may, of course, invite others to be on the air in your absence."

I looked up at him incredulously. "You already have someone in mind, don't you?" He said nothing. "How long have you been waiting for this kind of opening, Trevor?" Before he could say another world, and before I could begin slinging nasty epithets at him, I picked up my purse and stood up. "Never mind. We're done."

~

I was home by 10:30 in the morning, with the rest of the day stretching out in front of me like a yawning cavern about to swallow me up. I was still shell-shocked as I climbed the stairs to my bedroom and dropped onto the bed, where I stared up at the ceiling for a while. I didn't know how long I'd been there when I heard my cell phone ringing from the depths of my capacious handbag.

It was Andrew. "How'd it go?"

"Not well," I said.

"So, Trevor had the balls to fire his most popular host."

"Not exactly," I said, sitting up and looking at my watch. I was shocked to see it was just past noon. Had I fallen asleep? "I'm on sabbatical."

"A sabbatical? That's a fantastic outcome, Erica. You can spend your time doing things you never have time for."

"Like what? Cooking?" I said wryly.

Andrew laughed. "I certainly hope not! Maddie and I value our health."

"Very funny." I knew we'd have plenty of time to discuss my circumstances and the possibility of me needing a lawyer, a subject that was on my mind, so I changed the subject. "You still on campus?"

"I am, and I have a meeting with my publisher at two, so I won't be home until after I pick Maddie up from drama class."

"I can do that, Andrew," I said, wondering where my car keys were. I hardly ever drove in the city.

"No, Erica dear. I think it might be best if you just spend the afternoon getting used to having the luxury of time. But I do have one piece of advice."

"What's that?" I said, wondering what I'd have for lunch.

"Do not under any circumstances watch this afternoon's show and stay the hell off social media. Got it?"

I got it. I just wasn't sure I could comply.

After I hung up, I changed my clothes and wandered downstairs into the kitchen. I made myself a cup of coffee and toasted a bagel that I then smothered with peanut butter. I sat at the breakfast bar with my laptop in front of me. *Well*, I thought, *I can at least check my email.*

There was a formal email from human resources detailing my "sabbatical" and how much money they'd pay for the six months. *Geesh*, I thought, *the folks in HR must have whiplash from moving so quickly on this*. It usually took them weeks to get anything done. Trevor must have put the screws to them. The skeptic in me wondered if he'd been planning this all along.

Then, there was an email that Trevor had forwarded to me. It was from someone representing Laura-Lee Cox—her agent, perhaps. In that roundabout, jargon-heavy legalese that accountants and agents seemed to like, they were demanding an apology (of course) and a meeting (what?). Despite the legal-sounding vocabulary, there didn't seem to be any mention of a lawyer's involvement—at least at this stage. I was relieved.

There was also an email from Sam asking me what I'd need from my dressing room, that she would courier anything I needed, and when we could get together. I responded to her, telling her to box up everything that looked like it belonged to me, send it along and call me on the weekend.

As I popped the last piece of bagel into my mouth, I picked up my phone that I'd placed on the counter beside me. I clicked it on, and my finger hovered over the Instagram button just as the landline in the house rang. It had to be either the guys who mowed our lawn, tended to our flower beds and did our snow-clearing, or it was my mother. They were the only people who didn't call our cellphone numbers. I walked over to the opposite side of the kitchen, where the wall phone hung just below a black-and-white photograph of Andrew, Maddie and me on a trip to Paris. As I looked at the caller ID, I shuddered just a tiny bit. It was my mother. I had wondered how long it would be before she tuned into my latest escapade and decided to weigh in. I took a deep breath, fixed a smile on my face, hoping it would help me convey a warmer tone than I felt, and picked up the receiver.

"Mom. How are you?"

3

# How to Embrace the Luxury of Time...Without Going Crazy

*One of the main perks of being unemployed is*
*that Mondays aren't really so bad*
~ Author Unknown

MY MOTHER, MAUREEN FLANAGAN, had put her second husband, Charles Davidson, in the ground (or rather in an urn on the fireplace mantle) eighteen months earlier. They had been married less than three years when Charles had unexpectedly and, rather inconveniently to hear my mother tell it, died of a heart attack—while on a cruise ship in the middle of the Mediterranean. My father died when I was a teenager (another heart attack), so Mom and I and my brother Phillip had been a tight little family for all those years between Dad and Charles. But Mom and I have always been two very different people—at least, that's how I saw it.

At age seventy-eight now, Mom had finally completely retired from her professorship in philosophy (she taught and wrote about ethics and political philosophy) after spending her years since her formal retirement ten years earlier guest lecturing and writing books. The last time I'd seen her, she told me she had finally given it up and intended to ignore her professor emeritus status on campus. But once a philosopher, always a philosopher.

For my entire childhood, Mom had tried to imbue me with a sense that there's more to life than what we see on the surface—that I should think beyond what I could see. For example, I had

35

always wanted to be a writer. Indeed, I'd always been a writer, from the very first short story I wrote in fourth grade to my feeble attempt to write a book when I was seventeen. Mom had applauded my exploration of a future as a writer because she believed a writer could only write well by digging far beneath the surface. When I was in my senior year in high school, I told her I was applying to journalism school so I could pursue a career as a journalist. I can still hear her sighing dramatically and quoting Oscar Wilde: *The difference between literature and journalism is that journalism is unreadable and literature is not*. As far as she was concerned, journalists were pseudo-writers. So, you can imagine how she reacted years later when I told her I was leaving on-the-ground reporting to be an afternoon television personality. Not well. Now, here I was.

"How am *I*?" Mom said. "How am I? More to the point, how are you? And why are you at home at this hour of the day?"

"If you didn't think I'd be home, why did you call?"

"Erica, don't get snippy with me. I called to leave you a message to do something for me. But, now that I have you on the phone, tell me what happened yesterday. One of my friends, Audrey—you remember Audrey—called last evening to tell me I should go online and watch your television show from yesterday. You know that I never watch that kind of thing, but I made an exception this time since she seemed to think it was important. I now wish I hadn't. Erica, you know I've never really understood or approved of this career choice. You have so much potential. But I must admit you went even more overboard than usual with yesterday's antics. What were you thinking? Of course, the young woman is a fool—that is inarguable—but calling her out in that way on television seems a bit beyond the pale even for you. I hope you've had a substantial discussion with Madeline about this. She's at that vulnerable age, you know. She could go in any direction from here."

"Oh, Mom, you know Maddie. She probably has her head on straighter than either of us."

"Don't deflect, Erica. What has been the aftermath of yesterday's debacle?"

I was hardly deflecting since she was the one who brought up the subject of Maddie, but I chose not to say that. It would only prolong the irritation I could feel building.

"They've put me on sabbatical."

"Sabbatical? Television personalities don't get sabbaticals. Is that a euphemism in your industry? Have they fired you?"

I sighed. "No, Mom. They haven't fired me. They've put me on leave for six months."

There was a moment of silence on the other end of the phone. "Six months? You have six months to do what? What are your plans? I never had a sabbatical without a complete plan."

I knew that. University professors were required to have sabbatical plans before the university granted them one, even if it was a contractual right of the professoriate. I, on the other hand, had no plan.

"Well, Mom, I've been on sabbatical for," I checked my watch, "two and a half hours, give or take."

"Well, Erica, I hope you come to some decisions soon about how to spend your time. You used to be a good writer, so maybe it's time you wrote that book you wanted to write when you were seventeen. You know, this is quite a gift. Time, I mean. Use it wisely, my dear."

"I'm going to try to, Mom." At least she didn't ask me if I was being sued for defamation, and since she wasn't much for social media, she probably hadn't seen the memes or the nasty comments. It was just as well.

"Oh, by the way, the reason I called is that I was wondering if you had time this weekend to help me with a few things around here."

"As it happens, I do," I said wryly. "What do you need?"

"Oh, just come over on Saturday afternoon. I'll show you."

So, I had my first sabbatical plan.

~

I spent the rest of the afternoon listlessly roaming the house. What in the world was I going to do with myself? I had worked all my adult life, with the exception of the three months after Maddie was born thirteen years ago. And I spent all my time then devoted to a little human whose welfare rested on my shoulders. So, this "found time" was a new and unwelcome experience.

At three o'clock, I couldn't help myself. In complete defiance of Andrew's wise advice, I turned on the television and sat back to watch the show. I hadn't been watching for fifteen minutes when I turned it off. There they were, my three co-hosts and the guest host (we often had guest hosts) who had been planned far in advance, sitting at the counter, chatting as if nothing had happened. They completely ignored the fiasco from the day before. A mere twenty-four hours later, and already I'd been erased.

I sat back and clicked my phone. *In for a penny, in for a pound,* I thought. I decided I might throw caution to the wind and see what was happening on Instagram. I wasn't a big social media butterfly, so the accounts I followed were inevitably ones that Trevor and the production team asked us to follow because of some guest or another. It was mandated as part of their show prep process. I followed authors (of course), certain retailers, cooking accounts and lots of over-fifty women who were "style influencers." Imagine that! Since I was the eldest among the group of co-hosts (and writers and most of the production team besides Trevor himself), I had been tasked with following the over-fifty spaces. Of course, they also wanted me to follow retirement lifestyle accounts (read: old people's homes), although I refused to do that in case the algorithm began thinking I was ready for one and started bombarding me with smiling centenarians leaning on walkers and sipping tea from fine china.

Before I started scrolling, I decided I might as well get comfortable. I made myself an afternoon coffee (I wanted a cappuccino, but I couldn't remember how to get the steam spout on our fancy coffee maker to work and was too lazy to look for the directions) and then took it into the family room. I flopped down into one of the massive leather chairs our interior designer had placed ever-so-carefully on either side of the stone fireplace. It had been at least several months since I'd even had time to peek at Instagram, and since we had a social media team who posted on our accounts for us (I know, you thought celebrities actually did their own posting to connect with you, didn't you?), I had no need to pretend I cared. As I started taking a closer look at my Instagram feed, I was increasingly horrified at what I was seeing.

First, there was an over-fifty woman (over sixty if she was a day) giving chapter and verse on how older women should style denim jackets. I was having a hard time, though, getting past the fact that her *au natural* hair hung limply down past her shoulders, giving her the aura of a denim-clad witch. I looked at her recommended outfits and was left wondering what made her think she had a shred of style talent. The fact that she'd been a model in the 1980s did not, in any material way, make up for the fact that she looked like a frump. So, sue me.

Then there was another one—over seventy, to be sure. This one was tall and very skinny—so skinny that she could wear a paper bag and look good if you ignored her odd expressions. She did have some great ideas, but she showed them in some bizarre "reels" set to inexplicable music to which she danced as each piece of clothing magically appeared on her as if out of mid-air. It was cringeworthy. Then there was one that I quite liked—except for the jerky movement of this foot in front of that one, the head turn this way and that way. Why in the world did they do that? What happened to the still photos Instagram was made for in the first place? This woman was an attractive, over-fifty woman with a good sense of style, but I was embarrassed for her. Then there were the rest of them shilling for companies that gave them free stuff. You know the ones. They waxed rapturous over cheap sweaters and faux-silk scarves—with links to buy embedded below the videos. I noticed the little red dot on the heart at the top of my home page and realized I'd probably been tagged in posts. I was happy to see just my usual feed. I ignored the little red dot. I didn't care what they were saying. I would keep telling myself this for as long as I could. Then I threw the phone on the table and sat back to sip my lukewarm coffee. I had an idea.

Maybe I could be "an influencer." There certainly seemed to be room in the over-fifty social media space for someone with a brain. *Yes,* I thought, *why can't I use my current fame—or infamy—to my advantage? I'll be a style influencer. I can critique all those weird trends out-of-touch stylists tried to foist on women—especially women my age and older.* I could spend my sabbatical developing a following outside of the requisite one I had because I was on television. I could be my own "brand."

I was suddenly energized. I went to my little home office upstairs at the back of the house overlooking the garden, where we had converted an oddly tiny room into a small office for me. We had long ago decided Andrew needed a larger office, given his work since "retirement," so he had taken over a larger room, and I was happy with my own small space. I fired up my computer and began researching how to create an Instagram brand. The more I researched, the more discouraged I became. No, strike that, the more bored I became. My problem was that I had no interest in following Instagram accounts, so I could hardly expect others to follow mine. Besides, I wasn't a style icon. But my main problem was that being an influencer would mean I'd have to engage with other people—all day, every day. I remembered Mom liked to quote Sartre. *"Hell is other people,"* he'd written. He was so right.

~

I spent Friday puttering around my office and organizing the stuff Sam had collected from my dressing room and sent via courier as requested. I knew I'd return to the station in due course, so I hadn't asked her to bring everything, only items that might result in a bit of decluttering. I found my car keys and drove myself to our local Canadian Tire store to find some clear boxes for storage.

I had been in the store for only a few minutes, mesmerized by the array of merchandise, when I began to feel like I was part of the display. I had forgotten how much I had enjoyed wandering around these mega-stores back when Andrew and I had needed things to set up our house. But this time, something was off. As I chose a few storage containers and headed to the cash line, I realized people were staring and whispering. I had to get out of there as quickly as I could. As I drove home, I wondered how long it would take for people to forget about what happened.

The following day, I arrived at my mother's house promptly at two in the afternoon. After we had spoken, she sent me a text with precise timing. Mom still lived in the house where I'd spent my teenage years, and it would always be home to me despite my mother's philosophical bent and my pragmatic approach to life that was so different from hers. At least she knew how to make oatmeal chocolate chip cookies, something I'd never been able to master. A plate of these mouth-watering cookies was on the kitchen table when I came in through the side door that led directly into the kitchen.

"For later," she said when she saw me eyeing them. She beckoned for me to follow her, which I did after hanging my coat on a hook by the door.

As we emerged into the hallway, something wasn't right. The place seemed different. Paintings and mirrors were missing from the walls, and the table in the foyer, where Mom usually had a large bouquet of fresh flowers, was covered with piles of books.

"What's going on, Mom?" I said, alarmed at what seemed to be the devastation of my family home.

"Yes, well, Erica, we need to talk before we get started."

I followed Mom into the living room, where boxes containing what looked like hordes of objects wrapped in newsprint were scattered everywhere. "What is going on?"

"I'd ask you to sit down, but we have a lot to do, so perhaps we could talk as we wrap up these bits and pieces and put them in the boxes."

As we worked side by side, Mom told me the story. First, she was selling the house. I had hardly gotten over that shock when she told me she'd already found a condo she loved and was downsizing—or rightsizing, as she put it. She would be donating everything we were wrapping and putting into cardboard boxes, and by the way, did I want anything? I was speechless.

"So, my realtor says the house has to be ready for staging by the end of next week," she was saying while I tried to digest the news that she was selling my home. "And the week after that, Anthony and I are going on a cruise."

I turned toward Mom so abruptly that I hurt my neck. "Anthony? Who is Anthony?"

Mom sighed. "Erica, if you could get your head out of your navel, you'd remember I told you about Anthony. Anthony Duncan is a former colleague from the university. His wife died last year, and we've been seeing one another for a few months. We ran into one another at a function for retired faculty. Do you ever listen?"

I vaguely remembered Mom saying something about someone she'd had dinner with, and the name Anthony Duncan rang a bell. "Mom, isn't Dr. Duncan that Jungian psychoanalyst you said was a quack?" The conversation when Mom had talked about Anthony Duncan years earlier was beginning to float into my consciousness. "I distinctly remember a discussion about pseudoscience, and perhaps the word charlatanism might even have come up."

Mom shrugged. "I've learned a thing or two about Jungian analysis since then, Erica. And besides, we can all evolve. Perhaps you might give it a try with all this found time you have."

Normally, I would have risen to the bait, but this time, I had other more pressing matters on my mind. A horrifying thought had just crossed my mind. "You're not buying the condo with him, are you?"

"And what if I were? What difference would that make?" Mom watched my face for a reaction that I tried to mask. Then she went back to her packing. "But no, I'm looking forward to decorating it and living in it alone. I've been clattering around in this big house alone for the past three years, and that's long enough. I need a change of scenery."

I was slightly mollified and meekly followed her upstairs when she asked me to go through boxes she'd managed to bring down from the attic, which she said was now empty. I was grateful for that. However, I was a little less grateful when she told me to go ahead of her into the guest bedroom, where I could begin going through the boxes. As I walked in through the door, my horror grew.

The pile of boxes was four deep and reached almost to the ceiling.

"Mom! What the hell? What have you been keeping?"

She shrugged as she came in after me. "I have no idea what's there, Erica. I haven't looked in those boxes in years. I only know I can't sell the house without going through everything. Some of your father's things might be there, and I want to see them before we pitch anything."

I settled in, and Mom left me. Two hours later, I'd gotten through a creditable number of boxes, finding old photo albums, files from Mom's PhD dissertation, which she'd successfully completed two years after she had married my father and no less than fifty-six years earlier, and masses of old dog-eared paperback books. There was everything from *The Godfather* to *Dune* and *Valley of the Dolls*. There was also an original copy of Betty Friedan's *The Feminine Mystique*, published in 1963, which Mom had bought when it first came out. It had been Mom's bible, so it was not much wonder she agreed with my opinions about that young author, if not my approach.

Friedan's work criticized the prevailing post-World War II suburban ideal of women being fulfilled solely by homemaking and motherhood. You may remember that when I mentioned her name on air, my two young co-hosts had acted as if they had no idea who she was. I suspect that was because they didn't. Betty Friedan argued that this ideal of women's fulfilment via domestic drudgery, often perpetuated by media and society, left many women feeling unfulfilled and trapped in their roles as housewives, leading to what she called "the problem that has no name." I wondered if the problem had a name in the twenty-first century. When I first read her early work back when I was in journalism school, something resonated. Anyway, I was keeping this one and a few others. All in all, it was a wonderful collection of 1960s nostalgia.

I'd just catalogued the books as Mom had asked me to do when I opened what I hoped might be my last box of the afternoon (there were still dozens). When I opened the flaps, I wasn't sure what I was looking at. It seemed to be old magazines. I started lifting them out one by one.

*Good Housekeeping*, January 1960. I looked at the photograph on the cover of a woman wearing a flowing negligee and holding her young child close. Several cover stories were highlighted: "Women Against Men, a Novel" and "Women Who Are Afraid to Marry." I picked up another one. This issue was also *Good Housekeeping* from the 1960s, with articles about how to make tomato aspic (if you don't know what that is, go look it up, then join me in gagging), how to be the best wife you can be, how to have glowing skin, and how to lose weight. So many how-to's! And there were more—many more such issues of *Good Housekeeping*. Then there were *Redbook* magazines, also from the 1960s and 1970s, *Woman's Day*, a few *Glamour* magazines and yet more vintage copies of *Good Housekeeping*. They were all in mint condition or close to it with a few dogeared issues. Perhaps these were ones that had been particularly well-read—but by whom? Surely not my university professor mother. I looked around at the remaining boxes and opened another and another. They were all filled with old magazines.

When Mom returned to ask me if I'd like coffee and a cookie or maybe even a glass of wine, I appreciatively accepted the wine offer and followed her downstairs.

"So, Mom," I said, gratefully taking the offered glass of wine, "what were all those old women's magazines doing in your attic?"

She had no idea what I was talking about, so I told her what I'd found. She sat sipping her wine for a moment before speaking. "Gosh, I'd forgotten I still had them. Erica, I believe you have stumbled upon one of your feminist mother's dirty little secrets. In the 1960s, before I married your father, and I suppose even after, and despite my higher education and career aspirations, I was a junkie for women's magazines that might teach me how to be a good wife."

I was flabbergasted. My mother, the star academic, wanted to be the perfect 1960s wife? It was impossible to imagine. Then I thought about that young wife-author from earlier in the week. Six decades had passed, and here we were again. I could again feel the anger I'd felt on Wednesday as I sat there castigating that Laura-Lee person. I asked Mom if I could have her stash of magazines. She asked me why I wanted them, and I told her I had no idea. I just knew I had to have them. She said yes, and I took them home.

~

Andrew, Maddie and I usually spent Sundays together, although recently, Maddie had begun chafing at this forced family time. I concluded that her apparent resistance was because she thought it was how thirteen-year-olds were expected to behave while secretly loving it. That Sunday after my meltdown, Maddie had a birthday brunch to attend anyway, so our usual activities would have to be curtailed. Her friend Kathleen was turning fourteen, and her parents were hosting a group of Kathleen's friends for brunch in a private dining room at the Four Seasons Hotel. I had expected the brunch to be all-girls since Maddie and her friends attended an all-girls school. However, Maddie had informed me that this wasn't the case. This party would be a first—there would be boys. I often worried about this phase of my daughter's life, given the way young girls portrayed themselves on social media—far too grown up for their age, as far as I was concerned. But what do you expect? I am, after all, a mother. Anyway, I wasn't too worried about this occasion since Kathleen's parents would be overseeing the festivities. Since Maddie wouldn't be home anyway, Andrew encouraged me to go when Sam called to ask me to have lunch with her. I know he wanted time to create his pizza masterpiece that was on the menu for dinner.

I was sitting at my dressing table, fluffing my face as best I could, when Andrew walked in.

"I just walked past your office door. What are all those cardboard boxes? Did Samantha bring them from your dressing room?"

I told them they contained my mother's secret stash of women's magazines. He was just as astonished as I had been to discover his erudite feminist mother-in-law's dirty little secret. She had been a closet "housewife."

"Kind of reminds me of that gag gift one of your co-hosts gave you a few years back in your Secret Santa Christmas thing." I had no idea what he was talking about. "The apron? Remember, it was one of those things women in the '60s tied around their waists when they dusted and cooked to keep their pretty skirts clean. This one had a red ruffle around it and the word "wife" emblazoned in red on white. How could you forget about it? I remember how we laughed—well, I did. Anyway, why do you have those magazines here?"

I stopped what I was doing and turned around. I had forgotten all about that apron and wondered what I had done with it. "I'm not exactly sure, darling. I'm sort of fascinated by them. I spent an hour looking through one of the boxes yesterday when I got home from Mom's, and I almost couldn't stop reading them. I know I have to do something with them, but I'm not sure what that might be. I do have an idea, though."

Andrew smiled and shook his head. "You wouldn't be my wife—the Erica I love—if you didn't have an idea or two. Are you going to share?"

"Not yet," I said. "It's really just gelling, but I'll let you know the minute I have something."

"Does this have anything to do with you trying to figure out how to spend your sabbatical?"

I shrugged and went back to my fluffing. "We'll see."

"Say hi to Sam for me," he said as he headed back downstairs, presumably to get out his pizza crust ingredients.

Sam was already at our table when I arrived at Sassafraz, a chichi restaurant in a chichi corner of the city called Yorkville, which was our current favourite lunch spot. Sam stood up, waving wildly when she saw me. As I reached the table, Sam lunged toward me, encircling me in a bear hug. "How *are* you, Ricky?" she said, seemingly full of concern.

As I extricated myself, I said, "I'm not dying, Sam. I don't have a fatal illness."

"Oh, honey, it's just that you really put your foot in it this time," she said, sitting down.

I noticed Sam had already ordered a bottle of wine, which was now chilling in an ice bucket beside the table. Sam poured me a glass and topped hers up. She had already started.

"It's been so weird in the studio, Ricky. It's as if nothing has happened. There's a bit of whispering, but it's like no one is prepared to acknowledge that we're now minus our biggest personality. You've always been our ratings star."

"Maybe," I said ruefully as I sipped my wine. "But to hear Trevor tell it, you'd have to believe I'm becoming more of a liability."

Sam's eyebrows popped upward. I told her about my conversation with Trevor about ratings and my personal "charm quotient" on its downward slide. Then we switched to the silver lining (as she put it—I was still having some difficulty imagining one). We started talking about my sabbatical—my "found" time.

"In some ways, this might be just what you need at this point in your life."

I knew Sam was talking about my age. She was three years younger, just turning fifty this year, and I knew she was having more difficulty with the thought of that milestone birthday than I had—and I'd had my moments.

Then I told her about Mom's secret stash of vintage women's magazines and how odd it was for her to have them. Sam had known my mother for over a decade and was just as surprised as I had been. Then I told her I thought they might be inspiring a project.

"Maybe I could write something about how these magazines mirror or maybe even help to create women's evolution in society. I could do a few magazine pieces. I miss writing."

"You do know that's been done to death, don't you?"

Sam's role as our on-set director might suggest to you that her job is to guide those of us who appear on-air to the best performance possible. Perhaps you think her duties would be confined to giving us direction about where to find our marks (where to sit or stand), when to open our mouths and speak and when to close them. Her job encompassed so much more.

Sam played a central role in pre-production planning, which required her to collaborate with the show's producers, writers, and other key personnel. Her input was always crucial to the final decisions about what stories we should and could cover, how they might be presented and who should do the presenting. Trevor often deferred to her in these essential aspects of our show. I often thought he considered her his connection to all things in the feminine and feminist world. Sam's broader interest in this topic had propelled her to graduate school, where she had been plugging away at her master's degree, one course at a time. All of this is to say that Sam was always more informed about what was happening in women's worlds than anyone else. If she said the idea had been done to death, I had to refrain from beating a dead horse.

"Maybe I could write a book?" I said meekly. "Everyone thinks I should write a book."

"Who is everyone? And what would it be about? Surely not women's magazines, Ricky."

"Well, Trevor suggested I should write a book and, as it happens, so did my mother."

Sam was clicking things on her phone. "Just a minute. I remember reading something in one of my courses a few years ago." She stopped for a moment and turned her phone toward me.

It was the cover of a book titled *Women in Magazines: Research, Representation, Production and Consumption.*

I think I blanched. "Dear god, Sam. You read that one?"

She nodded and sipped her wine as the server arrived to take our order. When the server had gone, I picked up Sam's phone and looked at it again.

"Seriously, did you actually read this book?" She nodded. "The whole thing?" Another yes nod.

"And it wasn't as deadly as it sounds," Sam said. "It was fascinating. Of course, it was written by a bunch of academics, but the gist of it was important to help me understand the female zeitgeist. You might find it interesting." Sam then took her phone back and tapped again. "Then there's this one." Again, she turned it toward me. The title of this one was *Cosmo Woman: The World of Women's Magazines.*

I sighed. "Well, Mom's collection didn't seem to have any *Cosmo* magazines, but I haven't been through it all yet."

Sam then showed me the cover of another book. *Decoding Women's Magazines: From Mademoiselle to Ms.* Then another. *Reading Women's Magazines: An Analysis of Everyday Media Use.* And *Women's Worlds: Ideology, Femininity and Women's Magazines.*

"Sorry to rain on your parade, Ricky. You know I'd be the last person to want to do that, but," she hesitated before continuing, "I can't think of a single reason for you to do anything remotely related to 1960s women's roles or old women's magazines. It's just not you. You have no reason that I can see to pursue this. Why does this topic even interest you? Where is it coming from? Domesticity is so not your thing, Ricky, and you know it. Last week's debacle seemed to cement that, don't you think? I'm sure I don't need to remind you that you were dripping disdain." Sam took a breath, then started up again, probably so I couldn't get a word in. "If you want my opinion," and I usually did, but I wasn't so sure this time, "you're just flailing around trying to force yourself back into a project. Take your time, Ricky. Enjoy the luxury of time." She finally stopped and tipped back her glass, draining every last drop.

"Okay, okay," I said, reaching for the wine bottle to refill both glasses. "I get the picture. The truth is, I don't really know why unless…" I trailed off, put the bottle back in the ice bucket, and took a sip. I was pondering. Finally, I said, "I was thinking about writing something the average woman would read. I was thinking about a dynamic, fascinating book about how women's roles are so much more than the domestic drudgery of the 1960s and '70s that would jump to the top of the bestseller list."

It was Sam's turn to roll her eyes. She shook her head firmly. "Never going to happen, my friend. I guarantee you no one—and I mean no one—would read it. Women aren't interested. *You're* not even interested." She stared at me closely.

As I sat there mulling over Sam's words, I began to examine my motives. "I have to admit this whole historical thing does sound a bit bogus."

"Erica Flanagan, what are you thinking?" Sam leaned in toward me. "I've seen that look before, and it usually means you're up to no good."

"Maybe," I said, then changed the subject. "Sam, doesn't it ever bother you that we've come so far as women and now there are so many younger women who just seem to want to take us back to the dark ages?"

Sam shrugged. "I've just never seen it as my problem, Ricky. What are you getting at?"

I couldn't yet put it into words, but I was feeling that anger I'd felt toward our author-guest the week before beginning to bubble up again. "Sam, I just know I have a point to prove."

Sam looked up as our server approached. "Well, Ricky, I don't know exactly what point you want to prove, but I saw something on Instagram a few weeks ago that might be worth considering. *It is better to prove your point with a period than with a million exclamation points.*"

I made a face at her. I was sure I knew what I was doing—and exclamation points were kind of my thing.

4

# When Opportunity Doesn't Knock, Beat Down its Door

*Women have two choices. Either she's a feminist, or she's a masochist.*
~ Gloria Steinman

SAM HAD WORK TO DO. I DIDN'T. So, when she left me at the restaurant, I stayed for a few minutes finishing my cappuccino, pondering the six months that lay ahead of me like an open door—at least, I hoped the door was open. As I got up to leave, I realized that the only one who could figure this out was me. I walked down the steps back onto the sidewalk and looked down the street to see if there was a cab coming. Then, as one turned into the block, I changed my mind and started walking.

The next thing I knew, I was walking into the revolving door of Indigo, the enormous book and tchotchke shop a few blocks away. The shop was busy. After all, it was Sunday, and what better way to spend an urban Sunday than in a bookstore that lets you sit and read, buy a coffee at the attached Starbucks and finish shopping for Christmas stocking stuffers under the same roof?

I passed by the tables laden with staff picks for books, running my fingers over the covers as I passed. How long had it been since I'd read an actual hardcopy book rather than a digital one? I was surprised how much I missed that feeling of opening the cover and flipping the pages, then laying it down on the coffee table and seeing its cover so that I could remember the actual name of the book. I cannot tell you how often I forget the title of the book I'm reading. Yes, I realize you can tap the top of the page, and it will appear, but it doesn't feel the same as seeing the cover with its design and the author's name right in front of you. I sighed and moved on.

I walked through that main floor past families with children in tow, young adults leaning up against bookshelves flipping through new titles and groups of teenage girls tittering around the tables laden with candles and throws. I took the wide, curving staircase down to the lower level. When I reached the bottom, I was in the middle of the magazine section. As I looked around, I seemed to remember that it used to be so much larger. There's something just a bit sad, isn't there, about how glossy magazines seemed to be going the way of the do-do bird like so much else. The woman who was the CEO of this particular establishment must have been a visionary when, a few years earlier, she had started putting in homewares and so much giftware, increasing the possibilities for her shoppers as book sales moved online.

It wasn't long before I found myself standing in front of a rack of women's magazines. Considering that most of the magazines still in print seemed to me to be targeted at women, that wasn't too difficult. And there it was: *Good Housekeeping*—still being printed even to this day after a hundred years in the business. I picked up the most recent issue, stared at the colourful, glossy photo of well-curated food, then opened it and started reading through the table of contents.

"How to paint a wall-to-wall headboard." How odd was that? It seemed to me that painting a wall-to-wall headboard amounted to painting a wall. And was painting walls part of housekeeping?

"Your ultimate guide to home office planning." I looked at the photos of home office spaces that clearly had never seen actual office work with their tiny chichi matching pen and paperclip holders and a bulletin board covered with well-placed sayings like "Carpe diem, seize the day" and "Together we do great things" instead of masses of post-it notes which covered the bulletin boards in every real home office I'd ever seen. Although, I did remember once seeing an office print that held definitions. The one

I particularly liked was "Fuckity fuck fuck." But I suppose that wasn't in line with *Good Housekeeping's* editorial policy. I flipped the page.

"How to give your brain a 'spa' day." That one had possibilities. Who knew that modern domestic drudgery included spa anything, although it had never occurred to me that it required much brain power. Perhaps I could learn a thing or two. Moving on.

"Everything you need to know about cookware and kitchen tools." As I leafed through that article, I realized I had no idea there were different kinds of cookware—non-stick, ceramic non-stick, stainless steel, cast iron, copper. Kill me now.

I moved on to the current issue of *Woman's Day*, another one that appeared in Mom's stash from so long ago. The first article I happened upon was "Learn how to cook with coffee." That one made me stop and think for a moment. Was that even a thing?

And since it was near Christmas, there were articles for festive things that had never occurred to me. "Festive DIY décor ideas for every room in your house." Every room in your house? Who decorates every room in their house? There was so much I didn't know about modern women. Of course, then there was an article titled "How to make a holiday cookie cutter wreath in three simple steps." I cannot begin to describe how hideous that was.

Then, there were the recipes. So many recipes.

I turned to a magazine I knew my mother had read in her youth because she had subscribed to it for years, and it had arrived in our mailbox like clockwork month after month. It was and is the doyenne of Canadian women's literature: *Chatelaine* magazine. I happened to know its initial issue had appeared in 1928. How did I know this useless piece of trivia? Because we had interviewed the current editor a few years earlier. It seemed that in addition to domesticity and all that entails, they now prided themselves in "empowering" women. I remembered the editors telling us about their focus on issues like climate change. Did they still do recipes, I had innocently asked. The answer was yes, but the editor added the caveat that it was only a small part of their focus. As I picked up the current issue, I thought, *Let's just see about that.*

"The only holiday cookie you need." "Delicious ways to use leftover bubbly (if you have any!)." "The best red lipsticks for all skin tones." "How to shuck an oyster." "How much red wine is too much red wine?" Climate change, my ass. Geesh, not even *Chatelaine* can convince me that young women don't need a wake-up call. I thought I'd need more than a bit of red wine to get through this one. Was there any hope anywhere?

I thought maybe Oprah would be a bit more high-minded. Nope. Her magazine ("O," in case that one passed you by) was full of makeup, gifts, more makeup, more glowy skin stuff. I put that one back and turned around.

Behind me, in a much smaller section, were magazines aimed at men. Most of them seemed to be about health, fitness, weightlifting, and a few about cars. My eyes landed on a copy of *Esquire*. I flipped to the table of contents.

"It's time to drink champagne like you drink beer." I had no idea what that meant, but it sounded more interesting than making a wreath with cookie cutters. Car of the year. New best restaurants. Best grooming products. Not a single recipe.

I put it back and picked up *GQ*. "29 ways to dress like the life of the party." Of course, this was essentially a fashion magazine, so we can expect that one, and it did have possibilities for Andrew. Then there were lots of articles about watches.

*Men's Health* magazine. "Best whiskey sour recipe." Okay, a recipe in a men's magazine—but for a cocktail. "Seven things that can happen to your penis over time." Hmm. That one sounded intriguing, but on the other hand, I wasn't sure I wanted to know. Did men?

So, in the men's magazines, there wasn't a single recipe in sight (barring ones about drinks). There were no articles waxing poetic about how to clean the dust bunnies from under a bed—no décor tips for creating that sexy atmosphere for the boudoir. And there were certainly no articles about organizing your life around your kids' activities. The other little observation I made was that the more serious magazines, like *Newsweek*, *Time* and *The Walrus*, were shelved among the men's interest magazines. I guess they figured women wouldn't be interested in such high-minded things as current affairs. And if they were, they'd damn well have to search for them. What is wrong with this picture?

The truth struck me. I was right. Women seemed to be falling back into the pit of domesticity that I'd tried my best to avoid. I left Indigo with a pile of up-to-date women's magazines and an idea.

~

Andrew, Maddie, and I ate breakfast together the following morning, an event of great consequence since it had almost never happened. However, I was determined that this sabbatical would find me taking on a new schedule in addition to working on my new project. As I sat at the table with them, I could almost feel myself wanting them to move more quickly so I could get on with my day. I wanted them to go; I had a lot of work to do.

I hadn't yet said a word to anyone about what I had in mind that morning. I needed a lot more ammunition, but I planned to have it before Andrew and Maddie returned at the end of the day. As luck would have it, Monday was the one day of the week that Andrew spent the entire day on campus.

As soon as they were gone, I settled into my office and started my research. Ten hours later, as we sat at the dinner table, I said, "I have an announcement to make." Both Andrew and Maddie looked up from their dinner (which, no thanks to me, consisted of delicious left-over meatloaf that Andrew had made accompanied by garlic mashed potatoes and a salad—again, no thanks to me).

"Shoot," Andrew said. Maddie nodded.

"I'm going to start a blog."

Silence ensued—as they like to say these days, crickets. You could hear a pin drop. Nothing. One might even go so far as to say I read incomprehension on the two faces before me.

"Did either of you hear me? I'm starting a blog. Any comments that might help?"

"One word, honey. Why?" Andrew said when he finally found his tongue.

"Wrong word, Dad. The one word is NO. No, no, no. *Why* doesn't even matter," Maddie added. "No one reads blogs. No one even writes blogs. And I don't need anyone in school to have any more reason to make fun of me because of something my mother's doing. Blogs are for weirdos who need someone to tell them that the earth is flat and stuff like that."

"There you would be wrong, my child," I said, pulling my phone onto the table. "As it happens, 77% of internet users read blogs. And food, lifestyle and travel blogs are the most popular."

Maddie rolled her eyes. "That leaves you out, Mom. You don't have time to travel, you don't have a lifestyle, and you don't cook. Are we over this yet?" Maddie rolled her eyes again before stuffing a large piece of meatloaf into her mouth. She chewed, swallowed, and said, "Blogs are dead, Mom."

I looked at Andrew, who shrugged and nodded toward Maddie. "What she said," he said before taking another bite.

Maddie had put her fork down and folded her hands in her lap. "Okay, Mom. Let's say you did have a blog. You have nothing to write about—or at least nothing anyone wants to read about."

Andrew reached out and patted my hand. "We're not trying to be negative," he said and held up his hand since he could, no doubt, feel a rant coming on from my side of the table. "We really aren't, Erica. It's just that we think your time might be better spent on doing something you might get more reward from."

"Yeah, even my TikTok channel is going nowhere."

The fact that my daughter even had a TikTok channel (whatever that would be from a thirteen-year-old girl) was news to me. I was mildly alarmed. "What exactly is your TikTok channel about?"

"That's just it. It has no direction, so I think I'm going to delete it and stick to Instagram reels. At least I can practice my photography. I think I'm going to branch out from just fashion stuff."

I don't know why, but that sounded so much better to a mother. Instagram over TikTok? Sure, but what did I know? I was just happy she was planning to take down any of her social media forays.

Anyway, I would show them. I would start my blog and use it to prove my point about women today. My idea was simple and clever—perhaps even ingenious. At least, I thought so. I would master domestic drudgery and prove that focusing your life on domesticity isn't a life.

The more I thought about the idea, the more I could feel my inner activist bubbling to the surface. I didn't even know I had one, but when the cause is righteous, it might be the only way to proceed. My plan was simple. I would do my research in women's magazines of yesteryear and compare them with today's versions that, as far as I could see, hadn't come nearly as far as they thought they had. I would then take on the domestic drudgery challenges, master them (because any simpleton can do them) and outmaneuver all those young women proselytizing about the good wife's role—you know, that one where the man's home is his castle, and it's the wife's role to make him feel like a king. Yeah, that one. Take that all you #tradwife people.

And since everyone had to eat, that's where I'd start.

~

Over the next few days, I did my research. I went through Mom's old stash and found that I was right: so much of what the new magazines were still writing about was the same topics the old magazines—most often run by men—fed to women more than six decades ago. At least back then, there was no attempt to dress it up in the guise of empowering women. It was simply how to be a reasonably good homemaker, or even better, an ideal one if you could manage that.

Tucked in among Mom's magazines (that I had, as it happens, planned to recycle in due course), I found a couple of vintage and very dog-eared cookbooks from back in the day. I put those aside.

Food. There would be no better place to begin. I knew I was hopeless in the kitchen, but the thrust of the articles was that any woman could (and should) learn to cook. Up until that moment, I had zero interest in learning anything remotely domestic, but all that was about to change.

One of the cookbooks I saved was called *The I Hate to Cook Book* by a woman named Peg Bracken. Who is or was this woman? She sounded like someone I should know. She could have written it just for me! I wondered why this book, published in 1960, had never had a comeback. I'd make a note to find out and do something about that.

As I began reading, I realized that Peg Bracken did, in fact, like to cook, but only when she felt like it. Her motivation to cook once in a while was something that came from inside her rather than from someone outside telling her that since she was a woman, it was her job. That sentiment resonated with me. In the introduction, Peg says, *"Some women, it is said, like to cook. This book is not for them."* I loved that!

I loved her overall philosophy. For example, one recipe suggested you *"let it cook for five minutes while you light a cigarette and stare sullenly at the sink."* Except for the cigarette, I had experience in the latter—staring sullenly into the sink. In another recipe for something she called the "Hootenholler Whiskey Cake," the first instruction was to *"take the whiskey out of the cupboard and have a small snort for medicinal purposes."* Drinking while cooking was an aspect of the process that had eluded me until now, and I thought it might need to be applied in the twenty-first century.

~

By the time the following Friday rolled around, I was starting to lose my conviction that this blog thing would amount to much. And all this found time? It was already beginning to wear on me. As I stood in front of the kitchen sink at noon, spooning banana yogurt from a tiny plastic cup into my mouth, I realized this was me. This was who I truly was. I was the woman who stood in front of the kitchen sink, mindlessly shovelling in whatever prepared food she found in the refrigerator. I was not the one who planned menus and then executed the preparation flawlessly—or as close to flawless as possible. Who was I kidding? I was the woman who didn't have the interest or the inclination to do anything to make her household better, brighter, more inviting, as all the magazines suggested. I didn't even have the motivation to cook when I had the time. How could I possibly prove to all those young women they were on a retrogressive path?

I rinsed out the plastic cup, tossed it in the recycling bin, and put my spoon in the dishwasher. I'm not a total household slob. Then, I wandered out of the kitchen feeling listless and untethered.

As I rounded the corner from the hallway into the living room, I was startled—I mean really startled—to see someone standing in front of the fireplace. It seemed to be a woman, and she was holding a framed photograph that usually sat on the mantle.

"What the hell?" I said, sounding less frightened than I felt at the prospect of an intruder in my home. But since she was about my height and a few pounds slimmer, I wasn't as frightened as I might have been.

The woman jumped and almost dropped the photograph. She turned abruptly, the picture still in her hand. "Who are you?" she said.

"More to the point," I said, daring to take a step closer, "who are *you*?"

"Why are you in my house?" We both said it simultaneously. What?

She put the photograph back on the mantle and smoothed her skirt. I suddenly noticed her wardrobe and hoped it wasn't a homeless person who had wandered in—although I was sure the door was locked and she looked well, if oddly, dressed. She then smoothed her dark hair—a sort of bouffant hairdo that brushed her jawline with a slight flip-up, reminding me of a 1960 pin-up girl. But her clothes were certainly not pin-up style.

She was wearing an impeccable short-sleeved white blouse with an open collar. Resting on her slim neck were two strands of pearls. Her skirt was something blue and flowy, and it brushed her calves. She was wearing a small watch with a leather strap and kitten-heel pumps. But the most mesmerizing part of her outfit was the apron tied around her waist. It was white with a red flounce and the word "wife" emblazoned on it. I stared at it, wondering where I'd seen it before, and then I realized it was the gag Secret Santa gift I'd received a few Christmases ago at the station. What the hell? Who was this?

"I am so sorry," she said as she sank uninvited into the deep cushions of the sofa. "Of course, this is your house. I only meant…" She sighed as she trailed off, emanating an exhausted vibe.

Despite her innocuous appearance, I wasn't sure I liked the idea of a stranger appearing in my house and now taking up residence in my living room.

"Please," I said as I stood there a few feet away from her, "who are you, and what are you doing in my house?"

The woman sat up straight with her ankles crossed in that very lady-like position. "I am so sorry," she said again. "I'm Elizabeth Crocket, and the rest of it is a long story." She sighed again. "But you can call me Betty. And you are?"

Given my recent infamy, I was a bit surprised she didn't recognize me. But I concluded she wasn't a pop culture aficionado. "I'm Erica Flanagan, and I think you better tell me that long story."

Then I stopped and thought about her name for a moment. Where had I heard it before? Betty Crocket. No, that wasn't right. And why was this woman, who looked like she had just stepped out of a 1950s or '60s advertisement for a household appliance, now in my house?

"To tell you the truth, I'm not exactly sure why I'm here, but I have a feeling I may just be looking for a place to take a bit of a rest," she said. "But it does seem like a long way to go to do that—so maybe there's something else." She looked around the room. "Anyway, I'm here now. It might be best to sit down before I tell you the rest of the story." She gestured to the chair opposite the sofa she was now occupying.

Why I followed this unknown woman's directions, I don't know, but I did as she asked and sat in the chair opposite her.

"If I'm going to be completely transparent, I have to tell you this isn't the first time I've been here," she said. "By which I mean it isn't the first time I've come back, but it is the first time I've been back inside the house." She looked around. "And I must say it is looking well-loved, although some of the décor is puzzling." Her eyes focused on the opposite wall, where there was a large, colourful abstract painting.

I was becoming more and more muddled with every syllable she uttered.

"This is the first time I've ever talked to anyone."

"You're going to have to be much more concrete," I said, "if you don't want me to call the police."

She shrugged. "I think it's safe to say that doing so won't do either of us any good," she said. "I believe you will have a bit of difficulty understanding what I probably need to tell you. But here goes." She took a deep breath. "This is the second time I've needed to escape my life for a short period of time, and this seems to be the only place I can go. I may need to beg your indulgence so I can stay a while."

None of this made any sense to me. "What are you escaping?"

She waved her hand as if to swat away my question. As she did so, I noticed her impeccable red manicure and a flash of a gold bracelet. "Oh, you know. Just things about life. I'm sure you need to escape once in a while. Anyway, I was trying to explain why I'm in this particular house. Your house. You see, Erica, this used to be my house." She looked around. "Of course, it looks very different now from what it looked like when I lived here."

"When was that?"

She thought for a moment. "My husband and I moved in about a year after we were married in 1941."

I tried to process this piece of information while wondering how old she could possibly be. She looked at least a decade younger than me, making it impossible for her to have lived here that long ago. She couldn't have even been born then. Despite the oddity of how she came to be here, I was fascinated. "And when did you move out?" I said, playing along with the absurdity of the situation.

She shrugged. "That's just it," Betty said, "we didn't. At least, not yet."

I could feel a chill run up my arms and neck, making the hairs stand on end.

"I'm sorry, Betty, but you couldn't possibly have lived here in the 1940s. None of this makes any sense." That's when I began to wonder if she had walked away from a psychiatric institute of some kind.

"Hmm. I don't suppose it does." She thought for a moment. "Erica, you strike me as a very logical, rational woman. Am I right?" I nodded, and she continued. "You will find this very difficult to understand, but I believe it's important. I suppose it's a bit like time travel in science fiction, but it's not really that. You may be one of those people who thinks that today is the only time there is. You would be wrong. It's more like multiple timelines that occasionally converge."

I was beginning to think I needed to call someone to take her away.

"Hear me out," she said, twisting the gold bracelet I'd noticed. A single charm hung from it. "As I said, I'm here because I need a break—or at least that's what I thought."

"A break from what?" I was beginning to feel a touch of hysteria under the surface of my calm.

"A break from my domestic life. In 1960. Just once in a while. I promise I won't get in the way."

I started to laugh. "Okay, you're pulling my leg now. This is like the storyline from that novel I read a long time ago. *Our Lady of the Lost and Found.*" Betty looked puzzled. "Where the Virgin Mary appears in a woman's living room with her suitcase, looking for some rest and relaxation as a break from all the adoration? Of course, you've read it."

Betty shook her head. "Sorry, Erica. I don't know that one. I don't have much time to read anymore, although before I was married and had children, reading was like oxygen to me. I used to love it. When was it published? I could look for it in the library."

"About twenty years ago." I have to admit I didn't know a single person who actually borrowed books from a library anymore.

Betty seemed to be calculating. She shook her head. "No, that won't work. It's not been published yet." I was about to protest when she held up her hand. "Erica, I know this is a lot, but trust me, I believe it's what we both need right now. Just let me stay a while."

I got up to retrieve my cell phone from the hall table and returned to the living room. "Look, Betty, I don't know what you're trying to pull here…" but I was talking to the ether. She was gone.

~

By the time Andrew and Maddie got home later that afternoon, I had already downed two glasses of wine, something very out of character for me. But after my encounter (was that what it was?), I was shaking so badly that I needed something to calm me down.

"We've brought Chinese, Erica," Andrew called from the foyer. I could not have been happier.

Andrew walked into the living room and found me sitting on the sofa with my legs pulled up under me, an empty wine glass on the coffee table. "Erica? Have you been drinking?"

I nodded. "Andrew, we need to talk." I looked toward the doorway. I didn't want Maddie to hear any of this. "Something happened today, and I need to discuss it with you. Let's wait until Maddie goes to bed."

Although I was a bit jittery and off my game, I made it through dinner and evening activities. When Maddie finally went to bed, and we were alone, we holed up on the couch, sipping decaf coffee.

"Erica, you're certainly not yourself this evening. What's wrong? What on earth happened today?"

I wasn't sure how to begin. "I was doing some research for my blog," I said.

"So, you're going to pursue that project? You know, Erica, you don't need a project. You could spend your time doing something you haven't had time for in the past. I know you always have to be doing something, but maybe it's time to learn to take it a bit easier. You could take a yoga class or learn to play tennis. You don't need to be constantly in relentless pursuit of something. You've accomplished a lot."

I wasn't sure how to respond. I had not intended to discuss my apparent obsession with work. I shook my head. "Let's not go there right now, Andrew. There's something else I need to talk to you about."

"I'm so sorry, darling. Please tell me." He put his empty mug on the coffee table.

"I think I had a hallucination today."

Andrew just sat there, staring at me.

"Did you hear me?"

"Yes. I'm just trying to process this. Tell me about it."

And, so, I did. When I told him my apparition's name was Betty Crocket, he started laughing.

"Don't laugh. This is serious, Andrew. Stop it."

"Erica, darling, think about it for a moment. Betty Crocket? Seriously? Can't you hear Betty Crocker there? You've been so focused on this bonehead idea about domesticity that your imagination is in high gear."

I rolled my eyes. "Andrew, you're not taking this seriously. It was as if she was really here. We sat here and had a conversation. I'm so confused." Then I told him about her weird explanation of a timeline and that she'd lived in this house before—or maybe still did. I didn't know what to think.

Andrew sat back. "Okay, honey, I hear you. And I might have been on the right track about you needing to take a step back from a relentless focus on work. Let's face it: even your on-air meltdown was just a symptom of your need to step back. This sabbatical is a great idea. But I do think you should talk to someone—someone professional."

That was the last thing I wanted to do.

"You remember Peter Sparrow, don't you?" Andrew said, taking out his phone.

I did remember him. He was an old friend who Andrew used to play golf with back when he played golf. Peter had been a prominent psychiatrist, but I doubted that he was still practicing since he was a decade or older than Andrew—more my mother's age. I did remember how I enjoyed talking to him, though. I found him unconventional in his thinking and an excellent conversationalist.

"He's not still practicing psychiatry, is he?" I said. "Because I don't need a psychiatrist." At least, I hoped I didn't. Although, if anyone else had told me they'd had a conversation with an apparition, I would have suggested that route—and perhaps medication.

"He's retired now but still sees the odd patient just for counselling." He looked down at his phone. "Yes, I have his number. I'll give him a call if you'd like. And I think you should go."

I hadn't seen Peter in some years, but I'd always liked him, and I was still spooked by my afternoon's visitor, so I agreed.

~

Less than a week later, on a Wednesday afternoon, I got into my car and drove the fifteen minutes to where Peter lived and continued to see the occasional patient.

Dr. Peter Sparrow lived in a three-story detached brownstone-type house in an area of the city called Cabbagetown. A black iron gate at the sidewalk opened onto a grey flagstone pathway leading to a porch with another black iron railing. Like most of the houses in Cabbagetown, currently home mainly to the *nouveau* version of Yuppies, the front yard was filled with a plethora of shrubs and deciduous trees that were now devoid of leaves as well as a stand of tall cedars and spruce trees. I figured it must be stunning when everything was in full flower in the summer.

I rang the doorbell and waited. Now I stood shivering in the cold wind because I had left my scarf in the car, which I'd had to park a few blocks over because no one who lived in this area had a driveway, and everyone parked on the street.

I looked around at the red-brick townhouses lining this street and thought about its history. In the 1840s, Cabbagetown had been home to Irish immigrants who had fled the potato famine and landed in Toronto, so poor they had to grow cabbages (and presumably other things) in their front yards. The snotty British, who had arrived years before and were the elite of the city by that time, had derisively named the area Cabbagetown. I wondered how surprised those old snobs would be now to see the gentrification of the streetscape and that to tell someone you lived in Cabbagetown was to tell them you could afford a house upwards of a few million dollars.

I heard footsteps inside and wondered how Peter Sparrow had fared over the years.

The door finally opened to reveal a tiny, grey-haired woman wearing a housedress and an apron. I was startled since I hadn't been aware Peter had remarried—if this was, in fact, Mrs. Sparrow. As far as I recall, Peter's wife had died sometime during their golfing days.

"Mrs. Sparrow?" I said. "I'm Erica Flanagan."

The tiny woman tittered a bit. "Oh, my Ms. Flanagan. I certainly know who you are. I wouldn't miss you on the telly every afternoon," she said, her light British accent becoming more pronounced with every syllable. "I was right miffed with you when you scolded the jolly, pretty young thing back a while. Haven't seen you lately." She smoothed out her apron and stepped back to make space for me to enter. "Oh, and I'm not any Mrs. Sparrow, mind you. The doctor is quite single. I'm Doris, Dr. Sparrow's housekeeper." She led me into the living room. "Just take a seat if you can find one, and I'll be back with himself in a jiffy."

I only had to wonder for a moment why she suggested I could take a seat if I could find one. I looked around what was probably a spacious living room with a large bay window overlooking the front yard. I suspected there was a fireplace over on the far wall, but stacks of boxes entirely obscured it. There were boxes everywhere. I was still looking for a place to sit when Peter appeared at the door.

He was taller than I remembered, now with silvery white hair that shone in the overhead light. Although his hairline was receding, that did nothing to obscure the fact that he was still a handsome man. His most striking feature, his vivid green eyes, belied his age. I was momentarily mesmerized by the unexpected youthful sparkle of his eyes and the smile.

"Erica Flanagan! How long has it been?" Peter walked toward me, his arms outstretched, enveloping me in a brief bear hug. He then stood back and looked. "You still look as radiant as when I first met you. And I understand from what Doris tells me you still have that rebellious streak. I'm sorry to say I missed your on-air shenanigans, but I'm told they were explosive."

"It's lovely to see you again, Peter. Thanks so much for humouring me."

He peered directly into my eyes, and I felt like he could almost see my thoughts. I was both flattered and wary.

Then he looked around. "I do apologize for the mess. I'm about to start a renovation, and this lot is about to get carted off to one of my storage lockers. They say psychiatrists have their own issues, and I may be a bit of a hoarder, but I assure you there are places in this house where we might sit and have tea. I understand from Andrew that you might need an objective ear."

He led me to his bright breakfast room at the back of the narrow house. Doris had laid out tea and what appeared to be authentic English scones accompanied by clotted cream, butter and marmalade. It looked downright mouthwatering. I suddenly felt hungry.

Peter and I sat at the table, and I was more than happy he hadn't asked me to sit on a couch of some sort. This was less like a psychiatrist and a patient than it was two equals having a chat. I started talking.

Peter listened closely to my story, making me feel comfortable to reveal much more to him than I had planned to do. He asked me to start from the beginning, so I told him about my career trajectory from on-the-ground reporter to television personality to persona non grata. He asked just the right questions. Then, I told him about my current project, a part of my story I had not intended to share. Something about those eyes made me feel I needed to unburden myself. Unlike everyone else who knew anything about what I was doing, he seemed intrigued with the project.

"You know, Erica, we don't always take a straight line to our destiny. In fact, it's a lot more fun if we don't. Have you read Emerson?" I had, but only a bit, and I couldn't remember much of it. He continued. "Emerson's view was that the purpose of life is not to be happy but to be useful, honourable and compassionate. But others, like Eleanor Roosevelt, believed the purpose of life is to reach for and experience new things."

I thought about these two different perspectives on the purpose of life—if there even was one. "I've always been more on Emerson's side of the argument," I said. "I guess I've always believed that the purpose of life is to accomplish as much as you can as fast as you can." I thought about my recent change of direction and wondered how that would play out.

Peter sat back and contemplated me for a moment. "You haven't told me why you're really here, have you, Erica?"

"It's just that now that I'm here, it seems a bit embarrassing." I took a deep breath. "Here goes. I think I've had a hallucination of some kind, and I can't figure it out."

Then I told him about my experience finding an apparition in my living room and our ensuing conversation.

"Tell me how you felt when this Betty—whoever or whatever she was—told you she had lived in your house and was a homemaker somewhat like the ones you're trying to eviscerate with your work."

I tried to put myself back at that moment in time. "I thought she was crazy."

"Erica, I didn't ask you what you thought. I asked you how you felt. They are two very different things." Peter then remained silent, permitting me a moment to think.

"I suppose I felt uneasy. How else could I have felt? I mean, there was this person in my house, and I had no idea who she was or how she had gotten in."

"Erica, when you heard her talk about being a 1960 homemaker, how did that make you feel about your project?"

"I suppose, in some ways, it made me think my project might actually be important." I looked at Peter, who continued to listen silently, his face an inscrutable mask. "The truth is now, though, I don't really know how or why it's important. It just feels that way."

"Erica, what do you think is the real reason you want to do this project?"

I was puzzled, and at that moment, I was unsure of the answer. "I suppose I want to add something to my legacy."

"And you don't think any of this has to do with a deeply buried desire to do what those homemakers do?"

"What? No, of course not." I was horrified.

Peter sat back in his chair and thought for a moment. "Erica, you and I used to have interesting conversations at those golf club dinners where everyone else just talked about their golf score." I did remember. He continued. "I always knew there was more to you than the goal-driven, rebellious young woman who wanted to change the world through her journalistic skills. So, I'm going to tell you an important truth. The easiest person to fool is yourself."

I was trying to process that thought without getting my back up when Peter continued. "I'll share with you something Goethe said. *Most people spend the greatest part of their time working in order to live, and what little freedom remains so fills them with fear that they seek out any and every means to be rid of it.* You are now free, Erica. Will you fear that freedom?"

I had no idea.

When I left Peter's house, I knew I'd take him up on his offer to come by regularly to tell him how the project was progressing.

When I walked back into the house after our conversation, I threw my keys onto the hall table and walked into the living room. I sat on the sofa where "Betty" had sat and looked at the painting she'd noticed. I had to admit its stark modernity didn't fit with the house's traditional architectural elements like the coffered ceilings and intricate wrought iron around the fireplace. Then I saw something shiny on the floor.

I bent down and picked it up. It was a gold chain—a bracelet—with a single charm. As I dropped it into my palm, I noticed the charm was a tiny gold spatula. I picked up the spatula and held it between my fingers. *A golden household implement*, I thought. A shiver coursed down my spine, and the air around me seemed to grow unnaturally cold. My hand shook as I looked down at the bracelet and remembered seeing it on Betty's wrist. This couldn't be happening.

# 5

# You're Gonna Love This Recipe...or Gag Trying

*I don't think any day is worth living without thinking about what you're going to eat next at all times.* ~ Nora Ephron

MY MIND WAS RACING AS I LOOKED DOWN at the little puddle of gold in my hand. It was impossible that my "visitor" could have left it here since she had been a figment of my imagination, but I couldn't explain what I was looking at, so I decided to ignore it.

I put the bracelet in my desk drawer and closed it firmly, hoping it wouldn't be there when I looked again. I then tried to put it out of my mind. The following day, I sat in my home office surrounded by the boxes full of Mom's old magazines and books and wondered what I would do with them. The spectre of the 1960s housewife was haunting me, and I couldn't seem to shake it. I mean, who in their right mind sees apparitions of 1960s housewives in their living rooms? Who has conversations with hallucinations? Was I losing my grip?

I picked up a copy of *Good Housekeeping*. Among all the pristine old magazines in my mother's stash, this one was different. It was a dog-eared copy of the August 1960 issue—as if it might have been read over and over. I wondered what was in it.

On the cover was the headshot of a beautiful young girl, perhaps about fourteen years old, her long hair held back off her face with a black velvet headband. Her innocent smile played perfectly with her white collar and cuffs, and I wondered what lurked behind that chaste smile, all so reminiscent of a pious

71

convent girl. The cover stories were the usual: diet, family dilemmas and salad recipes. I flipped through the pages listlessly, unsure why I was looking inside. I would have to take the whole lot of these to the recycling depot this week. Then, my flipping stopped suddenly when I reached a dog-eared page.

The article on the page was called "I Say Women Are People, Too." The author was Betty Friedan, none other than the mother of modern feminism—three whole years before she wrote her manifesto. And it was in *Good Housekeeping* magazine, no less. My mother, an early feminist, if ever there was one, must have stumbled upon this in the years before she was married since she and my father weren't married until 1965. It was difficult to imagine, but she must have been reading these magazines when she was in grad school. I cannot even comprehend the dissonance in the mind of a young 1950s woman reading magazines about domestic drudgery alongside the research papers for her doctoral dissertation. I looked over at the corner of my desk where I'd piled up the books I would keep from Mom's stash. The original 1963 copy of Betty Friedan's book *The Feminine Mystique* was on the top. I looked back at the magazine article and started reading.

When I came to the following passage, I stopped. *"The image of woman that emerges from this big, pretty magazine is young and frivolous, almost childlike; fluffy and feminine; passive; gaily content in a world of bedroom and kitchen, sex, babies, and home…where is the world of thought and ideas, the life of the mind and spirit? In the magazine image, women do no work except housework and work to keep their bodies beautiful and to get and keep a man…"*

I closed the magazine and sat back, shivering. The image of Betty Crocket appeared in my mind's eye, and I wondered about what she represented. Indeed, that housewife thing was going on, but there seemed more to it than that. At the same time, I was still stuck on what I would do with myself and my sabbatical. It was becoming increasingly clear that if I didn't soon figure that out, I might well lose my mind.

I was still brooding about the blog idea, but what it would be about (other than my desire to skewer twenty-first-century domestic drudgery and the young women who thought it was their destiny) was still a bit foggy. There had to be more substance to it, or I'd soon run out of things to write about after the first rant. But life went on.

It was now only a few weeks before Christmas, and I still had some shopping to do. Christmas dinner had been planned months ago when I placed my order at Pusateri's, one of those high-end gourmet markets that are so ubiquitous in certain areas of big cities. So, there was little to do on that front.

Later that week, when I finally had a handle on the Christmas shopping, I was sitting in my office, pondering life, when my phone dinged. It was a text from my mother.

**Just on my way home from the airport. Wonderful cruise, BTW.** (Mom always wanted you to know she was hip to the texting jargon—does anyone say "hip to" anymore?). **Not going to be able to bring anything on Christmas Eve. Kitchen all packed. See you then. LOL.** Was she giving me lots of love or laughing out loud? I could never be sure.

*Oh god*, I thought. *Christmas Eve.* I'd completely forgotten about it. Every year for the past dozen or so years, Andrew, Maddie and I had hosted a small Christmas Eve gathering. Mom would be there, of course. We would be joined by Sam and her husband, and two children (did I mention that Sam was one of those superwomen with a job, a part-time grad school gig, a husband and two children, and she did all her own cooking?), as well as my friend Evelyn, a lawyer, her husband and her two children. Matt and Marcus also came when they weren't away on a Christmas cruise, which they were not this year, so we could expect lots of merriment and a Christmas sing-along with Marcus at the piano. Those two loved nothing better than a party. And they always brought extravagant gifts for all the kids. Then there was the food.

I usually ordered platters of hors d'oeuvres and mains from another nearby gourmet grocery store where the eyewateringly high prices were exceeded only by the scrumptiousness of their offerings. I counted on Mom and Sam to bring desserts. Evelyn was a bit like me—hopeless in the kitchen—so she brought wine and lots of it. The one major problem, though, was that I had planned to place the order the minute I heard from Matt that they'd be coming, but with so many things on my mind, it completely slipped my mind. Not only were we at half capacity for desserts because of Mom's pending move, but we were at zero for anything else.

I went into my office and fired up my computer. I opened a spreadsheet and started making a plan for the event. There wasn't much time. I sat back and looked blankly at the computer screen. I opened my drawer to find a notepad and a pen and noticed the gold charm bracelet. *Damn*, I thought, *it's still there.*

I lifted it from the drawer and stared at the tiny spatula. *I wonder*, I thought, an idea forming in my head. *Maybe this is a sign. Maybe I do need to do that blog. Maybe I could do the food. Maybe doing food for a Christmas Eve group could be my first blog adventure.* Food was, after all, the first thing I'd thought about when the idea of the project had begun to gel. The spatula had to be a sign, didn't it? I closed the drawer.

I looked at the pile of current magazines I'd bought at Indigo and pulled the top one over in front of me.

Since it was a December issue, there were plenty of articles about how to host the perfect festive event and recipes for what to serve. Of course, there were. What could be more domestic than hosting a festive event and being responsible for the food? Perhaps I'd always been a bit domestic (minus the cooking, cleaning and decorating). After all, I'd been a good hostess over the years. That had to count for something, didn't it?

All that aside, my imagination was on fire. There would be a blog, and it would start now. I clicked over to the only blog platform I knew about and opened an account. I was mesmerized by the array of options for layout. Realizing that I had lots to accomplish, I opted for the simplest one they had and created a header. But what would I call the blog?

I sat back, tapping my pen on the notebook on the desk in front of me while I stared at the blank page of the blog. Several thoughts flitted through my mind, and I wrote each one down so I could see how they looked.

"Down the Domestic Rabbit Hole." Not bad, but I thought I could do better.

"Erica's Good Housekeeping." More personalized, but not catchy enough.

"Adventures in Domestic Drudgery." Almost there, I thought, typing this one into the header on the blank page to see how it looked. *Hmm*, I thought, *that's not quite it*. Then I had it. I started typing furiously.

~

## *ERICA DOES DOMESTICITY*

*Hi all. Erica here. Erica Flanagan? Remember me? I'm the one who made that girl cry on television. I'm the one you loved to hate. I'm the one who told the world that "From Good to Better to Best: Becoming the Wife You Always Dreamed of Being" was a piece of lunacy possibly concocted by insecure men who find it easier to deal with women when they're barefoot and occasionally pregnant. Because, let's be honest, no one dreams of being a domestic drudge. I didn't. You didn't. Okay, then, here's what I'm going to do. Stay with me, and I'll take you on my adventures into domestic drudgery. Come along with me, and at the end, we can compare notes. Up first? Baking for a family event!*

~

I spent the next two days planning what I'd bake. I scoured online recipe books, but they just made me crazy with all their pop-up ads and stories about how to do this and that. Just give me a recipe. I can figure it out myself.

I finally decided my first recipe would be a Christmas cherry cake. I managed to wade through enough ads on one recipe site to find an appropriate recipe. The pictures were lovely, and I seemed to remember the taste of cherry cake from my childhood when my grandmother Nora, who hailed from Newfoundland (and still lived there—she was pushing a hundred), would make a similar cake filled with cherries and wafting the homely aroma of almonds, filling the house with that Christmas smell. She never failed to take over Mom's kitchen when she arrived for the festive season, as she did every second year until turning ninety years old and deciding she'd had enough flying to last her a lifetime. I considered calling her to ask for some tips on making the cake, but I knew her well enough to know that she would laugh uncontrollably at the idea that her granddaughter, Erica, had visions of making a cake. And that wouldn't bode well for her precarious continence. Nora was still mentally as sharp as a tack, but there were parts of her that were showing—or leaking, as the case may be—her age. So, I passed on that idea.

I made a list and went shopping for the ingredients. Before I ventured to the supermarket, though, I took out the ingredient list to make a list. There was one ingredient that I couldn't remember ever seeing before, although I may have heard of it. It was something called evaporated milk. Did such a thing really exist? I put it on the list and headed out to the supermarket.

I had my head buried in one of the massive refrigerators, searching for this elusive ingredient, when an employee, a young man, came along and asked me if everything was okay. By this time, the glass door was completely fogged. When I told him I was looking for the evaporated milk, it was all he could do to stifle the laughter I could see bubbling just below the surface as he said, "You know it comes in a can, don't you, ma'am?" I did not. Since when did anything with "milk" in the title come in a can? When I mentioned this to Sam sometime later, she said, "Coconut milk?" I didn't know that either.

Once I had everything on the list, on Saturday, a week before Christmas, I assembled everything I thought I'd need—pots, pans, bowls, spoons and spatulas. When I retrieved the spatula from the drawer, I felt a shiver as I remembered the gold charm.

Once I had everything out of the cupboards and the instruction book for our Mix-Master (which I had never found any reason to use before) queued up on my iPad, I started taking photos for my blog. What was a blog without pictures?

"Good lord, Erica. What are you doing?" Andrew wandered into the kitchen.

"I thought you and Maddie had a Christmas shopping date this afternoon," I said, noticing he didn't seem to be ready to leave. I wanted them out of the house for my inaugural domestic adventure. Every year, the two of them went to the mall together, ostensibly to find something for me for Christmas, but I think they just liked the father-daughter bonding thing. I had wondered if Maddie might not think she was getting too old for this, but she had still seemed keen when I asked her about it at breakfast.

"Oh, we're going soon," Andrew said, peering at the baking implements, the plastic box of candied cherries and the Mix-Master. "Are you sure you should be doing this, Erica? Do you really think we should be leaving you alone?"

I made a face at him. When I finally told my little family that I planned on a minor foray into domesticity, Andrew had been (not unexpectedly) skeptical. He and Maddie had both cautioned me against any further consideration of blogging (I neglected to mention that this might be a tad too late) and had wished me well. I hadn't explicitly mentioned baking.

"OMG, Mom," Maddie said dramatically as she swept into the kitchen. "What. Are. You. Doing?" She immediately whipped her phone out of her pocket and started filming just as I began to speak.

"Stop that right now, Madelaine! I do not want to be immortalized on your phone. And do not get any smart ideas about sending videos to your friends."

"Oh, Mom. Why would my friends want to see this? It's just going to be for us. I mean, it really should go down in family history, don't you think? After all, it might never happen again."

As she smiled, her eyes sparkled. "Come on, Dad. We have shopping to do!"

Once they were gone, I donned my apron—I found the old gift Andrew had reminded me about and realized it was what I'd pictured on my Betty Crocket person. Before I began, I went to my office and lifted the little bracelet from my desk drawer, depositing it in my apron pocket. At least it might be a good luck talisman. Then I returned to the kitchen and sat for a few moments (maybe more than a few), reviewing the recipe I'd wrestled off that internet site while sipping a glass of wine. I figured it was the only way to get this done. I smiled and started humming.

The humming lasted only a few minutes until I started following the instructions about chopping the glacée cherries. Before I had half a dozen chopped, everything was sticking together. The cherry pieces were stuck to the knife, to each other and to me. My hands were so sticky I thought the knife was glued to me for posterity. I was almost in tears by the time I had them all chopped. Maybe this hadn't been such a good idea.

I put those aside and moved on to the Mix-Master to cream the butter and sugar together. Before I could begin that step, though, there was much to be learned. The instructions for the machine seemed to have been written by someone whose grasp of the English language was less than impressive. It took me half an hour to figure out how to use the damn machine. Then it wasn't long before I realized I probably should have waited until the butter was softer before trying to get it to mix in with the sugar. I just turned the contraption up—full speed ahead and damn the torpedoes. And if flying bits of butter were torpedoes—well, you get the picture. Then, I added the eggs, one at a time, as the recipe suggested. I turned on the machine again.

Before I knew what was happening, splotches of eggs were all over the walls. Then, when it came time to add the flour, I had no idea what it meant to fold something into another thing, so I just put some of the flour in the bowl and turned on the machine again. That was the precise moment when Maddie and Andrew, who had clearly returned from their mall adventure, walked back into the kitchen. It had taken me the entire afternoon to get to this point. Maddie whipped out her phone as quickly as she could, and the hilarity began. I glared at them.

"Dear god!" Andrew said, looking around. "What happened?"

I couldn't give up now, so I plastered a smile on my face and said, "Just a little problem with the Mix-Master. Nothing to worry about. No need to be concerned. I'll let you know when I'm finished." I shooed them out of the room and turned to Maddie. "And put that away!"

I had finally looked up what it meant to fold one ingredient into other ingredients so I could finally get the cherries in. I then wrestled the batter into the pan and the pan into the oven. I was sitting at the breakfast counter in the middle of the mess, covered in flour, watching the cake rise (sort of) and sipping on a second glass of wine when I felt like I was being watched. I turned abruptly, expecting to see Maddie with her phone out again. It wasn't Maddie.

"Need some help?"

I was startled yet again to see Betty Crocket leaning against the kitchen door frame, this time wearing a light pink pullover sweater and a pencil skirt, again with an apron (a different one) tied around her waist and the double strand of pearls lying on the neckline of her sweater.

"Please don't take this the wrong way, Erica, but it seems you might need a bit of baking guidance." She sighed and walked toward the counter, her hands behind her back and bent down to peer into the oven. "This is a fancy one. Does it have a light inside?"

I got up from the table and pecked at the spot on the front of the oven that said, "oven light." I supposed that was it. I was right. The interior of the oven came immediately to light.

"Ooh," we both said simultaneously.

The cake looked like a pack of mad dogs had attacked it. The top had risen (a good thing, I'm told), but it was lumpy and odd-looking. It did look like someone, or something, had already taken a bite out of it. I was sure this one wasn't one for the party crowd.

"How much longer is it supposed to bake?" Betty said, standing back and crossing her arms as she continued to gaze at the mess in the oven.

I checked the timer. "Five minutes, I think."

"Okay, I'll wait." Betty then sat at the counter on the stool adjacent to mine and looked around. "This is quite a mess, Erica. But I don't suppose you're any stranger to cleaning up a mess, are you?" She looked at me knowingly, her blue eyes seeming to penetrate my tough exterior. At least, I thought I was projecting a tough exterior.

"How do you know anything about me?" I said defensively, thinking of all the messes I had gotten myself into and out of throughout my life.

"Oh, you'd be surprised at what I know about you," Betty said, turning her attention to the cake in the oven. "I think it might be ready to come out."

I got up, picked up the oven mitts I'd been smart enough to have at the ready, and took that sucker out of the oven, almost dropping it onto the wire rack Betty had just put on the counter. How did she even know where to find one?

"Let's let it cool for a few moments," she said, sitting back down. "Now, what were we saying? Oh, yes, we were about to discuss what I know about you."

I sighed and sat back down. If I was going to have a conversation with my ghostly hallucination, I might as well try to get something out of it.

"Forgive me for prying, but I glanced at some papers you had left on that desk in that tiny office. I'm not very familiar with computer things—for obvious reasons," Betty said, clutching her pearls gently, "but they looked like pages that might have been printed from something on that screen."

After my initial horror at the thought of someone creeping into my office uninvited, I realized how silly that was since I was talking to a hallucination (wasn't I?). I remembered I'd printed off some of the news stories that had haunted me for a few weeks after last month's on-air debacle.

"The pages I read said you are a famous television personality. Impressive," Betty said. "One of them also said you are a famous bitch." Betty smiled. "I don't get to say that very often. I must say you don't seem very bitchy to me under the current circumstances." She waved her hands around the kitchen, pointing out the obvious. "Anyway, it seems you have some kind of disdain for those of us who spend our lives on domestic activities. That seems to have gotten you into a lot of trouble."

I started to interrupt her, but she held up her well-manicured hand, and I stopped. She looked around, taking in the mess and the seriously messed-up cake on the wire rack. "I also recognize that baking isn't something you know a lot about, but, for some reason I have yet to figure out, it seems important to you that you learn how to do it. How am I doing?"

I sighed again and wiped a bit of flour off my hands with a flour-drenched towel, to no avail. "I suppose that about sums it up."

"I have no idea how I'm supposed to get a rest from my homemaking activities by being here with you, but there you have it." Betty got up and expertly removed the cake from its tube pan using a second wire rack.

*What a great idea*, I thought. *Why didn't I think of that?*

She then proceeded to take a knife from the magnetic knife rack and jumped when it came loose. "What a wonderful gimmick that is! I must see if I can get one of those for my kitchen."

"You're not going to cut it, are you?" I said in a panic. "I wanted to be able to show it off intact." I suppose I still had hopes of salvaging it for company rather than admitting defeat.

Betty looked at me, raised her eyebrows and proceeded to cut it in half. "Erica, you are not going to serve this to your family or anyone else you know and love." It wasn't a question or even a statement. It was a command.

I looked at the sad sight before me. After initially rising, the cake had fallen in the middle, and all the cherries had dropped to the bottom. I remembered my grandmother's cherry cake having cherries all through it.

"You didn't rinse the cherries, did you?" Betty said. "And you didn't toss them in flour, either." I nodded again. There was a lot more to this baking thing than met the eye.

"Well, not all is lost," she said. "Let's get this cleaned up first." She looked around the kitchen. "You don't happen to have a cake mix, do you?"

We certainly did. Our part-time housekeeper, Alice, was the queen of the cake mix cake. Angel food, Devil's food, white. She made them all right out of the box. I went to the pantry, and Betty followed me. We found a box of cake mix, a can of pineapple rings and a bag of dried coconut.

I held the box up in front of me, the "Betty Crocker" brand label clearly visible.

"Don't get me started," Betty said, reaching for the box. "I was Betty long before I was a Crocket." Then she giggled. "It is a bit funny, though, don't you think?"

Before I knew what was happening, Betty and I had the kitchen cleaned up, and she was expertly mixing the cake, instructing me how to line the bottom of a cake pan with precisely placed pineapple rings and helping me to sprinkle them with coconut, brown sugar and melted butter. We whipped it into the oven, and when it came out, she turned it upside down, and it was the most beautiful thing I'd ever seen. I was almost in tears.

Betty smiled. "You did it, Erica."

"*We* did it, Betty." God, I was now referring to my hallucination by name.

"You know, Erica, I'm not sure how helping you make a cake gives me a break from my housewifely duties, but I do know this. *Anyone who has never made a mistake has never tried anything new.* Of course, Albert Einstein said it first."

"*The more you learn, the more you realize how much you don't know,*" I said. "Also, Albert Einstein."

"Who are you talking to, Mom? Maddie said as she rounded the corner and came into the kitchen.

I felt a moment of panic. What would I say about Betty's presence?

"Oh, and what's that smell? Its…" Maddie trailed off as she noticed the coconut pineapple upside-down cake on the counter. "OMG. Can we have that for dessert tonight?"

Before I could answer, I remembered that I'd have to do some explaining about Betty. I turned toward where she'd been standing beside the oven, but she was gone. Vanished, just like any good hallucination.

I turned to Maddie. "Yes, darling daughter. We can have it for dessert tonight." I figured if they liked it, I might be able to make one for the Christmas Eve crowd.

Once again, she whipped out her phone and did a few video clips before dancing out of the room. Her mother had baked!

The pendant lights above the breakfast counter caught on something shiny. I picked it up. It was the bracelet that I'd put in my apron pocket. *How in the world did it get here*? I wondered. It was the same bracelet—I was sure of it—but now it had two charms. The spatula was still there, but next to it was what appeared to be a tiny gold feather duster. I slid it back into my pocket.

6

# Eating off the Floor? How to Make Your House Gleam (or at Least Glimmer a Bit)

*My theory on housework is, if the item doesn't
multiply, smell, catch fire, or block the refrigerator
door, let it be. No one else cares. Why should you?*
~ Erma Bombeck

"ERICA DARLING, YOU'VE OUTDONE YOURSELF!" Andrew said later that evening at dinner as he asked for a second piece of cake, something that was unheard of in our household.

"Yeah, Mom, we didn't think you could do it," Maddie said as she scooped the last morsel from her dessert plate.

I wasn't sure how to feel about this. On the one hand, I was flattered and frankly delighted. On the other hand, I was slightly insulted that my family didn't seem to have any faith in my abilities. Secretly, I had started to believe them. And why did I feel so guilty? Because "Betty" had helped?

"There was such a mess in the kitchen earlier, we thought you'd had some kind of a baking catastrophe, but I have to admit, you really pulled this one off. Have you had enough domesticity now?" Andrew stared me down.

I had wondered the same thing myself. Had I finished this thing? Of course not. In fact, I'd barely begun, and, after all, I had my blog followers to think about. The fact that I didn't yet have any readers didn't faze me in the least. *If I build it, they will come, or something like that,* I thought. Tomorrow, I would start writing about my baking success. I was almost sure of this.

Just as I had hoped, the cake was such a hit with Andrew and Maddie that I made another upside-down cake the next week so I could serve it for dessert on Christmas Eve—and this time, I did it all by myself. I was determined to impress my guests with my newly acknowledged abilities, proving that I wasn't domestically challenged, and if I wasn't domestically challenged, then no one was. Being a housewife was an illusion—not a real thing if anyone could do it. With all the preparation for the Christmas festivities, I hardly had a moment to consider that I'd had another hallucination. But then there was the matter of the cake and the bracelet. There was no acceptable explanation for either—yet. But that would have to wait.

~

Christmas Eve was finally upon us. As one festive song or another said, the Christmas rush was through. *Sure*, I thought, *all except for the six presents I still have in my closet for Andrew and Maddie that I haven't wrapped yet. Oh, well. I can do that after everyone has left.* At six-thirty that evening, as our first guests, Sam and her family, arrived, I had no idea I would not be getting to that much before two am.

I was proud of myself as I thought about taking the cake I'd made out of the refrigerator and placing it in the middle of the dessert table in due course. However, the less said about my attempt at puff pastry canapes, the better. As a result, I made a late, in-person visit to our local gourmet grocery and begged the manager to fill our usual order. After giving me chapter and verse on how this was too much to expect, he relented, and the trays of food had arrived at five-thirty just as my mother had walked up the front steps.

"Cutting it a bit close, aren't you, Erica?" Mom said, taking off her coat as Andrew helped the delivery person take the trays into the kitchen.

What could I say? When Mom was right, she was right. I didn't care. At least the food had arrived before the guests.

By seven pm, the party was in full swing. As expected, Matt and Marcus arrived with armloads of presents for the kids and bottles of various liquors and mixes, which Marcus immediately took into the family room, where Andrew was set up to mix a few drinks and pour champagne. Another thing I loved about Matt and Marcus on Christmas Eve, apart from the ugly Christmas sweaters that they took so seriously, was that they always came with a special drink recipe.

Once I had checked on the buffet set-up and was assured we had enough clean plates and silverware, I wandered into the family room where Andrew and Marcus were standing behind the bar with an array of bottles and glasses in front of them. Everyone was gathered around, including the kids, while Marcus explained the featured drink of the night.

"It's called a Santa Clausmopolitan," Marcus said as he poured vodka into a cocktail shaker that I could see was filled with ice.

As he did this, Andrew was busy running limes around the rims of the martini glasses that were lined up like Christmas soldiers in straight rows. As Andrew finished each glass, Maddie dipped the rims in sugar. Then Marcus added cranberry juice to the shaker with the vodka and poured a copious amount into another shaker to which he had not added vodka. As usual, Marcus wasn't leaving the kids out of his masterpiece. He then poured some triple sec into the adult version and lime juice into both. He then passed the shaker for the kids to Ethan, Sam's son, who shook that sucker like he'd done it a million times before. He reminded me of that scene in the movie *Cocktail* when Tom Cruise goes to town with his shaker. I wondered where Ethan had learned that.

After Marcus and Andrew poured drinks, it was time for Christmas carols at the piano. Marcus took his drink and sat at our baby grand, and suddenly, the house was filled with music and laughter.

He usually stuck to carols to which everyone knew the words, and even the most self-conscious teenagers—Maddie and Ethan, to be specific—reverted to their younger selves and belted them out with the rest of us. No one cared if we were off-key. Then, when Marcus started to play (and sing) "Grandma Got Run Over by a Reindeer," everyone practically rolled on the floor laughing. It was Mom's cue to sing. It never ceased to amaze me that this seemingly prim, sensible, accomplished woman wasn't afraid to show her silly side once in a while. Throughout the years, Mom and I always seemed to have our differences, but every Christmas, I remembered why I loved her so much.

An hour later, we all gathered in the dining room for dinner. Despite having a large dining room table, it could accommodate only ten people for a sit-down meal. That meant we had to have a buffet and sit in the family room or kitchen, which was really one enormous room, balancing plates on our laps. As soon as everyone had gone through the buffet and found a place to perch, Mom would always say, "Well, isn't this a savage mug-up," in her best Newfoundland accent, mimicking my grandmother, Nora, who hated nothing more than she hated eating with a plate on her lap. Scratch that. She hated eating off a paper plate even more, but she wouldn't have had to worry about that in our house.

"By the way, Mom," I said, "how is Nora?"

Mom gazed heavenward and said, "Still with us and still talking. I've not heard about any reindeer accidents yet this year." I stifled a splutter that threatened to become wild laughter. Mom put her fork down and looked at me. "And before you ask me why I'm not visiting her over Christmas, it's because she told me not to. It seems she's too busy in that retirement facility." My grandmother Nora, who, as I mentioned almost a hundred years old, still had very much a mind of her own. We'd all get on a telephone call with her after dinner tomorrow, but the less time spent dwelling on that, the better. Nora wasn't an easy woman. It was Christmas Eve—we could think about her tomorrow.

Once we had finished our main course, Maddie helped me to set out the desserts. I had an array of fancy Christmas cakes and squares from the gourmet shop and warm madeleines that Maddie said she'd take out of the oven. I placed my upside-down cake in the middle of the table on a footed cake plate I'd borrowed from my mother. I'd never needed one before, but now I was thinking I should have put that on my Amazon wishlist. But to tell you the truth, Andrew probably would have ignored it, thinking I'd made a mistake putting it there.

As everyone crowded around to make their dessert selections, Sam nudged me. "You didn't make that one, did you, Ricky?" she said, pointing to my upside-down cake. I was shocked at how proud I felt as I told her that, yes, indeed. I had made that one. "I'm having a piece of that," she said, elbowing her way past Marcus and Matt, who were admiring the Yule log delivered by the gourmet shop.

The shop's pastry chefs had outdone themselves this year. The log was iced to perfection. If you didn't look closely, you'd think we'd put an actual log on a bed of fluffy white icing resembling snow. Pieces of holly with bright red berries were tucked under the log. On the top of the log were mushrooms—made from marzipan. And I knew from experience that when we bit into that log, we wouldn't be tasting a log. We'd be luxuriating in dense chocolate cake rolled around chocolate whipped cream. Calories be damned! I was having my annual slice.

After dinner, the kids left for the basement entertainment room. It wasn't huge, but when we did the renovation, we had turned half the basement into a laundry room and storage area and the other half into a home theatre of sorts. Maddie had Christmas movies cued up for all of them, and I knew the popcorn machine (Andrew was a popcorn addict and had to have it when he watched a movie) was ready to roll.

We adults retired to the living room where Andrew and Marcus had laid out trays of *digestifs*. This year's array consisted of limoncello that Matt and Marcus had brought home from a trip to Italy they'd taken in September, Grand Marnier that I happened to know had been in our liquor cabinet for at least five years (it was still good, wasn't it?), and pisco. This last offering was something I'd drunk only in a mixed drink—a Pisco Sour—years before when I was in Chile on assignment. According to Marcus, it was really a type of brandy and should be taken neat. I was willing to try despite the copious amount of wine I'd already imbibed.

Marcus had also brought along some biscotti, which he had placed on a plate in the middle of the coffee table. It was a nice touch, but I don't think anyone could eat another bite. I was still basking in the admiration showered on me for my domestic accomplishment. I wondered if it might not have been a bit overblown. It was, after all, just a cake—I hadn't achieved world peace.

The conversation on Christmas Eve usually centred around the past year. We'd been catching up on everyone's work, trips, and kids (if any) when finally, Matt said, "Any news of fall-out from last month's on-air incident?"

Everyone stared at me expectantly. I was momentarily irritated that Matt had brought up the subject, but then I remembered that I was among friends. If anyone could understand my position, it had to be this group. "I've heard nothing," I said, sipping the surprisingly tasty pisco.

"Well, then," Matt said, raising his glass, "let's drink to Erica's wide-open future!"

We all drank to my wide-open future, and I was left thinking, yes, my future might well be wide open. I only hoped that wasn't going to be a problem for me.

It was just after midnight when everyone was finally gone. As usual, Matt and Marcus were the last to leave, and as usual, they were insisting that they would stay to help us clean up. Andrew and I were just as insistent that we had a system and would get it done in a flash. So, they said good night and Merry Christmas, and Maddie blearily made her way to bed, leaving her parents alone to tackle the mess.

"Drink?" Andrew said.

"Why not," I said. And so, it was two am before I had a moment to finish wrapping Christmas presents. I suppose this is what Christmas domesticity is like—if you squint a bit!

~

The success of the upside-down cakes had spurred me onto another session in the kitchen. This time, I asked Maddie if she'd like to help, and she seemed more than happy to get her hands dirty. I had never noticed that she was so interested in cooking and baking, although I'd seen her in the kitchen with Andrew or Alice a few times over the past few years.

The day before New Year's Eve, Maddie and I combed through Mom's old magazines that I hadn't managed to put out with the recycling yet. Maddie found a recipe for Swedish meatballs that had been popular in the 1960s, researched it online to bring it up to date, and together, we cooked it.

As we stood over the Swedish meatballs simmering on the stove the day before New Year's Eve, she confided in me that she'd always been interested in cooking but that she'd gotten the impression from me that successful women didn't spend their time wasting away in kitchens. They were out in the world doing important things, and Maddie certainly intended to do important things. When she said this, I was momentarily speechless. I had taught her that? Of course, I had. As we worked together side-by-side in the kitchen, though, I began to wonder if I should have.

When we were finished, Maddie and I divided the meatballs into containers—one for us and one for Mom. I had asked Mom to spend New Year's Eve with us, but she said she preferred to see in a new year alone. So, the following morning, New Year's Eve, Maddie and I went over for lunch. We took along the meatballs that would be my New Year's surprise for my mother, who, despite the success of the Christmas Eve cake, remained skeptical about my project.

As we sat together in her tiny but beautiful dining room, Mom spooned Swedish meatballs onto her plate. "I remember making these when your father and I were first married in the 1960s. I don't know why I ever stopped making them. I loved them, and so did he." Mom took a bite, then another and another.

"Perhaps there is hope for you after all," Mom said, smiling as she reached for a second helping.

I smiled and couldn't think of a single comeback at that moment. I wondered where Betty was.

Betty. That made me wonder what I was going to do about my apparition. Being the logical journalist I'd been trained to be, I had a plan. My first stop would be the city archives. I planned to find out if there had ever been anyone named Crocket who had lived in this house. I know what you're thinking. You're thinking I was really losing it if I even considered the possibility that anyone named Elizabeth Crocket had ever really lived in my house. But I was desperate. Stay with me here.

~

By the end of the first week in January, I had expected to hear about any legal issues that might result from my momentary lapse on air. It was getting close to two months after the fact, and I had heard nothing. I was beginning to wonder if Laura-Lee and company had given it up. I didn't dare call Trevor in case I upset the balance of the universe.

Once Maddie was back to school and Andrew had embarked on his new semester, I trekked to the city archives to see if there was any mention of a Crocket family who might have lived in our century-old house in the area of the city called The Annex.

Once I had found myself a worktable and a friendly archivist to point me in the right direction, I started my research by figuring out a bit about the area where I lived. I wondered why I'd never had an interest in this before. Is it the case that people generally don't care about the history of where they live? Do we never think about who might have lived in our old houses before us? What their lives were like? Why they had ultimately left? I suppose, like me, they simply had other things to occupy them. I now had the time.

I first learned that the area where I lived was called the Annex because when the city of Toronto, as it existed in the middle of the nineteenth century, was looking for land to the north to expand, this was the first parcel of land to be annexed. That struck me funny since where we lived was now almost at the heart of the city. Most of the houses were built between 1890 and 1910. When Andrew and I bought our red-brick two-story twenty years earlier, our realtor told us it was built in 1908, making it well over a century old now.

Like many houses in the neighbourhood, ours was British Queen Anne Style, which had a resurgence in the late nineteenth century. And like many houses with that design, it had a steep roof, several large dormers and an asymmetrical front façade. We also had a large front porch. The house had a round corner tower with a conical roof. Andrew and I had fallen in love with it at first sight despite its crumbling interior. A total renovation later, and we had lived happily in our neighbourhood ever since. But all this interesting research wasn't getting me any closer to knowing who had lived in it.

I consulted with the archivist again and discovered that some fascinating people had lived in the neighbourhood, if not in the house. Chief among them was Timothy Eaton, a scion of Canadian business and founder of the Eaton's department stores that had been such a part of my youth. I remembered the iconic art deco-style flagship store on Yonge Street with its marble and granite staircases and floors upon floors of remarkable merchandise. It was one of my favourite places to escape to as a teenager growing up in Toronto. It was still a fixture on Yonge Street, but long gone was the department store. However, its original seventh floor, designed by a French architect named Jacques Carlu, remained intact and was still currently one of the poshest event spaces in the city—called, unsurprisingly, The Carlu. As interesting as this trivia might have been, it still didn't get me any closer to discovering what I'd come to find out. I turned to the list of archived real estate transactions—deed transfers, to be more specific.

There, about halfway down the screen I was peering into, was a transaction dated Wednesday, June 7, 1939. It was for the purchase and sale of the house at our address. The deed had been transferred to Edward Crocket and Elizabeth Crocket. I was stunned on two counts. First, the fact that the name was Crocket was mind-blowing. Second, I wondered when women could even have their names on deeds. A quick online search told me that here in my home province, women had been awarded property rights as far back as 1884. So, Elizabeth Crocket had been a real person. This revelation was too much to believe. I sat back in my chair, my heart racing. Surely, I must have read this somewhere before. If not, how could my apparition have this exact name? This was impossible. I continued searching.

Finally, after combing through decade after decade of records, I found what I'd been searching for. There on the screen was the next deed transfer for our house. It was in October 1989—fifty-three years after the first one I'd found. The Crockets owned the house for fifty-three years. It was then sold to the people we'd eventually bought it from. I have no idea why this seemed important to me, but it did. It appeared that a woman named Elizabeth (Betty) Crocket had lived in my house for more than half a century. Then I thought of something. I took a closer look at the second deed transfer. There was only one name of a previous owner—Edward Crocket. What had happened to Betty? I would probably never know. But it still bothered me.

I felt strange as I drove home with the printout of the real estate transaction in my briefcase beside me on the passenger seat. My head was telling me that this was impossible and that I ought to book another visit with Peter Sparrow as soon as humanly possible. Some other part of me (my heart, perhaps?) told me to take a different view. Was it telling me to open my mind? This incident was too bizarre to be anything the logical, rational, reasonable, bitchy, snarky Erica Flanagan would open her mind to. There had to be some other explanation.

I managed to put all that aside for the next few days to concentrate on writing about my first domestic adventure for my blog. When I reached the end of the piece, it occurred to me that I ought to tell them what was coming next. I'd read somewhere that it was one approach to hooking readers—to get them to come back for more. So, I wrote, *Join me next month as I take you on my journey through the domestic drudgery of house cleaning and tidying. And remember what Phyllis Diller, that irreverent comedienne extraordinaire from the middle of the twentieth century, once said, "Housework can't kill you, but why take the chance?"*

~

House cleaning and all that went along with it would be my project for January. I was delighted to learn that this was, in fact, the usual focus of the January issues of women's magazines. I congratulated myself on being so intuitive about my topic. I was in the midst of planning my attack on the details of domestic drudgery when Sam called to remind me we hadn't seen one another since Christmas Eve and could we meet for a drink. I happily said yes.

When I arrived at Sofia, Sam was sitting at the bar. Since Sofia was also a restaurant of some note, we had planned to have a drink and then grab dinner. Sam always seemed to manage to escape her family duties and look spectacular. This evening was no exception.

She was wearing a black jumpsuit, black boots and a fabulous (enormous) red pendant. When she saw me, she waved me over and picked up her glass. She made her way toward me, gave me an air kiss and nudged me toward our table.

Once we were seated and I had a drink in hand, Sam said, "I read your blog, Ricky."

I smiled in anticipation of the accolades I expected to come my way. "And so?" I said, prompting her to continue.

"Well, I don't quite know how to say this, but it was..." She trailed off, her eyes floating up to the sky as if she might be trying to access just the right words.

I was beginning to get worried. What was not to love about my blog piece?

"Ricky, what can I say? It was, in a word, boring."

"Boring? It was boring? Sam, it was full of clever quips and even a few tips. What's boring about that?"

"Everything. Erica," Sam rarely used my full name. "I guess I expected it to be quirky and bitchy and to paint a real picture of how the perfect upside-down cake emerged. I've known you for a long time, and you've never been good in the kitchen. I find it hard to believe it happened the way you described it. Surely, there was more drama. More humour. Surely, the whole thing didn't come together so perfectly as your piece suggests."

I was chastened—but only slightly and only for the briefest of interludes. Then I was full-on bitch again.

"I don't know what everyone expects of me. Maddie said almost the same thing." While that was true—Maddie *had* said that, and Andrew had not disagreed—what I didn't tell Sam was that Maddie also said I should have written about the mess I was in when they arrived home. Andrew then mentioned seeing a discarded cake in the organics bin. It had never been my intention to make that part of the process public. Was I being disingenuous? Maybe, but it was my blog, my story, and I'd tell it any way I wanted.

"All I'm saying, Ricky, is that if you expect to garner any readers, you'll have to find something more than the bland story about making the perfectly turned-out cake on your first attempt." Sam emptied her wine glass. "Oh, and just a suggestion: You might consider writing weekly. Readers usually lose interest when the blog comes out only sporadically or monthly."

Several things irritated me about Sam's conclusion. First, I felt there was no way I could tell my public the whole truth about my ineptitude. That wasn't what this was supposed to be about. Second, she had a point about the frequency of my posts, although since I didn't actually have an audience yet, it hardly seemed to matter. Finally, and most importantly, and something I wasn't prepared to mention to my friend at this time: she was entirely correct about the whole thing. My blog *was* boring.

~

I'd done my research and was ready to start the next phase of my domestic drudgery adventure. I would do the housekeeping without Alice's help for a week (I gave her a week's vacation that she was long overdue), and I would declutter. I had enough sense to realize these were two different things. I was going to be sure not a single item in our house was there unnecessarily. I would purge us of all the unused, unloved and unnecessary items that accumulate in everyone's house. Of course, that meant minus Maddie's or Andrew's belongings. They'd made me promise; although I fully intended to talk Andrew out of a bunch of things I knew he didn't need to keep any longer. But before I could get to the decluttering, there was cleaning to be done.

I had a checklist I'd found online. The first thing on the list was to gather my cleaning supplies. I was more than a bit puzzled about the array of bottles and other cleaning-related items perched on our utility closet's shelves. I had used only one of them before—it was something called an all-purpose cleaner. I couldn't think of a single reason why that couldn't be used for everything. Hence the name. If an all-purpose cleaner couldn't be used for all purposes, then surely the name should be changed. Is that not simply logical? I might have to take that on as a project. The array of other bottles just confused me.

The second item on the list was to clear the clutter, but I didn't think this referred to the overall decluttering project. I realized it meant that before one cleans, one must tidy so that one might reach the dirty spots. As I further reviewed my checklist, I realized I was right. Thankfully, I lived with two people who weren't slobs, so there was little clutter (with the possible exception of my office, which was professionally and willfully untidy. I wouldn't bother cleaning in there).

Next, I was supposed to dust and vacuum, then wipe mirrored and glass things, disinfect just about everything (maybe the all-purpose cleaner wasn't going to work after all), sweep, mop, blah-blah-blah. So mind-numbing and so time-consuming.

I'd managed to get as far as the wiping mirrored things before collapsing. I was exhausted. The rest would have to wait.

"Giving up already?"

I was startled out of my slouch on the living room sofa. "What?"

"There's a lot more to do," Betty said. "And when you're finished, you'll have to start again. That's the nature of housekeeping, you know. You just get it done, and you have to start all over. It's never actually finished. Oh, and I noticed that pile of laundry that needs to be ironed, but perhaps you don't consider that part of housekeeping." Betty stood by the front window, leaning against it while examining her nails. "I must get a manicure," she said. "Housework is so hard on the nails, as I'm sure you're discovering."

I looked down at my nails before I even had a chance to be alarmed about Betty's arrival—again.

*"Housework is a treadmill from futility to oblivion with stop-offs at tedium and counter-productivity."*

"I'm having difficulty believing that's original," Betty said.

I sighed. "Caught again. Erma Bombeck," I said while Betty frowned. "Never mind. She didn't write her first book until 1965."

Betty took a tiny spiral-bound notebook and a pen from her apron's pocket. "I'll have to write her name down. I might as well get something out of these encounters since you're not really helping me achieve my objective to rest from my homemaking job." Betty looked around at the living room, which was tidy as always. "You know, Erica, most homemakers have a weekly agenda."

"An agenda? You mean like a schedule for housekeeping duties?"

"I mean that exactly," Betty said, sitting in one of the chairs flanking the fireplace. "You know, Monday is for laundry, but not linens. You leave that for Thursday. Tuesday is for doing the marketing and cleaning the kitchen. On Wednesday, you clean the bedrooms and the bathroom. And so on for the week. The weekends can be devoted to ensuring your husband and children are content. You must also find a time slot to get your hair and nails done. You can never look like a fright. And, of course, cooking is a seven-day-a-week endeavour."

I was exhausted just considering the idea of a housekeeping timetable. "You know, Betty, I read somewhere that in the 1950s, women spent about forty-two hours a week on housekeeping."

She shrugged. "I suppose that's true. It is, after all, a full-time job, Erica. But that doesn't count childcare, does it?" She checked her nails again and patted her perfectly coiffed hair. "So, what's next on your homemaking agenda?"

"Decluttering."

"Didn't you already do that before you started cleaning?" She looked around, "Besides, I must say your house is not very cluttered to begin with. Why declutter?"

"These days, the word means something a bit more involved than simple tidying. Didn't people in the 1950s and 1960s ever have to declutter? You know, get rid of stuff—those things that clog up your house, things that accumulate over time?"

Betty shrugged. "It seems to me if you tidy every day and examine unused articles as you go along on a daily basis, nothing has the opportunity to accumulate. How does this happen?"

I was wondering the same thing. Maybe there was something to this regular housework stuff. Even at the risk of playing into my own fantasies, I got up from my chair and said, "Come with me. There's something you need to see."

I marched Betty to my office and sat her down in front of my computer. I moved enough stuff off the desktop to assuage her tidy sensibility, prompting her to remark about the difference in the tidy quotient between my office and the rest of the house. I chose to ignore her. I turned it on, and she was delighted. "What is this? Is it a television? Oh, I think I've seen something like this on a news show about the future. What am I looking at?"

I explained to her, as best I could, about computers, their ubiquity (she was skeptical when I told her everyone had at least one at home these days), the workings of the internet and how we could see what people are doing all over the world. She was wide-eyed as I homed in on Marie Kondo's website. Betty giggled in delight as I clicked here and there through the site, asking me to stop occasionally so she could look at a photograph or read a headline. I explained to her that Marie Kondo had a method of decluttering that people all over the world had adopted.

"All over the world?" she said, wide-eyed.

I smiled. It was like opening up the world to a child.

"Stop there!" she said as my pointer ran over an article titled "How to Keep Shared Spaces Tidy." She pointed excitedly at the screen. "I think you need to see that one," she said.

Before I knew what was happening, Betty had taken the mouse away from me and clicked from one article to another. She was a fast learner.

"Make a plan, then bring everyone together?" Betty looked confused. "What nonsense is this? Who wrote this? Why does a housewife need to bring everyone together? You just do it. This idea is just plain stupid, if you'll pardon my language." She read further. "*I believe that tidying is a celebration, a special send-off for those things that will be departing from the house, and therefore I dress accordingly.*" Betty looked pensive. "Well, I suppose that does resonate."

It certainly didn't resonate with me. Dressing up to tidy? That might have been a bridge too far even for my project, but it did give me some ammunition for making my blog more interesting. I had always thought that donning one's most comfortable and tatty clothes was the best attire for a decluttering job. Suddenly, I had an idea.

"Betty, I think I should start my decluttering with my closet. I have a lot of clothes I don't wear."

"Why would you have clothes you don't wear?" She seemed horrified. "Unless, of course, you attend many cocktail parties and need a selection of frocks that you wear only occasionally. I suppose that does add up to a lot of rarely used clothing, now that I think about it. After all, I understand not wanting anyone to see you in the same dress twice."

I rolled my eyes. "Yes, of course. I attend *so* many cocktail parties."

"Do I detect a modicum of sarcasm?"

"You do," I said. "Perhaps more than a modicum. Anyway, clothing accumulation is a bit of a long story, and I'll tell you about it as we go along. But what do you think? Should we try some of Marie Kondo's techniques for making our homes clutter-free?"

Betty shrugged. "I suppose we could, but it's getting a bit late in the day. How long do you think it will take?"

I swatted away her idea. "Not long. I've heard her techniques are very efficient."

So, I picked up my iPad (we were definitely going to need to consult MK herself as we moved through this project), Betty followed me upstairs, and I took her into my walk-in closet. As I opened the double doors fully, Betty's eyes almost popped out of her head. She backed up into the bedroom and then farther back into the hall before returning to stand in front of the door, staring at the racks of clothes and shelves filled with shoes and handbags, all jumbled and pressed together to make room for more and more.

"Erica, what have you done? This tiny room was the nursery attached to the master bedroom. What is it? Whatever am I looking at? Is it a shop of some sort? Do you sell things from your home?"

I almost laughed, but it must have looked that way to her—as it would to many people of lesser means than we had. I explained to Betty the attraction of the walk-in closet, a concept that was new to her. I was puzzled at first, but then I realized that this was a relatively recent innovation in the homes of regular people. Royalty had been using dressing rooms for centuries, but the average working person was lucky to have a small closet with a rod for hanging clothes. I explained to Betty that it was pretty standard these days.

"But why so many things?" Betty held her right hand over her mouth as her left hand ran over the clothes and handbags. "Are these all yours?"

I nodded, and she continued her perusal of the contents of my overflowing closet. I had never considered what this might look like to someone who hasn't experienced the walk-in closet and was suddenly embarrassed. I was embarrassed by the sheer excess demonstrated by the number of "things" I had in that closet and the utter chaos that spoke to a lack of consideration for them. Was I so blasé about how much I had that I failed to appreciate them and look after them?

"How can one person have so many things?" Betty said. "I mean, do you need all these?"

I was no longer confident that I did.

"I do love a nice dress and always like something new for an occasion," Betty said, "but I would never be able to find anything if I had to face this every day." She turned away from the mess and looked at me. "There must be a point when you have enough."

That stopped me in my tracks as I remembered my philosophical period in my early forties when I was seized with the idea that I'd become conversant in ancient Asian philosophy. I remembered something Lao Tzu, a Chinese philosopher from around the year 500 BCE, had written—something I had glossed over because I couldn't understand how it could be true. "*He who knows that enough is enough will always have enough.*" I was beginning to think perhaps I should consider this.

"What did you say?" Betty said.

I hadn't realized I'd said it out loud. I repeated it.

"Well, I don't know anything about ancient Asian philosophers, but whoever he was, you should listen. Dear god, Erica. No one needs this many things. I think I'm now beginning to understand the need for this decluttering."

So, we got to work. According to Marie Kondo, "*Gathering every item in one place is essential to this process because it gives you an accurate grasp of how much you have.*" This edict that required me to remove everything from that large walk-in sounded like a bridge too far, but Betty seemed to think MK might have a point.

"Maybe if you do take everything out and pile it up on your bed," Betty said, "you might get a better idea of just how overwhelming this looks to me."

As I eyeballed the morass, I feared it wouldn't all fit on the bed. Well, anyway, there was a whole bedroom we could use.

Betty helped me as I removed every purse and every pair of shoes from the closet. Then we started on the clothes. Rack after rack, we took them out, discovering as we went along items that I'd completely forgotten about.

"I'm exhausted," Betty said as we stood there looking at the enormous pile of clothing on the bed and shoes and handbags on the floor. The bedroom was a complete jumble of stuff. "I don't think I'm up for any more work today," she said.

Just then, I heard the front door open and a voice call up the stairs. "Mom? Are you here, Mom?"

I gasped as I considered what I was going to do. Andrew and I would have to sleep in the guest room tonight—and maybe even longer if I didn't do something with this mess. The pile was enormous. And then there was Betty. I turned to her just as Maddie appeared in the doorway, but she had disappeared.

"What the hell, Mom?"

"Maddie! Language!"

"But Mom, what are you doing? This is insane."

I could hardly argue with her on that count. "I'm starting a decluttering process," I said. Then I remembered I'd also left a mess in the utility room, cleaning supplies in a jumble on the kitchen counter and the vacuum in the middle of the living room.

Maddie had her phone out and was filming the mess from every angle.

"Maddie, stop that! I'm just going to leave this here and get at it later."

"Mom, I didn't know you had a Gucci hobo bag," Maddie said, putting her phone down long enough to pick the vintage Gucci from the pile. "Wow, can I have this?"

I thought, *why not*? One less thing to consider in the decluttering process. Maddie picked up the bag and headed toward the door. "I can't wait to see Dad's face when he sees this." Maddie turned for one last photo op. "BTW, Mom, what's for dinner?" She snickered and was gone.

I moved a pile of shoes from the single chair in the bedroom and slumped into it. I was still there fifteen minutes later when Andrew appeared at the door.

He stood in the doorway, his arms folded and looked around. "Well, I guess we'll be sleeping in the guest room for a few days." He was nothing if not pragmatic. And I loved him for it.

~

After I explained to Andrew and Maddie over takeout dinner what I was trying to accomplish, I spent the next day trying to follow Marie Kondo's often weird online instructions. As I did so, I kept looking over my shoulder, almost hoping Betty would appear again. I wasn't having any luck talking to myself.

I was fascinated by some of Marie's ideas and perplexed by others. I was on board with the idea that *"we should be choosing what we want to keep, not what we want to get rid of."* It was such a novel approach. Instead of looking for what to throw away, I should consider what I wanted to keep. And I tried to approach my closet clean-out with that in mind. As I examined each item, I wondered if it was a metaphor for life. *Should I take the time I have now (on my sabbatical) to consider what I want to keep in my life?* Then, Marie's idea that we need to keep only things that "spark joy" initially caused me to snort derisively. Really? Could a sweater "spark joy?" Well, why not? Was wearing things that didn't cause me to feel joy—or happiness or enjoyment or pleasure—any way to live my life?

I sat down to consider this idea. But what I was really trying to do was to brush aside a growing impression that kept floating to the surface. It was about my career. If I were honest with myself, I would admit that my job had stopped sparking joy a few years ago, which was the precise time when my bitchy persona started to appear. I had rationalized that at the time as an evolution in my on-air role. Was I kidding myself? Was this my wake-up call?

I found myself again wishing Betty were here to give me her clear-eyed view—a view that didn't seem to be tarnished by today's mind-boggling array of ideas and opinions. As I sat there, considering how I was beginning to enjoy my hallucination, I realized I might be developing a problem. I reached for my phone that I'd placed on the bedside table and clicked Peter's phone number.

~

The minute I walked into Peter's house two days later (after I'd finished a half-hearted de-clutter of my closet that I knew I'd have to do again), I immediately felt calmer. Something about his demeanour and the quality of his voice made me feel safe and relaxed. He was almost hypnotic.

I gratefully accepted a cup of tea and then told him about the recurrence of my hallucination. I told him some of the details of our "conversations" and then waited for him to speak.

He sat silently for a disconcertingly long time (it felt long, anyway), and then he said, "How do you feel when Betty is with you?"

"How do I feel?" I thought about that for a moment. "I suppose I feel like I've lost my marbles. Imagine me, Erica Flanagan, talking to an apparition. That's how I feel."

Peter shrugged. "I'm not so sure you're being honest with yourself. Remember what we talked about the last time you were here."

I did remember. Peter had said the easiest person to fool was yourself. Was I fooling myself? Maybe I could try that answer again.

"Okay," I said. "Maybe chatting with her—whoever *she* is—makes me question some things about myself. But, Peter, I know myself. I'm fifty-three years old."

"Is that supposed to mean something? Being fifty-three years old?"

I could feel my eyebrows arching. "Well, of course. I'm a grown woman. I know who I am."

"Do you?"

I was beginning to feel irritation creeping up my spine. "Yes, Peter, I do."

"You know, Erica, people who are so adamant about knowing themselves often find new and interesting aspects of themselves if they look hard enough." He looked at the notes he had jotted on the tiny spiral-bound notebook on his lap. "Didn't you tell me Betty made you think about the idea that enough is enough?"

I sighed. "Yes." Then, I repeated Lao Tzu's quote to Peter.

"Yes," he said, "I know that one. But the one I like to suggest to patients is this: *Enough is never enough for those for whom enough is never enough.* And what do you suppose happens to people for whom enough is never enough?"

"I suppose they just keep grasping for more." Even as I said the words, I realized I didn't like the sound of them.

"So, you *are* learning a few new things about yourself. Tell me something, Erica. When you called, you said you needed help to eliminate your hallucination. Are you sure you really want to get rid of it?"

I looked at him, not understanding what he was getting at. "Well, of course I do," I said. "Isn't a hallucination a harbinger of mental instability of some kind?" I didn't dare tell him I was beginning to wonder if she might not be real. Surely, that would make me completely insane, yet I could feel the bracelet I'd placed in the pocket of my jeans. "Aren't there ways to rid people of their hallucinations?"

Peter sat back, steepling his fingers. "Hallucinations are complex, Erica. It's first important to understand them before attempting to eliminate them. Many factors can contribute to their appearance—sleep deprivation, medications, specific neurological conditions and, yes, mental illnesses like schizophrenia and bipolar disease. I have no sense from you that you suffer from any of these medical conditions, and you haven't mentioned medications or that you're having trouble sleeping. So, we have to look for other reasons." He stopped for a moment as if he were trying to figure out how to say something. "Has it ever occurred to you that your so-called hallucination might just be trying to tell you something?" I hadn't considered that and wasn't sure I wanted to. He continued. "Perhaps you should consider listening."

~

I had been sitting at my desk for fifteen minutes, staring at the blank screen, when I realized this wasn't getting my blog post written. I couldn't get Peter's words about listening to Betty out of my mind. I knew he might have a point, but I had no idea if she'd ever appear again. I jerked myself upright from my slouch and started tapping keys. My audience (wherever they were hiding) needed me. Today's post was about housework.

~

## ERICA DOES DOMESTICITY

*How much time do you spend cleaning your house? How important is housecleaning to you? According to the ideal wife brigade, nothing short of floors clean enough to eat off will do. Perhaps they subscribe to the notion that cleanliness is next to godliness *rolls eyes*. Once upon a time, a man by the name of John Wesley—an eighteenth-century religious person, in case you missed his bio—gave us that bon mot.*

*I prefer funny woman Erma Bombeck's observation on the same topic. "Cleanliness is not next to godliness. No one ever had a religious experience out of removing burned-on cheese from the grill of the toaster oven." Amen to that.*

*Of course, no one likes a dirty house—especially a dirty shower, in my view—but does that justify the kind of time commitment needed for germ-free accommodation? I think not. Anyway, as unaccustomed as I am to housecleaning, I gave it a try.*

*Make no mistake about it: housework is backbreaking. That's why I suggest you sit down with your significant other, if you are lucky enough to have one, and get out a spreadsheet. Pour a glass of wine or beer or whatever makes you happiest (maybe a CBD gummie will do it for you) and start planning. Divide up the work. Women were not built for housework any more than men were. No one was. It's just that someone has to do it. It might as well be a joint effort.*

~

When I finished the blog post, I got up to make myself a coffee. I reached into the pocket of my jeans to take a closer look at the bracelet. It was gone. But I knew, beyond a shadow of a doubt, that I'd put it there. I felt a shiver up my spine.

7

# Step Away From that Toss Cushion (You're One Step Away from a Total Makeover)



*Interior design: where 'good taste' and 'what on earth were you thinking?' collide.* ~ Unknown

I TOOK SAM'S ADVICE AND STARTED BLOGGING weekly. I gave updates, tips, tricks, and thought-provoking (at least in my view) reactions to everything domestic. Still, I had few readers. No one seemed to care. Even at that, without any external encouragement, something told me I should persevere. So, I did.

It was a frigid February. As much as I loved to get out for a walk each day (a joy of the sabbatical life I had discovered and somewhat grudgingly accepted as a good thing), it was often too cold and windy to go far. As a result, I'd taken to cutting my walk short and dropping into a small coffee shop on Bloor Street for a coffee and a muffin to bolster my resistance to the cold. To tell you the truth, though, I just did it because I enjoyed it—despite the minor feelings of guilt that crept into my consciousness once in a while.

It was an especially cold and blustery Thursday afternoon. I was seated in the window watching the few people braving the ice pellets and thirty-kilometre-an-hour northwest wind bend into the onslaught, shoulders hunched against the elements. I was enjoying the warm ambience of the wood-panelled walls and red-and-white-checkered tablecloths while making some notes about where to go next with my sabbatical project. I'd dabbled in the most high-profile elements of the housewife's role, but others demanded consideration.

I had learned a few things about cooking and cleaning, but I was really stuck on the decluttering aspect. Although I was still inclined to feel a resonance with the bumper sticker sentiment of "a clean house is the sign of a wasted life," I had begun to obsess about clutter after my visit with Peter. I had spent far too much time over the past week mulling over his suggestion that I should listen to my hallucination, knowing that what he really meant was that I needed to pay attention to what was in my own head. At that moment, sitting in the coffee shop with only my own thoughts for company, I realized that what was in my head was clutter.

I had completed the closet decluttering project by asking Andrew to help me take eleven bags of cast-off clothing to the drop-off depot. As we made our last trip to the counter, Andrew said, "I had no idea you had so much clutter in your life, Erica. You've hidden it well." This from the only person in the world who I believed actually knew me.

It would have been so easy to accept his observation as a superficial commentary on the state of my wardrobe, but it felt like so much more. I could almost see beneath the layer of words and suddenly realized he was right. I had so much clutter in my life.

These were the thoughts flitting through my brain when I felt a bump on my shoulder just as I'd lifted my cup from the table. I turned to see a tall man, perhaps forty years old with deep circles under his sad eyes, wearing a lightweight athletic jacket, his dark face above his black beard a mask of fright. "Oh, madame, I am beyond sorry. I hope you are not hurt."

Of course, I wasn't hurt, but I had spilled my latte, and an increasingly large, dark splotch was creeping toward the edge of the table. I could feel a tickle of irritation inching its way up my neck. My first thought was, *Can't you be more careful*? Then I turned.

The man was trying to settle two small children and a woman wearing a hijab—likely his wife—at the table. Not a single one of them was wearing a jacket that would come even close to protecting them from the wintery mess outside. The children looked at me with wide eyes that looked every bit as frightened as their father's. The mother just looked up at me sadly.

I have always been someone who prefers to be left alone when in a public space. I'm not one of those women who strikes up conversations with strangers. I like my own space and my own company. With that in mind, I have no idea what came over me as I turned to the father and said, "Are you sure your children have heavy enough jackets?" It was absolutely none of my business, but something compelled me to speak.

The father looked at me, his sad eyes telling a deeper story. "Madam, I believe you are entirely correct. The problem is that we have only just arrived in the country and have nothing heavier. We were required to leave most of our belongings behind." Although he spoke with an accent, his English was perfect.

"Do you have anyone helping you?"

He smiled. "But of course. Your government has been more than wonderful to have even permitted us to finally arrive here after two years in a refugee camp in Pakistan." He sat up straighter. "I was proud to have served your military for three years as a translator in Afghanistan, and now they have permitted us to come to safety."

The translating job explained his impeccable English, but I was less convinced of their safety, given the weather conditions. I felt a wave of something I don't believe I had ever felt before. It was so foreign I couldn't even put a label on it, but it compelled me to a completely uncharacteristic action.

I reached into my purse and took out my wallet. I didn't usually carry a lot of cash, but Maddie's school was having its annual fundraiser silent auction and fun night (kill me now) later in the week, and they would take only cash for many of the activities. I pulled out a wad of twenties, folded them and put them in his hand. "It would be my pleasure if you would take your children three blocks east and go into that Winner's store. They will have winter jackets and boots for all of you."

"But, Madame, I cannot take this," the man said, looking at the money I'd pressed into his hand.

I smiled and shook my head. "Now it's yours." I left my spilled latte and picked up my purse before that tickle of tears in my eyes became anything more. Erica Flanagan could certainly not cry in public. "I wish you the very best of luck."

There was nothing like ice pellets hitting you in the face to make you cry for real.

~

When I arrived home, a package had arrived from Amazon. In it were two books I'd ordered the moment I'd finished my decluttering. I had been leafing through Mom's old magazines (I still hadn't gotten rid of them) as well as the magazines I'd picked up two months earlier at Indigo (they, too, should be hitting the recycling bin one of these days), and noticed all the articles about home decorating. I hadn't been aware of it but doing your own decorating—and lots of it—seemed to be a thing among those for whom their homes were the centre of the universe. So, it seemed an appropriate continuation of the last topic. I'd start blogging about do-it-yourself decorating. But first, I needed a plan.

As I sat in the living room, staring at our professionally decorated space, I realized this task could be a challenge. If I truly wanted to redecorate, Andrew could probably be convinced to support the decision (he loved me that much!). Still, we'd finished our latest décor project only two years earlier. Our house didn't need redecoration. Then I thought about Mom, who might need it more than we did.

My mother had finally moved into her new condo about a half-hour walk from where we lived. I thought that I might be able to convince her to let her condo be the canvas for my latest creative foray. It would be a few weeks before I could get to her, though, because she was now away on another cruise. Retirement was undoubtedly beginning to suit her. I needed another approach in the meantime.

The books I'd ordered were about decorating. I sat at my desk, flipping through the first one, and as I stared at glossy photo after glossy photo, I concluded that doing any major decorating was out of the question. However, as I scrutinized the details of the pictures and articles, I realized there were more minor aspects of this whole home décor thing I could tackle. I made another trip to Indigo, this time picking up home décor magazines—and new issues of *Good Housekeeping, Woman's Day* and *Redbook*. I figured that should get me going.

Once back in my office at home, I started trolling through social media sites and was astounded by the array of accounts devoted to décor. I fell down a decorating rabbit hole when I discovered Instagram's obsession with everything home-décor-related. It wasn't long before I could identify several decorating things that seemed to be all the rage—bookshelf décor and toss cushions were chief among them. I could do this. And I'd prove that spending time on these frivolous matters was just another way for a woman to waste her talents. In fact, during my research, I stumbled on several online articles focused on what seems to be a trend—this obsession with home decorating.

The writers of the articles had identified behaviours that suggested people (women in particular) might have a problem. One article even proposed that an obsession with home decorating meant you had self-image problems. *Yes*, I thought. *I'm on the right track, proving this is a problem for women.* I even remembered something I'd read years ago. Charles Shultz, the creator of the *Peanuts* cartoon characters, once said, "*Decorate your home. It gives the illusion that your life is more interesting than it really is.*" That could have been Instagram's motto! Maybe that's what it was all about. Women without interesting lives just had to do it. I made a note and carried on.

Even the tongue-in-cheek article seemed to have a few truths. I particularly liked the observation that you might have an incurable obsession if you would prefer to sit on the floor to watch television rather than settle for a sofa that isn't perfect. As I sat back and thought about this one, it occurred to me that I might fall into this category—and what is so wrong with needing it to be perfect? So, maybe their observations had flaws. I moved on.

I would focus on redecorating our bookshelves and adding toss cushions to our sofa and maybe even our bedroom. My first stop would be our local discount homewares store.

I was astonished at the sheer number of knickknacks and cushions on offer. I got myself a cart (I used to make fun of women trolling these stores with carts, and look at me now) and started. Two hours later (two hours!), I stood in line at the cash with a cart filled with "things." I wondered how I'd lug them all home. But I managed. I would start my decorating with the cushions. But that would have to wait until the following day.

When I arrived home, I jammed all the bags into my tiny office and closed the door. I then spent the evening with my little family. We were just finishing dinner when Andrew said, "Erica, I know that look. You're planning another foray into domesticity, aren't you? Haven't you punished yourself enough yet?"

I just smiled—with enough self-awareness to know that when he asked if I'd punished myself enough yet, what he really meant was: had I punished them enough yet? I told him my next project would be fun. He and Maddie both rolled their eyes.

I started bright and early the next day. After two cups of coffee, I was hopped up enough to begin in earnest. It would be a new chapter. First, I did some research to be sure I got a really good sense of what this decorating with cushions was all about. Did you know there are rules for arranging cushions? Who knew? I certainly didn't, but when I discovered them, I started to consider their value.

First, although the rule seemed to have variations depending upon whose opinion you trusted, you are supposed to have only three to five cushions on a sofa. *Well*, I thought as I arranged the first three, *that's just plain stupid. Why bother with spending time on arranging if you only use three?*

The next rule said to always start at the outside and move toward the middle. That rule appealed to my logical mind because I figured that you couldn't do it any other way since they overlapped. However, once I had three (or four) on one side and realized they didn't look right, I had to start shoving cushions in between. I finally took them all off and started over.

Then, there was the rule about not putting a cushion the same colour as the sofa first in line and always using odd numbers of pillows. You know—three or five, but not two or four. Really?

The next rule was about what kinds of colours or patterns go where. Did you know that you have to use a big one here and a small one there, a fun-coloured one here, and a neutral one there? What the heck is a fun colour if it's not neutral? In my world, beige, taupe and black were fun colours. Then you must place a fun texture here (again, what in the world is a fun texture?) and a large-scale pattern there. The rules were mesmerizing. It wasn't much wonder people seemed to get carried away with this cushion thing. The final question returned me to where I started: Can you ever have too many cushions?

If you had asked me that before I started my experiment, I would have said, of course, you can have too many cushions. Only a moron would think there were no limits on what is tasteful. However, once I got going on it, I wasn't so sure.

By the time Andrew and Maddie arrived home, I had already spent more time than I care to admit placing and replacing cushions on the sofa and the chairs in the living room and had spent at least an hour in our bedroom. I was sitting opposite the sofa, looking at my latest arrangement, when they walked in.

Maddie's eyes nearly popped out of her head. She immediately reached for her phone. "OMG, Mom! You're now one of those weird cushion ladies."

I began to protest when Andrew interrupted. "Well, at least you haven't taken to filling our bed with cushions that have to be moved every night to get in." I started to bite my lip. Andrew noticed. "You haven't, have you?" Andrew examined the two plump, furry cushions on the chair by the fireplace. I do have to admit they didn't leave much space for sitting, but they looked divine. "I'm beginning to think you need a part-time job, my dear."

I pouted and picked up a cushion from the sofa, then another, replacing them here and there, fluffing as I went. "That's not the supportive husband I've become accustomed to, Andrew."

"Sorry, honey. It's just that I'm not seeing *you* in these projects. They are so *not* you."

I was beginning to wonder what was me and what wasn't. My feeling about the delightfulness of cushions on armchairs was starting to freak me out.

"Dad, maybe we should leave her alone. She might make a breakthrough." She picked up a furry cushion, never once stopping her video. "I mean, this one's nice, isn't it?" Then she started to giggle as I grabbed it from her and put it back on the chair, giving it one of those decorator chops. *Dear god*, I thought. *When did I learn that one?*

I was surprised that Maddie was so supportive. She seemed to have morphed from seeing my new project as an embarrassment to embracing my domestic side. I had never considered the possibility that having a domesticated mother might be a good thing for her. I'd have to do some research on that.

A few minutes later, after I'd gone into the kitchen and Andrew and Maddie had gone upstairs, I heard a deep-throated wail. I knew exactly what was happening. Andrew had just walked into our bedroom and was confronted with my artistic foray into principal bedroom cushion tossing. I couldn't help snorting with laughter.

~

The next day, I planned to begin focusing on bookshelf décor. Who knew that bookshelves even had décor? I had always considered bookshelves to be precisely what they appeared to be: shelves for books. How could I have been so wrong?

Once I'd reviewed dozens of photographs of decorated bookshelves in the magazines, in the décor books and in the dizzying array of suggestions online, I felt I had enough background to get at it. But I also realized I was missing a few items, so off I went back to the discount home décor shop.

I wandered the aisles again without focusing on the cushions this time and saw things I'd missed before. I was especially drawn to the aisle where the shelves on both sides were filled with little signs with *bon mots* like, "Today is the first day of the rest of your life," and "live, laugh, love," and my personal favourite, "rosé all day." Some of the frames were shabby chic, while others were sleek and modern. I especially loved the lightbox ones with their bags of letters so you could change your inspirational saying from one day to the next. That looked like so much fun.

I ended up buying a half dozen (or more) without the slightest idea where I'd put them. I knew only that I had to have them. Then I saw this "welcome" mat.

*We don't have a*

## WELCOME

*mat at our door*

*(because we are not liars)*

I could get behind that sentiment at this point in my life. So, I bought it.

I took my new toys home and got out my books, magazines and my laptop for help. We had several bookshelves in the living room, filled with—you guessed it—books. Since the shelves were, in fact, full, I'd have to find a place for half of them because I figured the other half of the shelves would be for shelf dressing. I was also planning to sprinkle my little signs throughout the house. I had one that said "Espresso yourself" that I loved and planned to put on the side table here in the living room. I have to admit feeling a bit embarrassed at how excited this made me feel.

I had also gathered the tchotchkes I'd bought earlier and a few older items I'd found around the house—you know, those things you accumulate and have no idea where they came from—and got ready to create.

I'd spent about an hour at the activity, placing and replacing items on shelves with and without a few books, when I decided it was time for coffee. Before I could get to the kitchen, I heard a voice.

"You still haven't learned, have you?"

As usual, I was startled and turned to see Betty again leaning against the far wall, her arms crossed. And as usual, she looked impeccable with her perfect bouffant hair, her crisp white blouse and her black skirt and low pumps. And, of course, her apron. This one was plaid—Nova Scotia tartan, if I wasn't mistaken. The tartan's blue added just a touch of glamour to her black skirt.

"Dear god, you startled me again."

Betty shrugged. "Perhaps you need a startle as much as I need a rest." She walked over to examine the shelf more closely. "You really have no idea, do you?"

"What are you talking about? I think this is going well."

"You would," she said almost too quietly for me to hear. But I did. "Again, Erica, when is enough enough?" She picked up one of the signs I'd wedged into a shelf space between a stack of books and a laughing Buddha statue. She looked at it. It said, "*It takes hands to build a house, but only hearts can build a home.*" She looked pensive. "I like the sentiment, but I'm having difficulty figuring out why you, of all people, would put it in your living room."

I think I was insulted. "Betty, I'll have you know I have a wonderful little family here. I know that's what makes a home." I took the sign she was still holding from her and looked at the shelf without it. It did look better.

"I suppose that's part of it, Erica. But where *is* your heart?"

"Where is my heart? I have no idea what you're on about," I said, feeling increasingly annoyed by my own hallucination.

"It might be time you looked for your heart." Now I *knew* I was insulted. She continued. "But we both know this project of yours is fulfilling something that's missing in your life and every time you embark on a new project, you go overboard—to make a point, if I'm not mistaken. Albert Hadley once wrote, *Make your home as comfortable and attractive as possible and then get on with living. There's more to life than decorating*. Of course, he was right. But his remark could just as easily be applied to anything done to excess."

"Who is Albert Hadley?"

"A famous American interior designer." Betty moved in toward the shelf and started pulling things off and replacing a few in different spots. Every so often, she took a few steps back and gazed, then moved back in to make another adjustment. Then she turned to look at me and said, "*What you are is what you have been. What you'll be is what you do now*."

"How do you know so much about these things?"

"Well, first of all, the Buddha said that. I cannot take credit for knowing that without help. Second, I suppose what you're really asking is how someone who is *just* a housewife—although I prefer the term homemaker—could possibly know anything requiring more cerebral commitment than what it takes to make the weekly grocery list." She walked to the sofa and sat down, but not before moving three cushions to make room. "Erica, you have a lot of preconceived ideas, I think. The truth is that I studied philosophy at university. I have a degree in existential philosophy." She stared at me. "That surprises you, doesn't it?"

You could have knocked me over with a feather duster—or just a feather. I'm not sure what startled me more: the fact that a housewife could be so highly educated or that I had trouble believing it.

"I met Edward, my husband, when I was in university. I did what we all did then—or at least, most of us. I made a choice to be his wife and to give up any idea of a career. You know, I wanted to be a professor. I think I would have been a good one. Instead, I teach my children." Her bracelet—that gold charm bracelet—jangled as she brushed a non-existent piece of hair off her forehead.

"That bracelet, Betty? May I see it?"

She shrugged and extended her arm. It was the same gold chain bracelet I'd seen before. Now, there were four charms on it: the spatula and the feather duster, both of which I remembered. There was also a book and a tiny martini glass.

"Beautiful," I said. Then I got up to survey what Betty had done. The shelves were beautifully curated, with not a thing that seemed to be out of place. It now seemed to me that perhaps less was more when it came to decorating bookshelves. When I turned to tell her how lovely it looked, she was gone. I then turned my attention to the remaining pile of tchotchkes and framed quotes and the second bookshelf.

I was taking things off the shelves and putting them back in other places when my little family arrived home. As usual, Maddie walked in and said, "OMG, Mom? What the heck?" And began filming.

When she saw the sign "Expresso yourself" on the side table, she made a face and said, "So uncool, Mom." Then she saw the lighted sign that came with its bag of letters so you could change it. "Mom! Those are so yesterday!"

I sighed. Maybe I was the one who was so yesterday.

~

# ERICA DOES DOMESTICITY

*Is it possible to be so obsessed with home décor that it obliterates all sense of reason or logic? I believe it is. And yet, it seems that to be an "ideal wife" or an "ideal homemaker," at least a minor obsession with the colour and shape of your toss cushions is obligatory—and I blame that largely on the gaggingly large number of home décor shows that have proliferated like fecund rabbits. The result is battalions of (mostly) women so focused on*

*the minutia of grout colour and drawer handles that they've lost all sense of proportion, of life, if nothing else. As I found myself sucked down into the rabbit hole that is modern decorating obsession, I discovered a few interesting tidbits.*

*Did you know that 60% of millennials and 40% of all adults look to social media before choosing a new sofa to replace that tatty one they've had since dinosaurs roamed the planet? That's what a Deloitte study said, anyway. And Forbes did an analysis that discovered that home décor decisions are increasingly influenced by what people think will look good on their social media feeds. Imagine! Living in a house decorated in a way that you might well not be comfortable with but that makes you look hip in the eyes of your followers. (Does anyone use the word "hip" any longer when not discussing the replacement of one?) My point is that we will all soon be looking to Gen-Z for our decorating advice. And some of these "influencers" will be those "trad" wives with nothing better to occupy their minds. God help us all!*

*And remember what one anonymous (for a reason) person once said, "If at first you don't succeed, rearrange the furniture!"*

# 8

# Don't Eat All the Cheeseball! Everyone Loves a Party

*A party without cake is just a meeting.*
~ Julia Child

THE WINTER HAD LONG AGO WORN OUT ITS WELCOME, and spring seemed far away despite the calendar saying it was only a few weeks ahead of us. I had vowed to stay away from afternoon television at all costs, but the day was so dreary, and I hadn't felt like blogging for a week. I needed something to jumpstart me. I walked into the family room and lay back on the enormous, feather-filled couch with its two chaise longues. I held the remote control in my hand and flicked on the television. It came to life with the face of that creepy Dr. Phil who was discussing something bizarre with a guest who must have been drugged to get on television to talk about the oddities of her life. I remembered reading about some of his strangest guests, a list that included a woman who thought she was pregnant with baby Jesus (despite Dr. Phil's ultrasound showing that she wasn't pregnant with anyone) and a woman who encouraged her daughter to have plastic surgery so she could pimp her out. Mom even installed a pole in their home so they could both learn to pole dance—at once athletic and entrepreneurial. I didn't think Dr. Phil would give me that jumpstart.

I clicked along to another channel. There was something called *The Talk*, which, of course, I was familiar with as a competitor to my own (former) show. In this one, a panel of peppy women and a couple of equally peppy men talked. Sound familiar? I continued clicking along.

I stopped at *General Hospital* for a moment and realized I wasn't interested in who was doing what to whom. All I could figure out was that soap operas were developed for people who gave a damn. I wasn't one of them.

Clicking onward, I landed on, you guessed it, *The Exchange.* There, staring out from the screen, were Jennifer, Veronica and Sylvie, coiffed within an inch of their lives. And next to them at the counter was—no, it couldn't be—Isabella Belanger Pelletier, recently divorced from Dominic Pelletier, our erstwhile prime minister who had recently lost an election. I had been replaced. And lest you think I am being overly dramatic (come on, Erica, you might say, she's just a pretty face with a famous last name, filling in for a while), you need to know that Isabella Belanger Pelletier was Isabella Belanger long before she was Isabella Pelletier. She was a well-known Quebecois television personality with the wit and style you would expect of someone who grew up in urban Montréal. Fluently bilingual, she had no accent when she spoke in either English or French, and she held a degree in communications. Perhaps most important of all, she had just turned forty and had extraordinary charisma (if you liked that kind of thing). I was doomed.

I clicked onward to one more channel, and Julia Child's face gazed out at her audience from a vintage rerun of her old cooking show, *The French Chef,* which was so popular in the ten years it aired between 1963 and 1973. Julia was talking about parties. And she was serving lamb. Then she said, *"Always remember: If you're alone in the kitchen and you drop the lamb, you can always just pick it up. Who's going to know?"* And I knew I had a new best friend. And I knew what was on the agenda for my next project: I would have a party, and I would do all the preparation myself. No caterer this time.

I spent the next two days making plans. I knew, however, that I'd have to have Andrew on board with this one. I couldn't have a party without his endorsement—or his bartending skills.

I combed the old magazines for ideas—theme parties were all the rage back in the day. I also poured over my new magazines for recipes as I considered whether to use decades-old party food recipes or more up-to-date ones. It occurred to me that my friends would be intrigued by the idea of a theme party like they used to do back in the 1960s, but they would not be as keen on the glommy party food that was so popular back then. With their dietary fetishes like gluten-free, vegan, and keto, and their current favourite foods like yuzu fruit (WTF?), cassava chips (barf), and oat milk (kill me now), I might have to be a bit more creative. Finally, I decided I'd have a combination of both old and new foods. Check that decision off the list.

Once I had made a few more decisions, it was time to discuss this with Sam. I'd get to Andrew eventually.

~

I called Sam late on Saturday afternoon when I knew she'd be home. First, we had to get Isabella Pelletier's appearance on the show out of the way.

"I can't lie, Ricky. She's good."

That wasn't exactly what I expected to hear from my best friend. "Have they offered her a contract?"

"I'm not sure, but I do know the top brass are considering all possibilities. There's even been some gossip about the show folding—"

I gasped. "What? It can't fold!"

"I suppose any show can fold. Anyway, there's also gossip about replacing it with a new format. I'm not sure what's going on. They're not saying much. To tell you the truth, if they don't tell us something soon, I, for one, will be looking for a new job."

"Sam! You'd leave *The Exchange*?"

"In a heartbeat, Ricky, if I don't like the new format. I may not have told you, but I've had another offer. In fact, two offers. But don't ask me about them. I can't tell you yet."

"Sam, I wouldn't want to go back without you there, but I would never stand in the way of a better position for you."

With that topic out of the way (sort of), I told Sam about my plan to have a party "like one they might have had in the 1960s."

"A party sounds wonderful right about now, Ricky, but I have a better idea. Why don't you have a 1960s-*themed* party?"

"I'm not sure I understand. Isn't that what I said?"

"No. You said you want to have a party *like* one they might have had back then—like a fondue party or a Hawaiian party. Am I right?" She was. "I'm talking about a twenty-first-century party with a 1960s theme. Even better—you could have a *Mad Men* themed-party! You could make the dress code 1960s attire and serve food and drinks like they did on *Mad Men*. That would be so much fun."

I could almost hear the wheels in Sam's head going around, deciding what she'd wear. I knew she was a great fan of the 1960s (and *Mad Men* in particular) and had a killer collection of vintage 1960s clothes. I had to admit that it did sound like fun. I also thought it might resonate a bit more with the guests, but we would have to suggest it would be an early-1960s party. When I told Sam this, I could hear the disappointment in her voice. There would be no mini-skirts, meaning she couldn't choose one of her Mary Quant dresses. It would be early 1960s—before the world went all hippie and crazy—and before mini skirts. An image of Betty Crocket flitted through my over-active brain, and for the briefest moment, I considered telling Sam about her. Then, I came to my senses and ignored it.

The more I thought about it, the more I realized this idea was how I'd get Andrew on board. He loved mixing drinks, and I was willing to bet he'd be fascinated by a party where he'd have to recreate popular cocktails from back in the day. I thought I might even be able to get him to research the drinks and stock the bar.

"Sam, you are a genius," I said.

After Sam told me she'd love to help, I got off the phone and made a few notes. I'd have to do a bit more research, and the moment I was ready, I'd spring it on Andrew.

~

Two days later, after fending off Andrew's (and Maddie's) badgering about what I was working on, I was ready to share my plan. When they arrived home the following Wednesday, I announced that, after dinner, there would be a family meeting in the family room. We were all expected to attend.

At seven-thirty, dinner was over and cleaned up, Maddie had finished what appeared to be her non-existent homework, Andrew had read the news on his tablet, and I had finished a glass of wine. I was ready.

Once we were all settled, I said, "We're going to have a party."

Maddie's smile could have lit up the block. "A party! Mom, that's great. Can I ask my friends?"

I hadn't considered that Maddie might like to invite friends. I had thought this would be an adults-only party, but I couldn't see how I could leave her out. I suddenly had an inspiration. "Maddie, you'll be too busy to entertain. I want you to make a movie about the party. Would you do that?"

"Wow, Mom! That would be super awesome!"

Andrew was a bit more subdued. He wasn't someone who loved parties to begin with, although we'd done our share of entertaining over the years. Recently, our Christmas Eve get-togethers were all the entertaining he wanted to do—and honestly, in recent years, they were all I wanted to do, too. "Erica, I can sense your enthusiasm, but what kind of party did you have in mind?" He was such a wise man (and knew me so well) to assume I had something particular in mind.

I told him my idea.

"So, I suppose this is for your blog project."

I told him it was and that I'd discussed it with Sam already. Andrew had always considered Sam to be a calming influence in my life. I was never sure why since I considered myself reasonably level-headed—most of the time.

"Okay," he said. "Tell us about your grand plan."

I pulled out my notes and began with my plans for the bar. I hoped Andrew would make martinis and Mai Tais and what I planned to be our signature drink of the evening: Singapore Slings. I could picture tall glasses of pinky deliciousness (as I remembered them) topped with little umbrellas, maraschino cherries and orange slices.

"Dear god, Erica. People will be sick before they even get a buzz on."

I had considered this, given the delicate constitutions of twenty-first-century Gen-Xers and millennials (and the odd Baby Boomer like Andrew), which constituted most of my guest list. "But I think they'll like them, don't you?"

Andrew shrugged, but I could tell he was on board already. He had taken out his phone, and I suspected he was searching for drink recipes. I decided not to interfere. I continued with my run-down of the planned menu. "I want to have a table of up-to-date party food—you know, the regulars like hummus and kale chips, a charcuterie board which I might order in," Andrew looked relieved, "maybe some avocado tarts if I can find a good recipe, cucumber canapes—you, know, things that our picky eater friends would eat."

"Mom, you aren't going to have any of that yukky yuzu fruit everyone's going nuts about, are you?" Maddie made a sour face that resembled the faces of people I'd seen actually eating said fruit. I assured her that yuzu fruit was a bridge too far.

I continued. "The most interesting part of the party will be the other table with 1960s party food."

"Didn't people eat the same things we eat now back then?" Maddie said. I had to believe she considered the 1960s as deeply mysterious as the Middle Ages.

"No, they actually didn't," I said. "Party food in the 1950s and 1960s was not the same as we serve these days. People would have been horrified about the prospect of kale chips—"

"They might have been onto something," Andrew said, interrupting me. As a proud member of the baby boom generation, he took a dim view of many current food fads. The kale mania topped his list, with the gluten phobia coming a close second.

"People weren't quite as fastidious about their food back then. Being a vegetarian was only for the weird outliers or people who lived in places where meat wasn't readily available. So, the 1960s food table will have," I looked down and began reading from my list, "Swedish meatballs, fondue, cocktail sausages, shrimp cocktail, deviled eggs, pigs-in-blankets, cheese balls…"

"Mom, other than the Swedish meatballs, I don't know what half those things are. Pigs-in-blankets? Sounds gross. And what's fondue?"

I laughed. "Don't worry. You'll love the pigs-in-blankets, and by the time we get to the party day, you'll know everything about everything. I promise." I looked back down at my list. "Oh yes. We'll also have some desserts. I'll make that Ambrosia thing and some gelatin things."

Maddie made a face, but I could see her mind was already considering how she'd film the food tables. We were good to go.

~

Over the next few weeks, we set a date for the party, and I made a guest list. I had considered doing the whole thing 1960s style, sending out hand-written invitations and the whole nine yards. In the end, I succumbed to a time crunch and, with Maddie's help, designed a killer email invitation. A week later, discounting those who were still in Florida or had previous engagements, everyone—all forty of them—said yes. The party was on.

I soon discovered that making plans for a party like this and executing them are two completely different things. I engaged Sam's help to make the grocery list and then set off by myself to procure everything I needed. After all, a '60s homemaker would have done it on her own, so I could do no less. It was overwhelming.

Once home, I realized I'd omitted several vital items—like the crescent-roll dough I'd need to make pigs-in-blankets—and gave into modern-day conveniences by ordering the missing items online and having them delivered. So, sue me.

When I got down to making a plan for preparing all the food, I realized my problem. Most of it couldn't be prepared in advance, so I'd essentially be spending the twenty-four hours before the party up to my elbows in cheese, dough, Jell-O and heavy cream. How in the world would I be a beaming, well-rested hostess (like in all those magazine ads from the '60s) after that?

These were the thoughts on my mind the afternoon before party day as I sat in the middle of a mess in my kitchen just after Maddie had blown through with her phone on video mode.

"Getting a bit overwhelmed?"

My head jerked up from the recipe print-out in front of me on the counter. It was Betty, impeccable as usual in a pale yellow, round-necked sweater, the neckline festooned with pearls, a brown and beige plaid pencil skirt, low-heeled beige pumps and a new apron. This one looked to me to be made from chiffon—that kind of lightweight fabric you can see through—and it was gathered into a wide, satin waistband that tied at the back. In general, I'd thought aprons were designed to be functional. This one didn't look like it would protect the skirt beneath it from very much.

"Nice apron, Betty," I said. "And yes, you could say I'm a bit overwhelmed. Thank you for noticing."

Betty looked down at her apron. "It's a party apron, Erica, if you must know. I wouldn't necessarily wear it for much heavy-duty work in the kitchen, but," she said, looking around at the mess, "I may have to make an exception today. By the way, if you're going to be the hostess at this party, you're going to need one of these entertaining aprons."

"Duly noted," I said. Wasn't I becoming lackadaisical about my hallucination?

Betty walked over to the counter where I'd finally managed to finish making something that resembled hummus. "What in the world is that?" she said, pointing to the large dish of hummus, her nose twitching.

I told her what it was, and she blanched at the mention of chickpeas.

"You couldn't possibly plan on serving that to guests, could you?" she said, horrified at the thought, or so it seemed. "It is a colour that I would suggest one never serve to anyone one likes." She turned to me. "You do like your guests, don't you?" I told her I did—for the most part. "My mother would have referred to it as a slightly sickly version of shit-brindle brown if you'll pardon my language. I feel I know you well enough by now to say that." I had no idea how she might react to kale chips, but I thought avoiding that topic for now might be better.

She turned around and looked at the counter behind her. On it were the following items: an open bag of miniature marshmallows from which I'd already eaten more than a few and was feeling bloated as a result, an open tin of mandarin oranges in syrup, a bag of coconut that had spilled when I opened it, and an unopened can of crushed pineapple. There was also a bottle of maraschino cherries that I had yet to tackle, a carton of whipping cream (which I had no idea how to turn from liquid to that fluffy stuff I supposed it had to be), and a container of sour cream.

"Oh," Betty said, her face lighting up, "you're making Ambrosia salad! I can tell from the ingredients. How wonderful. Is this your own version?"

"What do you mean?"

"Well, everyone's grandmother has her own version that you grow up with." I told her this would be my first foray into the delights of Ambrosia salad, and she immediately demanded a small bowl, a large glass bowl—or at least "one that looks like you could actually put on a serving table" for guests—and an eggbeater.

"An eggbeater? What's an eggbeater?" I said, getting up from my stool and opening a cupboard to retrieve bowls.

"It's just what it says it is," Betty said. "It's an implement to beat eggs, or in this case, to whip cream."

I whipped out my phone and Googled "eggbeater." The Merriam-Webster online dictionary said it is "a hand-operated kitchen utensil used for beating, stirring, or whipping." I was reasonably sure there was no hand-operated implement in this kitchen and told Betty this. I then looked at the image search and was certain I didn't have one, but I vaguely remembered seeing one in my grandmother's kitchen one summer when we were visiting her in Newfoundland. Betty then asked me what I used to make white sauce. My blank expression must have given her the answer. I had no idea what white sauce was.

"Never mind. Does anyone in this household ever make whipped cream?"

"I think my housekeeper does once in a while, and my husband makes it for Irish coffee occasionally. Then again, I'm not sure anyone actually whips anything. Doesn't it come pre-whipped?" Betty rolled her eyes heavenward. "I always thought they bought it whipped, but I knew whipping cream could be made into whipped cream, so I thought I'd be more authentic here and demonstrate my kitchen prowess." I sighed. "Stupid idea, no?"

"Stupid idea, yes," she said. "Well, there must be something — and not that big Mix-Master we used to mix that upside-down cake, either."

So, she remembered the Mix-Master. She had told me she used one, but hers was so much smaller and did so much less. I rifled through the kitchen and finally found an electric hand mixer. I'd never used it myself, but I now remembered seeing Andrew use it. I searched the drawers and found the metal beaters I'd seen attached to it. I quickly figured out how to affix them to the handle, plugged it in and turned it on.

Bettys was delighted. "Oh, my word! That is genius! Give me that thing," she said. And she was off. Only later, when I researched this little item, did I discover the patent hadn't been granted until 1961, so it made sense that she didn't have one.

Before I knew it, the cream was whipped, the canned fruits were drained and dumped in the large bowl, and the marshmallows and coconut had been added. After admonishing me for eating some of the marshmallows ("We need them all," she said), Betty then folded in the sour cream and whipped cream. Finally, she drained and rinsed the cherries and added them. The Ambrosia salad was finished, and it was a work of art—at least if you're a Jackson Pollock fan!

Together, Betty and I finished the Swedish meatballs and the gelatin-molded desserts. She gave me specific instructions for the fondue, which she said I shouldn't even attempt until just before the guests arrived. When we had finished, we sat down in the family room.

"Betty, you are a marvel. You know so much."

Betty sniffed. "I suppose you thought housewives didn't know much of anything."

"I suppose I did." I got up and poured two cups of coffee. I shook my head as I placed the two cups on the table. What was I doing serving coffee to my hallucination? I did need to see Peter again. Then I shrugged and sat down.

"There's something I've been meaning to ask you, Erica." She waited for me to nod before continuing. "Why do you have such disdain for homemakers? Was your mother not the slightest bit domestic?"

"I don't have disdain for housewives, Betty," I said, but I could see by the expression on her face she wasn't buying it, and at this point, if I were to be completely honest, I wasn't either.

"We both know you do," she said confidently. "Tell me. Did your mother work?"

"She did," I said proudly.

"Okay, but did she ever cook or bake or decorate your home? Or even entertain?"

I thought for a moment. "All of the above," I said.

"And you never acknowledged her for that?"

I suddenly realized I'd always been proud of my mother's career achievements, but I'd never once considered her accomplishments in our household. *My god*, I thought, *she did all of it—and without help.*

"You know, Betty, I'm fifty-three years old and never thought I'd ever learn anything new at this stage of my life. But you've taught me so much this afternoon."

"Perhaps more than you thought," she said. "There's an old Chinese proverb, Erica. *Learning is a treasure that will follow its owner everywhere.*" Betty turned her head slightly. "I think I hear someone coming down the stairs."

I looked toward the door, and when I turned back, Betty was gone. I looked at the coffee mug. It was half empty—and there was a small but distinct lipstick stain on the rim. It was Betty's colour.

~

It was finally time. It wasn't at all like me, but I was nervous as we finalized the details and got ready to welcome our guests. Andrew and Maddie were fantastic.

"Mom, the food looks terrific," Maddie said as we surveyed the dining room table laden with the 1960s cocktail foods. "I was really worried, what with all that mess in the kitchen yesterday."

I'd been worried, too, but I didn't mention this to her. As I looked at the table, I was proud of what I had accomplished (with only a little help from Betty). I can't lie, though. I was exhausted. The fondue, which I had just finished, had almost done me in. I hadn't been lying when I told Betty that Mom had done all of the homemaking things along with her successful career as a well-regarded university professor with a list of publications as long as my arm. She had done the daily work of caring for our house as well as my brother Phillip and me, and yes, she had entertained. And she had always looked like she enjoyed doing it. I had borrowed her three-tier cake plate that now held deviled eggs and cheese toasts and her fondue set. The Swedish meatballs were keeping warm in a large chafing dish and there was a platter of pigs-in-blankets—those mouthwatering cocktail wieners wrapped in crispy biscuit dough. I had used the refrigerated dough that came in a little cardboard cylinder like a toilet paper roll. You would think that a kitchen luddite like me would have discovered these handy timesavers years before, but alas, I had not. However, this item was destined to be a keeper in our kitchen. I loved them! The food was ready, the bar was stocked, and I was dressed. It was show time.

Sam and her husband arrived early to help, and by the time the party was in full swing, the forty partiers seemed to be enjoying themselves immensely, judging from the drinks in hand and the number of people hovering over the food.

I was astounded at how seriously they had all taken the theme. I suspect my guests had ransacked several of the vintage clothing shops in the area in an effort to come up with authentic early 1960s party attire. My female friends had gone all out. Most of them were in colourful cocktail dresses that fell to their knees or slightly above. Sam was in a sleeveless red sheath with a draped neckline in silk and perfectly matching red shoes. She looked fantastic. My other female friends were equally gorgeous in their silk, satin, lace, and chiffon. There were also lots of pearls, gloves, clutch purses, and heels. The men were more subdued but took the theme seriously and followed Don Draper's lead in their dark suits, white shirts and narrow ties. And they lounged attractively near Andrew's bar, holding martini and highball glasses.

The Singapore Slings and dirty martinis from Andrew's bar were the biggest hits of the evening, as was the music: Frank Sinatra and Johnny Mathis crooned from our speakers. Then, when The Four Lads began "Moments to Remember," someone started singing along and before we knew it, everyone was singing at the top of their lungs. It seemed impossible to me that this group of buttoned-down people could be making moments to remember.

By the time the party wound down, it was well after midnight, and Julie London was singing "Cry Me a River." When most of the guests had said their good-nights and Maddie had gone off to bed, Sam and her husband offered to stay behind to help clean up. As usual, we eschewed the help. Andrew and I thanked them for the offer and told them we would manage. Then, once they were safely bundled out to their Uber, Andrew poured one last martini—two, actually—and we sat down to observe the aftermath.

"I must admit it, Erica, this was a masterpiece." He had clearly enjoyed himself. "You know what surprised me the most?"

I shook my head as I sipped this lovely drink. It was only my second of the evening. I had decided a drunken hostess might not be the best look for the evening. Andrew continued.

"Did you look at the buffet tables?" he said. I had not. "The one with the hummus and kale chips is still full. Everyone loved those pigs-in-blankets and even that dreadful Ambrosia salad dessert. Several people remarked on how much it reminded them of their grandmothers."

I smiled and sat back. This was going to make the best blog pieces yet. I just hoped someone would read them.

~

# *ERICA DOES DOMESTICITY*

*I was disappointed recently to find yet another widely quoted line that had been misattributed for decades. Evidently, when asked how she had enjoyed some cocktail party she'd attended, Dorothy Parker, satirist extraordinaire, did not say, "One more drink and I'd have been under the host." I had always thought this conjured images of the cocktail party in its heyday of the 1950s. Indeed, I was even more disappointed to discover that the following little ditty, and extension of that quote, wasn't hers, either.*

> *"I like to have a martini,*
> *Two at the very most.*
> *After three I'm under the table,*
> *After four I'm under my host."*

*Despite not knowing who said what, I am beginning to think that throwing a party might be the most relatable of the obligatory tasks required of the "ideal wife." So, I hosted a party. At least, it's been the most fun part of this project to date—and between decluttering and scrubbing floors, here haven't been a lot of laughs.*

*After all the magazines I read and the television cooking shows I watched so rabidly (just for research purposes, mind you), I concluded that entertaining, yet another domestic duty for the ideal wife, is a joy. (Of course, it's important to keep this in context—you must remember that the #tradwives among us think cleaning toilets is a joy.) The joy of entertaining, however, supposedly emanates from weaving moments that linger in memory. It's supposed to be about crafting experiences that transport guests from the ordinary to the extraordinary. Do you suppose a Mad Men-themed party could do that? Well, if my entertaining adventure is to be believed, I think I might have nailed this one.*

~

I posted my new blog piece three days later after I'd fielded several dozen heartfelt thank you emails from guests who seemed to have loved the party. The genuineness of their gratitude started me thinking that perhaps entertaining isn't so much about the event itself. It was beginning to dawn on me that a party is more about the pleasure that lingers after in the telling and retelling and remembering the amusement. An hour later, just before noon, I checked my blog stats to see if anyone had read my piece.

"This has got to be a mistake," I said out loud to no one. I was alone in the house.

Since the day before, my subscriber numbers had skyrocketed. I suddenly had tens of thousands of followers and readers. *Wow, I thought, I'm really on to something. And to think Maddie said no one reads blogs anymore!*

I was so excited that I couldn't contain myself. I had to share this with Sam. When I called her, she was in a meeting, so I left a message and returned to the blog. I started reading the comments. I would have to try to answer as many of them as possible. I wouldn't be one of those blog writers who ignored their people.

I was still answering a few questions and comments when Sam called back.

"Hey, Erica. What's up?"

I told her what had happened. "Sam, it's unbelievable. I had hoped this would happen, but I'd lost hope it ever would. Maybe I am on the right track. This could be a book, I think!"

Sam laughed. "I think it might have more to do with Maddie's TikTok channel, Erica."

"Maddie's what?"

"Oops," Sam said. "You don't know about it, do you? Ethan told me about it, so I had a look." Sam's son was a year older than Maddie. "It's fantastic. Maddie is a natural on-air host. Wonder where she gets that? And you, well, let's just say you make for terrific content."

Content? *I* was content?

"Sam," I said slowly, "what exactly is on Maddie's TikTok channel?"

"It seems your enterprising young, budding filmmaker has amassed several hundred thousand followers posting videos of her mother on her domestic voyage over the past few months."

I thought I might faint.

# 9

# Parents Under Pressure: Ten Ways to Help Your Child Succeed (Without Making a Laughingstock of Yourself)

*I take a very practical view of raising children. I
put a sign in each of their rooms: 'Checkout time is
18 years.'* ~ Erma Bombeck

MADISON TAYLOR. WE NEED TO TALK. :) MOM. *There,* I thought, looking at my text, *that should get her in line.*

It would be hours until Maddie came home. After talking to Sam, I didn't know what to do with myself. But, of course, what would you have done? I immediately went to TikTok and searched for Maddie Taylor. I finally found it under an odd string of letters: @maddietaylorfilmserica.

I don't suppose you can ever imagine the horror I felt as I clicked on the first video and saw Maddie's face, close-up, whispering into the camera like a talking selfie.

"It's the Christmas season," she whispered into the camera, "and we're here in Erica Flanagan's kitchen. Yes, you heard me right. It's *the* Erica Flanagan, the most non-domestic woman on the planet. And I should know. I'm Maddie Taylor, and Erica Flanagan is my mother. And I'm going to take you into her newest project. Today, it's cherry cake baking."

The camera then moved from Maddie's face to a sweep of the kitchen. It took in the mess of cherries and flour spilled all over the counter and the half-empty bottle of wine and wine glass at the corner. Maddie had added little flashing arrows here and there to point out details to her viewers.

137

The camera then zoomed in to take in my face. It had little smudges of flour, and my tatty-looking button-down shirt looked like I had wiped my hands on it—more than once. I think that probably accurately depicted my behaviour. What puzzled me, though, was that I had been aware of Maddie and her phone camera, but I had no idea the extent of what she'd been filming.

I looked at the dates and saw that Maddie had posted that first video months ago—the first of many. My horror at what I was seeing only increased as I moved from one video to another and noted the astonishing number of views she'd garnered. The other striking observation I made was that the tiny films were really good. Maddie had a knack for this. Of course, I had perceived this, or I would never have asked her to film the *Mad Men* party. I just had no idea she was doing her own thing—publicly. Then I shook myself. Talent or no talent, this was unacceptable.

"What are you looking at?"

I turned abruptly, startled once again by the phantom voice over my shoulder. It was Betty. She was impeccable, as always. Today, she was wearing a short-sleeved green sweater and a black, full skirt that looked as if it might have a crinoline under it. This time, there were no pearls around her neck. Instead, she was wearing a wide, gold necklace that seemed to bring out the glints of gold in her eyes. And, of course, she was wearing an apron— this one was in a green checked pattern trimmed with a solid green ruffle the exact shade of her sweater.

"Oh my god, Betty. You startled me again."

"Sorry, but it's the only way I know how to make an entrance." She peered at my iPad screen, where I had Maddie's latest video cued up. "Whatever is that you're watching on the little screen? It looks like," she peered more closely, "your daughter. Yes, I'm sure it is. Is your daughter a television star? Oh, this is brilliant!"

"It's not brilliant at all," I said, wondering how I would explain TikTok to someone who allegedly lived in 1960. I tried, though, and was amazed at how easily she accepted it. I guess when you think it's perfectly normal to move from 1960 to the twenty-first century and back, learning about new things is par for the course. So, I explained TikTok as best I could, and Betty was intrigued, but she hadn't forgotten my sentiment about Maddie's online adventure as not being brilliant.

"Why isn't it brilliant, Erica? After all, you are a well-known television personality. Isn't this just an extension of that?"

I thought about that for a moment but wouldn't be pulled into that particular piece of vanity. The point was that Maddie had done this without my permission. Based on the reactions of her increasingly large number of viewers (not to mention the recent surge in my blog followers), I was something of a laughingstock. It seemed that a whole new online cottage industry had sprung up to skewer Erica Flanagan. Although I did notice there were pockets of support for me and my perspective that we should stop romanticizing the return of the 1950s housewife archetype. Surely, I was on the right track. Someone had to be.

Betty, looking every inch the perfect homemaker, was peering into the screen. "Erica, did your daughter do all this herself?"

When I told her that she did, Betty was stunned. I couldn't imagine how difficult it would be for someone like her (whoever she was—let's not forget that little mystery), yet she seemed to take it all in. As she watched the video, I could see her smiling. Then she giggled.

"Oh, Erica, this is marvellous. Your daughter is just terrific. You must be so proud."

Proud wasn't exactly how I was feeling. I walked over to the coffee pot and poured myself a cup. I asked Betty if she wanted one, and she said she'd already had far too much coffee today. I wanted to ask her where she got her coffee, but I thought that might take me down a path I wasn't ready for. After all, I hadn't seen Peter in a while, but I might have to after today's TikTok debacle and Betty's appearance. It seemed I was losing it.

I took my coffee mug to the counter and sat on a stool, staring at the iPad screen with my chin leaning on my hand.

"A penny for your thoughts," Betty said, smoothing out her skirt as she took a seat across the counter from me.

"I was just thinking about my project and this new development. Maddie had no business filming me without my consent." And yet, I was impressed with her end product. I sighed. "Raising kids is so hard. You never know quite what to do."

"It's always been that way for parents, Erica. These electronic things or whatever they are," Betty said, waving her hand toward the iPad between us, "might be new ways for children to amuse themselves—and I'm sure they have their own problems—but the need for guidance will never change. You know, Erica, you're doing this project about housewives—homemaker is the preferred term, by the way—but you seem to have forgotten that one of the most important parts of being that perfect homemaker is raising perfect children."

I hadn't given that aspect of being a housewife much thought. I thought about that odd stay-at-home girlfriend thing and how stupid I thought that was, but the one difference between real homemakers and those imposters was that real homemakers also raised children. Then I remembered that I'd noticed a lot of articles about child-rearing when I examined Mom's old magazines. I seemed to have made an unconscious decision to omit that from my project. Now, I wondered if revisiting that decision might be a good idea.

"Perfect children? How is that even a good thing?" I said.

Betty shrugged. "All I know is that a perfect homemaker is also supposed to raise perfect children. And if they're not perfect, it reflects poorly on the mother."

"Don't you mean parents?"

"I wish," she said. "But you need to understand that where I come from, fathers spend an average of twenty minutes a day with their children. And don't ask me how I know this, but I do."

I reached for my iPad and slid it toward me. I clicked a few keys, and the next thing I knew, I was looking at the statistics about how much time twenty-first-century parents spend with their children. Surprisingly, even working women spend more time with their children these days than they did before—as do dads. I told Betty this.

"Erica, you're missing the point here. It's not about the quantity—although I do have to admit, I find twenty minutes laughable—it's about quality. As an aside, I believe Edward spends too little time with the children. But let's not lose our perspective here, shall we? Twice twenty minutes is still only forty minutes. And perhaps if today's parents gave their children more freedom, they wouldn't need to fuss themselves about how much actual time they spend."

That thought thudded into my brain like a hammer, and then I was distracted from it by the mention of her husband. I remembered Betty had told me her husband's name was Edward. I also remembered the names on the deed to the house that I'd discovered in the city archives and shivered. I wouldn't go there. After that brain blip, I considered Betty's contention about time spent with children and realized I had no idea what was best. "I just wish there was some kind of manual for raising children," I said.

Betty brightened up. "But there is! It's been my bible since I first discovered I was expecting."

She had me there. A manual for raising children? Why didn't I know about this? "Tell me more."

"It's called *The Common Sense Book of Baby and Child Care*. It was written by a doctor—a pediatrician—named Dr. Benjamin Spock."

I might have rolled my eyes. The Dr. Spock baby book? That's how I'd heard people refer to it. Betty noticed my reaction.

"Roll your eyes all you want, Miss I'm-a-perfect-twenty-first-century-mother, but I believe you could learn a few things from Dr. Spock."

I knew I wasn't a perfect mother—in this century or any other—but I wasn't sure a book written in the 1940s could be all that helpful at this juncture. I had done some research a few years earlier for a parenting segment on *The Exchange*, so I knew a few things about Dr. Spock's work. First, I knew he was considered a revolutionary parenting advisor back in the 1950s and beyond. His advice was a departure from the traditional authoritarian, rigid parenting methods of the time. Dr. Spock had a far more flexible, empathetic, and nurturing approach than the approach taken by parents up to that time. He encouraged parents to trust their instincts and emphasized the importance of love and emotional support in child development. All of this sounded so terrific, and it seemed to have worked for a while. What had happened, though? Why did today's young parents seem to have regressed to rigid ways of bringing up babies? Of course, the world and, naturally, the rules were different now, but they were rules, nonetheless. I'd only recently heard that new moms were making up lists of rules for grandparents before they were even allowed to visit with their new grandchildren. I couldn't even imagine what might be on that list. What was the world coming to?

"You know, Dr. Spock focuses on the emotional well-being of children," Betty said. "He believes showing love and affection is essential for a child's development. He also says that there is no one-size-fits-all approach to parenting. And you'll probably be surprised to know that he advocates for a more equitable sharing of parenting responsibilities between mothers and fathers, challenging traditional gender roles."

As I listened to Betty's description, I was again impressed by how smart she was. Challenging traditional gender roles? That sounded more like something I might hear from a feminist warrior rather than a housewife. Betty had told me she had a university education—like my mother, some branch of philosophy if memory served—but I guess I just thought a housewife's brain goes to mush after a while.

As she spoke, I diddled through the online search results, discovering that Dr. Spock's book had sold over fifty-million copies by the time he died in 1998—and was still selling. I noted it was in its tenth edition and still on Amazon. Impressive!

"I remember one line from his book that I've never forgotten," Betty said. "Dr. Spock said, *Respect children because they're human beings, and they deserve respect, and they'll grow up to be better people.*"

Yes, of course, I thought. I do respect Maddie. But she needed to respect me, as well. Parenting would be the topic of my next blog post. But I still had to deal with Maddie.

~

I was expecting Andrew and Maddie to arrive home a bit late that day, owing to Maddie's after-school dance class, so I had some time to consider how I'd approach her.

It was now late March—I'd been on sabbatical for three months—and I had actually learned to make a few simple recipes I could serve to my family on a weekday evening. I was shocked at the sense of accomplishment this gave me. This turn of events was a situation Andrew found endlessly fascinating. He had never thought I'd learn to cook, much less have a genuine interest in it. I was puttering around the kitchen, tending to the chili I had simmering on the stove and thinking about how I would approach Maddie. Before I did, I'd talk to Andrew about it. I presumed he hadn't heard about her TikTok adventure yet, but I knew I might be too late to be the one who relayed the story. As I cleaned off the counter, I noticed that damn bracelet I kept finding—and losing. It was on one of the counter stools.

I picked it up and tried to get a tangible impression of how it felt in my hand because it seemed so real. Now, it had another charm—a tiny gold baby pacifier. I sighed and put it in the pocket of my jeans again.

When Andrew arrived home with Maddie, she went directly upstairs to her room, and Andrew came into the kitchen. After kissing me and tasting the chili (declaring it perfection), he said, "What's with Maddie? She seemed very quiet on the drive home."

"I have no idea why she'd be quiet unless she suspects she's about to be outed by her mother."

Andrew's eyebrows jumped upward. As it turned out, he had not heard about the TikTok affair, so I had the pleasure of being the first to inform him of his daughter's latest exploits. He immediately wanted to see a sample, and when he finished, he was laughing.

"There is nothing particularly funny about this," I said, annoyed that he didn't share my indignation.

"But Erica, it *is* funny." He reached for the bottle of malbec on the counter and proceeded to uncork it. "Maybe it's time for you to stop taking yourself so seriously. You do have to admit she's good at this, and she has captured her mother to perfection."

There was that word again. Perfect. Perfection. And me taking myself too seriously? Puhlease.

He continued talking, and I continued listening. Andrew was of the opinion that Maddie's online persona was just the synergy I needed for my blog. Synergy. That's what he said—as if I needed synergy from my thirteen-year-old daughter's parody of her mother.

"Do you remember Phyllis Diller?" Andrew said as he poured two glasses of wine.

I did remember her—she had died only ten or so years earlier. I remembered her as a comedienne with wild hair and a distinctive cackling laugh. I nodded.

"She once said, *Always be nice to your children because they're the ones who will choose your rest home.* You might want to remember that when you're talking to Maddie."

~

I decided that dinner might not be the best place to discuss the Maddie situation. Although I realized Andrew was usually my best ally in child-rearing issues, he wasn't in the right frame of mind as far as I was concerned, so I planned to do this solo. So, it was a few hours later when I knocked on Maddie's bedroom door.

"Come in, Mom," she said from the other side of the closed door. So, she had been waiting for me.

When I opened the door, she was sitting on her bed with her iPad in front of her. I could see it was cued up to her TikTok channel. The soft lights of her lightly pink-hued bedroom were low and cast an ethereal glow on my angelic-looking daughter. If she thought looking like an angel would disarm her mother, she was only partially correct. We had always had a close relationship (I suppose all mothers believe this to be true), and I hoped this would help us get on the same page.

I sat down on the end of her bed. "I suppose you know why we need to talk, Maddie," I said.

She shrugged. "I knew it was only a matter of time. But before you start in on me, Mom, just hear me out."

It was just like Maddie to try the pre-emptive strike. She'd been doing it ever since she smacked a classmate when she was in grade two. She'd gone to the principal's office and called me at work to tell me I would be getting a call and giving me her side of the story (there may have been an insult involved) before I could hear it from the school. I have to admit it was a clever approach for a young child.

"Go on," I said. There was no point in arguing with her at this juncture. She would only interrupt me as I tried to say what I had to say—but, make no mistake, I'd get to it.

"Mom, when you started this project—or whatever you call it—I thought it was so lame. I figured my friends and everyone else at school would think my mother was even more uncool than they had when they saw her make a woman cry on television. I started taking pictures and recording you because I wanted to be able to show *you* how lame it was. Well, you know I'm only thirteen, and my pre-frontal cortex won't be fully developed for another ten years, so I can't be expected to make the best decisions and control my impulses—"

"Now, you wait just a minute. Where did you get that nonsense?"

Maddie batted her eyes. "I read it in a *New York Times* article called 'Being Thirteen.' Here. Look." She clicked a few keys and turned her iPad around so I could see it.

It was my turn to roll my eyes. "Okay, so you have undeveloped impulse control, but does that give you the right to post things online without consent? I thought we'd talked about online activity, and you understood."

Her eyes started to mist up. *Oh, no*, I thought, *not the tears. She hasn't learned yet that I don't melt the way her father does.*

"But Mom, I only did it for you. And it worked. See." She clicked a few more times and then passed me the tablet open to a page of comments about her latest video. "Mom, everyone's so hype about you!"

"Don't you mean hyped?"

Maddie rolled her eyes this time. "No, Mom, I don't. The word's hype. It means excited. It means they think you're awesomely great."

I started reading the comments. They weren't half bad. My humorous antics did seem to hit a funny bone. The word "vulnerable" kept popping up. I cringed just slightly at the thought of me being vulnerable. It was a state I tried to avoid at all costs, especially when it came to my public persona. And if I'm being honest, and you were to ask Andrew, he'd probably say in my personal life, too. Vulnerability was akin to helplessness in my books, and I was not helpless. The odd thing was that they seemed to like this quality. The commenters seemed to like the fact that Erica Flanagan could let down her hair, so to speak. And they also really liked Maddie's commentaries. She had won. Her pre-emptive strike had let all the hot air out of my balloon.

"So, Mom, what do you think? Should we continue?"

"We? Continue?"

"Yeah, I mean, do it together."

I was puzzled. "Do you mean deliberately plan to show me off as a jackass?"

Maddie frowned. "Of course not. What I mean is that my followers love you, and we can do the rest of your project as a team. You do the stuff you have to do—and if it's funny, it's funny. If it's not funny, then it's not funny, but we'll do it anyway. My public wants this." She smiled. "*Your* public wants this."

So, that's how Erica Flanagan and Madelaine Taylor became a team—and a force to be reckoned with.

As I left Maddie's room that evening, I wondered how that little talk would stack up in the child-rearing annals.

~

# *ERICA DOES DOMESTICITY*

*It's tough being a parent. But do we have to raise perfect children? It seems that the newest generation of parents thinks so. And they think they've reinvented the wheel. I'm here to set that straight. Let's begin with a walk down memory lane—or, for all you millennials, a history lesson. Let's compare today's parenting with parenting in the 1960s.*

*Let's start with food since today's young parents are obsessed with every crumb that passes over their children's lips. They seem to believe food is the holy grail of child development—not to mention planetary survival. Back in the 1960s, baby food came in glass jars, or mothers made their own from scratch (take that, you millennial moms who think you invented homemade baby food). And they didn't even have baby-food makers, those stupid little food choppers that companies market to new mothers as essential kitchen gadgets. Today, we have organic, gluten-free, non-GMO, vegan, and artisanal baby food delivered to your doorstep, with names like 'Little Gourmet' and 'Tiny Foodie.' Oh, and don't forget, baby food bloggers have become a thing! The simple act of feeding a baby has evolved into a gourmet experience. And then there's the issue of ensuring good behaviour—or not.*

*In the '60s, disciplining a child was something parents just did. It was all about 'spare the rod, spoil the child,' and timeouts were unheard of. Now, we have something dubiously called 'time-ins' where parents and kids sit together to discuss their feelings. Just imagine discussing your feelings with a two-year-old. Show me a child who wants to have a parent share his or her feelings, and I'll show you a child on valium.*

*And if you try to spank your child, you risk getting reported to the 'Parenting Police.'*

*Now, about technology. In the 1960s, kids played outside until the streetlights came on. Today, we have playdates scheduled through smartphone apps, and children can code before they can tie their shoes. And teenagers can be online video stars with TikTok channels featuring their mothers. Let's talk more about that.*

# 10

# Make Your Own Shoes...Or Let Me Go Barefoot

*Why buy it for $7.00 when you can make it
with $87.00 worth of craft supplies?*
~ Unknown

I HAVE ALWAYS BEEN SOMETHING OF A LONER. You know that T-shirt logo that says, "Does not play well with others?" I'm the original poster girl for that slogan. I have always prided myself in getting the job done on my own. The very idea of teamwork makes me gag. I know what you're thinking. Erica Flanagan had to have been a part of a team to get *The Exchange* in front of an audience. You'd be right on that count—it did take a village. But as far as I'm concerned, my playing with others was confined to the bare minimum contact required to accomplish the objective.

I always cringed when I saw those little teamwork quotes on posters scattered around businesses, and our television station was no different. There were at least five in the break room, where the crew ate their lunch. There was one that said, *"Success is best when it's shared."* *cough* And another that said, *"Alone, we can do so little; together, we can do so much."* That one was from Helen Keller, who, I might be so rude as to point out, needed a lot of help in her early years. There was, however, one I found especially loathsome. *"Many ideas grow better when transplanted into another mind than the one where they sprang up."* Oliver Wendell Holmes, of all people, should have known better. Since he was at once a physician, poet and humourist, I have to conclude that this was one of his more humorous *bon mots*, written with his tongue firmly planted in his cheek. Really? My idea will be better if someone else develops it? Whichever way you looked at me, I was a do-it-yourself kind of employee, although that didn't always sit well with my "team" or, to be more specific, my boss.

Whenever Trevor had the brilliant idea that two or more of us could work on the same story, I always found a way to get myself out of it entirely or convince him that I would be the best one to do it—alone. Given this background, I can hardly be blamed for feeling a bit uncomfortable with the idea of doing a project as part of a duo—even with my own daughter. Who am I kidding? I was terrified. Suddenly, my solo sabbatical project was part of something else. Something bigger? That remained to be seen.

Anyway, it was now April, and spring was in full flower. Maddie had a week off after Easter, so we decided that would be our planning time. I already had several notebooks filled with material I'd gleaned about domestic drudgery from both the old stash of magazines and the newer ones I was now buying monthly. I seemed to have developed an odd magazine addiction. I couldn't pass by a magazine display without it beckoning me over and then coming home with at least one, and usually more than one.

By this point, I knew that domestic drudgery and the life of the housewife (homemaker if I wanted to be more politically correct) consisted of cooking (tried and true as well as new and exciting food), buying groceries (while being thrifty), doing laundry (and ironing it all so that there were knife-like pleats in everything), cleaning the house (to gleaming perfection) and raising kids (who are smart, polite, ambitious, caring, blah-blah-blah—just generally perfect, right?). The magazines, though, told a more complete story.

Since the 1950s (and perhaps even earlier—I hadn't checked), housewives were also expected to maintain the family's health and fitness (especially her own), be beautiful and stylish, always be "there" for their husbands, and make their houses beautiful—often by making things themselves because thrifty wives (see above) would do this. There seemed to be a whole thing about the superiority of doing all manner of things yourself—whether making your own furniture (yes, really, although I thought putting together Ikea furniture was enough of a nightmare) or creating the perfect Christmas wreath for your front door (made out of anything from pom-poms to cookie cutters, as I mentioned before). As I read through the magazines I had accumulated, I realized that I might have to branch out for my research, so I found myself glued to an online search engine for hours at a time. I would have to figure out the next steps in my journey through domestic drudgery so Maddie and I could move forward.

It was Maddie's idea that I (we) embark on an exploration of crafts and DIY, a world I had no idea existed before. Although we occasionally did DIY segments on *The Exchange*, I didn't pay much attention to them. I hadn't realized it was a complete industry unto itself. The more I researched, the more I discovered a saccharine world of scrapbooking and painting mason jars, where women (mostly) squandered mountains of precious time in the name of creating a hand-made, cheesy lifestyle. I guess I expected that anyone who did *it* herself actually did it herself. I had no idea that there was a whole supportive craft industry just waiting to take the DIYer's money for any manner of "stuff" that might be needed for the project. And the things people did themselves left me, Erica Flanagan, big mouth, speechless.

For example, why would anyone make their own shoes? Why would anyone even consider it? Was it a question of having too much time on their hands? *Who* in the world makes her own shoes? Certainly not me. Take me to the nearest Louboutin store, and I'll be in heaven.

After reviewing blog posts on sites dedicated to all things homemaker and trying to figure out this do-it-yourself culture, I began to understand that today's housewives have more time available to them than housewives of the past. At first glance, this extra time could explain why the DIY thing seems to be important in today's land of domestic drudgery. For example, today's laundry machines are more efficient and do more than they ever could in the past, and hanging clothes on a clothesline—a time-consuming activity if ever I saw one—isn't the norm. However, it does seem to be making a comeback to be promoted and swooned about. Vacuuming takes a lot less time with more efficient suction and the new vacuuming robots. All I ever have to do is tell Alexa what rooms should be vacuumed, and an hour later, wherever I am, I get a text telling me that it's done. Of course, stairs are a different story, but that's what housekeepers are for. As I said, though, extra time in the twenty-first century *might* explain this mania—except it doesn't. As I reviewed the vintage magazines, I discovered another factoid that might explain this crafty obsession. A housewife in 1960 was spending as much, if not more, time on DIY projects, but for very different reasons.

Many of the old magazines—*Good Housekeeping* and *Woman's Day* in particular—carried regular articles on these topics to help their readers accomplish even more for their families. Was all this crafting supposed to help save money? Knit your own baby clothes. Sew a quilt. Make yourself a new dress. It may have been a money-saving tactic six decades ago, but it most assuredly was not these days. Neither time nor money seemed to explain the current preoccupation with crafting among young housewives of the twenty-first century.

Today's online housewife sites had articles like "Ten ways to use a vase," "Eight homemade gifts from a knitted square," "DIY Mason jar tissue holder," and, my personal favourite, "DIY compost bin." Where do I even begin?

A vase is a vase. End of story. One "happy housewife" (her label, not mine) says to use it as a salad bowl, a fishbowl or a herb garden. Why wouldn't you just use a salad bowl? And what fish wants to be in a narrow vase? As for an herb garden—well, if you want to do that, go ahead. I didn't see the point. She also suggested giving a used vase as a gift. Well, I don't know who her friends are, but I'm pretty sure I don't know a single person in my circle of friends and acquaintances who would understand receiving a used vase as a Secret Santa gift. So, I moved on from that particular blog.

I still didn't have a project, though. I had to find something to show off my crafting skills, or I'd have nothing for my blog for the next few weeks, and Maddie wouldn't have new material for her videos. I had my laptop open in front of me on the kitchen counter and stacks of magazines on either side when I had the distinct feeling I was no longer alone in the kitchen.

"What now, Erica?"

When I looked over toward the sink, Betty was standing there, twirling the long strand of pearls around her neck over a red, V-necked sweater tucked into a black-and-red plaid pencil skirt. Her apron was black with red hearts embroidered on it. She was a vision. She moved closer, still clutching her pearls.

"What is this all about, Erica? I've not seen so many magazines here before. Are you still working on your homemaking project?"

I explained to her that I'd discovered housewives did crafts, and I thought I might make a pair of shoes. I know, I know. I had already shown disdain for this very project. She snorted in a most unladylike fashion—so unlike her.

"Oh, my word," she said, now in full-blown hilarity, "is this something you suppose homemakers do with their time?"

I shrugged. "I suppose it's kind of a specialty thing, but my research tells me crafts *are* a thing—and, frankly, always were."

Betty moved toward the counter and stood across from me. She began pulling magazines off the piles. One pile contained the modern magazines; the vintage ones were in their own pile. She was leafing through one of the more recent issues.

Betty snickered as she peered into the first one. "Here's a project for you, Erica. 'How to Turn an Old Rake into a Stunning Autumn Wreath.' Do you suppose anyone actually does this?" Betty was full-on laughing now. "Imagine," she said, "using your precious time to make a wreath, stunning or not, from a perfectly usable piece of gardening equipment. Maybe you should try that one—but I wouldn't expect miracles."

I was slightly insulted. "Are you implying that I don't have the skills to pull this off?"

"Whether or not you have the skills isn't really the point. Remember, Erica, that I've seen your home. You're not going to put a wreath that looks like this one anywhere in your pristine abode, are you? I don't for a moment believe a homemade wreath is in the cards for you." She picked up another magazine. "In any case, Erica, I don't know a single homemaker who does these kinds of craft things just for the sake of the craft itself. It's just preposterous."

I listlessly picked up a magazine from the pile of vintage magazines and began mindlessly flipping through it.

"You know," Betty said, sitting down on a stool as she watched me flip through one magazine after another, "there are some projects that my friends take on, but they all have a slightly more practical bent."

I looked up. "What kind of practical bent?"

Betty reached for one of the magazines. "I remember this one," she said. It was a copy of a *Woman's Day* magazine from 1959. "See this one? 'More Clothes for Less Money: Sewing Lessons.' It's pretty typical. Sewing clothing to save money is a big thing. Some of the magazines even have patterns included."

I'd heard that, but none of the ones Mom had accumulated seemed to have any. "I haven't seen any sewing patterns."

"I think your magazines are too new." Too new? "It's been a few years since I saw any patterns regularly. Now, we buy them separately."

I looked at Betty with renewed interest and said, "Do you make your clothes?"

She shrugged. "I used to make more of them, but I've tired of it. I've been developing new interests."

I had a new respect for Betty. I couldn't imagine anyone making clothes, although I'd heard there'd been a recent resurgence of interest in sewing because of the shoddy quality of clothing manufactured in sweatshops. For a moment, I thought how proud I might be to be able to say to someone when they asked me about a beautiful jacket, "I made it myself." However, the thought of making myself a piece of clothing almost made me lose the will to live. It was so not me. I suddenly remembered a "Cathy" cartoon I'd read years ago. The writer, Cathy Guisewite, a terrific humourist, had written, "*Each of us wages a private battle each day between the grand fantasies we have for ourselves and what actually happens."* This perspective on life had never resonated with me before, but I was beginning to get the picture.

Betty sat at the counter across from me as she seemed to be in the habit of doing. She looked thoughtful. "Are you a poetry fan, Erica?'

"Not usually," I said. "What did you have in mind?"

"I presume you're familiar with T.S. Eliot." I nodded. That was one name I *did* recognize. "Two lines from one of his poems come to mind. *Distracted from distraction by distraction—Filled with fancies and empty of meaning."*

Distracted. That had never been how I would have described myself in the past. I always seemed to be able to focus. But now, focus seemed to be eluding me. And I had to get my focus back to find the meaning. Christopher Columbus is reported to have said, *"By prevailing over all obstacles and distractions, one may unfailingly arrive at one's chosen goal or destination."* What exactly was my destination? Perhaps I was so distracted that I'd lost the plot.

Maybe Betty could help me discover this. But that conversation would have to wait. She was gone.

~

Two days later, on a Saturday morning, I was still no further ahead, but I had blog readers to consider. I had decided that if I were going to do some kind of craft, it would have to be something that had meticulous directions. Providing directions seemed to be a particular strength of the modern magazine articles. So, I sat in the family room, again with the magazines surrounding me, trying to make a decision. I picked up a recent issue of *Woman's Day.*

"How to Make an Edible Watermelon Table Centrepiece."

"Well, now that has possibilities," I said out loud to no one since I was alone in the room, sitting on the floor. I flipped to the article and began perusing the photographs and instructions. I snorted with laughter as I examined the pictures of the finished centrepieces. One of them looked like a smiling cactus, while another resembled a pair of demented dodo birds. "What would Andrew think of that one?" I said.

"What was that, Mom?" Maddie was suddenly over my shoulder, taking a video of the magazine I was reading.

I held up the magazine so she could train her phone on it. "How would you like to see that in the middle of our dinner table?"

Maddie laughed. "Dad would faint dead away, Mom. Maybe you should try it."

At least it had the advantage of being edible.

"How about this project, Mom?" Maddie had opened another issue to an article about making Easter crafts. That idea had possibilities. "The Cutest Crafts to Decorate Your Easter Table."

I took the magazine from her and rolled my eyes as they ran over the photos of the finished "cutest crafts." There were eggs that looked like they were growing little patches of green fungus. Evidently, they were supposed to be tiny topiaries. Even if I squinted, I failed to see topiaries, tiny or not. Then, the next photo showed eggs wrapped in pipe cleaners (did people actually keep stashes of brightly coloured, fuzzy pipe cleaners for craft emergencies?). The ends of the coiled pipe cleaners were fashioned into little loops so that each egg looked like it had bunny ears. How adorable. Not.

"So, Mom," Maddie said after turning off her phone camera, "are you going to do one of these?"

I told her I wasn't sure.

"You know, Mom, there are probably lots of other crafts homemakers do. Maybe you could try a different craft before giving up."

Such a wise young woman I was raising. "I'm not giving up, Maddie. I just don't seem to be drawn to any of these ideas."

"Why not try sewing? I've heard it's even making a comeback." Maddie looked wistful.

I had no idea where this was coming from, but Maddie seemed to be channelling Betty now. Sewing? Maybe sewing was a thing, but it did seem to be a bridge too far to consider making a piece of clothing when I had no idea where to begin.

How could I show the world that these domestic-related activities were just time wasters without a project I could complete from beginning to end? The following day, I scoured my online sources and reread the magazines, old and new.

I stumbled on an article that said a bunch of 1970s crafts were the new trends for the twenty-first century. Evidently, crocheted clothing was back. *Dear god,* I thought, *all that lacy crap? Not a chance in hell.*

Then there were the love beads. You know, the ones that the hippies favoured in the late 1960s. I'm sure they were all over Woodstock. According to what I read online, making love bead necklaces and bracelets was a new retro thing. It was, however, not my style. Then there were what they were now calling "pebble pets" that I had always thought were called pet rocks. The idea of a pet rock had never resonated with me. I wonder why. Then there was tie-dye—that could be nice but way too messy. Tole-painting? Gag me now. Too twee. Macramé? No home is complete without a macramé plant hanger or three, right? My house would have to go without. Sewing now seemed to have possibilities.

It seems that sewing is a rediscovered art form, and I am interested in clothing and fabrics, but making your own clothes? I still wasn't sure. When Maddie told me she'd often wondered how a sewing machine worked and how clothes went together, I realized I had no idea she'd been spending time looking at the seams inside her Lululemon leggings, wondering how they got to look like that. The more I thought about Maddie's suggestion about sewing and how she looked when she was thinking about it, the more I felt an idea forming in my mind. Maddie and I could learn to sew together. And yes, I was as surprised as you are that I'd consider this kind of a mother-daughter activity. Maybe I was changing, after all.

I was sitting in my office when I made this decision. I put "sewing machine" on Maddie's Christmas list I kept on my phone and turned on my computer to write about the sad state of my crafting abilities, wondering how I would redeem myself in the next project. That's when I heard the clapping.

"Well done, Erica," Betty said from her spot by the window. She was still wearing the same outfit I'd seen the last time she'd appeared. I was going to ask about it, given how much time had passed, but I thought better of it.

"What have I done well enough to warrant your applause?"

"You've admitted your lack of skill in an area and moved on. Brava!"

"I've often had to admit to a lack of skill, Betty, and I've moved on every time."

"I understand that's how it might look from your point of view, but Erica, this homemaking project—this fixation—seems to be something you can't see accurately."

I had no idea what she was talking about. I saw the whole thing more than accurately. How could I not? I was the architect of my own experience, of my own life. It had always been that way, and I told her so.

Betty laughed but without mirth. "You believe you're the architect of your life, but as the old saying goes, *if you want to make god laugh, tell her your plans*. You, of all people, should have embraced that by now."

~

## *ERICA DOES DOMESTICITY*

*Have you ever considered making your own shoes? Surely not. What about crocheting a doll-shaped cozy to cover your toilet paper rolls? That would be a big NO for me since I believe toilet paper rolls are best stored out of view in a cupboard (close to the toilet), not put on display wearing a hot pink ball gown and a tiara. So, is crafting brilliant—or is it bonkers?*

*Let's start by discussing crafting supplies—because, despite what people may say about working with what you have, there will be supplies needed. There will be many supplies needed.*

*I visited a crafting supply store for the first time in my life. I barely knew where to begin looking since there was so much "stuff." It was like a magical world where glitter and glue sticks mingle with embroidery thread and picture frames. And these materials aren't cheap. Yet, as I stood in the line with my new hot-glue gun (I know—what was I thinking?), I saw other shoppers with their baskets filled to the brim with every manner of supplies needed for myriad activities.*

*And let's not forget the DIY fails. You know, those Pinterest-inspired projects that end up looking like a sad, deformed twin of the original idea? Yes, that's where we all end up at one point or another.*

*Crafting is like a black hole that sucks you in. You innocently start a simple mason jar painting project on a lazy Sunday afternoon, and suddenly, six hours have passed, you've missed dinner, and you're debating whether your pet rock would appreciate a hand-knitted scarf.*

~

There was little doubt in my mind by this point. I was slowly going bonkers. I was willingly putting myself on a social media platform looking like a jackass; I was freely admitting to failure to embrace crafting, something that should be simple for someone as smart as I was; I was gamely planning a domestic activity with my daughter—albeit much later in the year (the sewing). But, and perhaps most alarming of all, I was still seeing a hallucination — regularly and apparently with no qualms about having a conversation with it. I needed to see Dr. Peter Sparrow again.

~

As usual, I immediately felt calmer when I arrived on Peter's doorstep. Since spring was upon us, the promise of his garden in the winter was coming to fruition. The trees were beginning to leaf out, and I could see perennials poking their heads up through the newly mulched flower beds. I took a deep breath, taking in the aroma. I'd always thought spring air was crisper and cleaner than other seasons. It always seems to carry a sense of renewal after the winter months. I found it invigorating whenever I had a chance to experience it. I now realize that it suggests the emergence of new growth. I was hoping for the same.

I wondered why I'd never taken the time to learn anything about gardening. I was one of those people who appreciated other people's gardens immensely but had never learned much more than the difference between an annual and a perennial. I had to know that to understand what our landscaping company told me when they arrived every spring.

Peter answered the door himself that day. He told me Doris was under the weather, and he'd given her a few weeks off. I missed her regular gushing over *The Exchange* and how wonderful it was to have *the* Erica Flanagan in the house. I realized what I probably missed was being *the* Erica Flanagan at all. I sighed and followed him into the breakfast room at the back, where he'd set out coffee and doughnuts.

He began by apologizing that he'd bought the donuts at the grocery store. I didn't care. I hadn't eaten a doughnut in years and didn't expect that hiatus on doughnut eating to end any time soon. Then I looked at them. I suddenly felt like I'd never seen anything so delicious. Peter must have noticed my face.

"This Boston Cream one is to die for, Erica. Life is short, right?"

I nodded and sat down, immediately taking the doughnut in question and placing it on the plate he'd laid out. As he poured the coffee, I bit into a little slice of heaven, closing my eyes as the velvety cream and chocolate glaze slid over my tastebuds, tickling them like they hadn't been tickled in years.

"Enjoying your doughnut, Erica?" Peter said as he sat down opposite me at the table. "Correct me if I'm wrong, but it's been a while, hasn't it?" I nodded, my mouth too full of sweet lusciousness to say anything. Peter sipped his coffee and bit into what looked like an old-fashioned glazed doughnut. He smiled contentedly.

Once we'd both had our moment of pleasure, Peter said, "Now, I always enjoy seeing you for any reason, Erica, but something specific has brought you here today, hasn't it?"

So, I told him about all the peculiar things I'd experienced lately, ending with particular emphasis on my continuing hallucination thing and how it was starting to worry me.

He sat back in his chair, pondering for a moment. "Erica, did you expect to have a doughnut when you arrived here today?" I had not and told him so. "Okay, you didn't expect that, yet here it was. You could have left it there, as I suspect you often do when faced with something you'd like to do or experience but feel somehow you shouldn't. How am I doing?"

He was doing very well. Of course, like any woman who wanted to succeed, I didn't give in to everything I wanted. I didn't give in to the temptation to eat too much, or drink too much, or get too angry, or get too sad. I told him this.

"You seem to have cornered the market on limiting yourself. Have you ever thought that you might also be limiting other things—things like love and sex and enjoyment?"

No, I had never considered that and wasn't prepared to do so any time soon. I was an intelligent woman. I had to keep telling myself that. Anyway, I had generally enjoyed my life even with all the parameters I'd set for myself.

"I'm quite a fan of Carl Jung's work," Peter said. "I'm sure you're familiar with him. He was an analytical psychologist whose work has influenced many psychiatrists like me, not to mention legions of lay fans. He once wrote, *When an inner situation is not made conscious, it appears outside as fate.*"

I took a minute to think about Peter's (and Jung's) words. I found it difficult to believe that I had an "inner situation" that needed attention—that there was anything about me of which I was not consciously aware. I considered myself, on the whole, quite self-aware. My whole current situation, being on a forced sabbatical, was one that I'd taken control of, and I was generally happy with the way I was handling it.

"Peter, I'm not aware of anything in my inner life that I need to pay attention to."

Peter just said, "Hmmm."

"My main concern is that I'm seeing things and hearing voices—or, at least, one voice."

"Erica, are you enjoying your encounters with this Betty? Do you ever look forward to them?"

I thought about that for a moment and realized that I did enjoy our little talks and I might actually miss them when she didn't appear. I told Peter that. I didn't dare tell him I had a bracelet that seemed to appear, disappear and reappear, and each time it reappeared, it had a new charm on it. I didn't tell him I could feel it in my hand—that somehow I knew it wasn't a hallucination.

"Okay, Erica. Here's what I suggest. For the sake of argument, let's consider Betty your shadow." I must have looked puzzled because he then launched into an explanation of Carl Jung's theory about how we all have shadows.

"Our shadow consists of aspects of our personality, emotions, and behaviours hidden in our unconscious mind. Sometimes, they're qualities, desires, or tendencies that we deny or are unaware of. When we don't acknowledge these as parts of ourselves, we can project them onto others. You don't seem to love your domestic side—"

I began to interrupt so that I could assure him I didn't have a domestic side. But he held up his hand and continued.

"Erica, I know you're going to say you don't have a domestic side, but again, for the sake of argument, let's say you have one deeply buried. Once you begin to recognize that you do have this hidden aspect and what you are doing to suppress it, you can be on a path to self-awareness. Why don't you see if Betty can help you to get on that path?"

I left Peter's house with a lot to think about. But one thing I knew for sure: I wasn't ready to eat doughnuts yet. That reminded me of one aspect of domesticity I needed to tackle immediately. It kept popping up all over those magazines, old and new, and it was one I'd dive into next. Diets and exercise were evidently also a domestic responsibility. No stone left unturned, I say.

# 11

# Dr. Who's 7-Day Wonder Diet? Make Mine a Double



AT THIS POINT IN MY PROJECT, I had concluded, without a shadow of a doubt, that the one thing that being a housewife—homemaker—had maintained as its consistent underlying theme was that to be the ideal homemaker, you had to be the "ideal" woman. And it doesn't matter one bit if you think no such thing exists (of course, it doesn't). That doesn't change the fact that every generation has had its own description. As I spent more time examining Mom's old magazines and compared them with today's versions and what the new housewives are writing on the Web, I began to discover that it wasn't enough that you could whip up boeuf bourguignon for twenty while ironing a week's worth of shirts and blouses, and at the same time polishing the floors and cleaning the toilets. No, there was more.

To be the ideal housewife, you also had to be slim (of course, that's not all you have to be, but I'll get to that later). We may not use that word these days, but the message is the same. Oh, don't give me all that stuff about what I like to call the Oprah Effect. You know what I mean. Remember back in 1988 when Oprah walked into the studio that day pulling a little red wagon piled with fat?

Yes, it had sixty-seven pounds of what turned out to be animal fat, and she did it to make a point. Oprah had lost that much weight.

I remember I was in my first year of journalism school, and we were all glued to the television hanging from the ceiling in the corner of the common room on my residence floor, watching it unfold. There was nothing university students liked better than afternoon television—talk shows and especially soap operas—when they should be studying. (I think that might have been the moment in my life when the seed of afternoon talk shows was planted—despite my protestations that I was going to be a "serious" journalist.) Anyway, I remember saying, "She is so going to regret this," and everyone agreed.

It was mere months later when Oprah told an American television host that it was the biggest regret of her career, but not for the reason I thought she'd live to regret it. No, she said it was the moment when her ego was at its biggest—when she had to show off. I thought it was because losing that much weight on a four-month liquid would surely return to bite her in the (even bigger) butt someday. As far as I'm concerned, that's when the "Oprah Effect" was born. Oprah is probably single-handedly responsible for this whole "love your body as it is" craze despite the diet industry continuing to promote all manner of new diet crazes. Did you know that globally, the diet and weight loss industry is worth in the vicinity of $190 billion? Yes, billion. And not only that, it's growing. But when I think about it, the dieting thing has always been underlying the ideal woman thing. And the ideal woman thing underlies the ideal wife thing. Stay with me.

I was curious about this phenomenon and took some time to research it before deciding how to fit it into my project. There had to be a hands-on project here somewhere, and I was going to find it. I discovered a study done only about ten years earlier that followed newlywed couples and discovered that over time, both husbands and wives were happier if the wife's body mass index was smaller than her husband's. I sat back, scratching my head over this one. Of course, that means that being slim is a relative thing (the bigger the husband, presumably the bigger the wife could be). Still, it also usually stands to reason that this will generally be true anyway since women have smaller frames than men. So, I wasn't sure how that helped me to understand the issue. I don't suppose it did. I was still on my quest to discover the definition of the "ideal woman."

I had been thinking about this for a couple of days when I decided to take a closer look at how the perfect housewife stayed the perfect *slim* wife over the years. I took two boxes of Mom's magazines into the living room and put them beside the large wicker basket I now had filled to overflowing with more recent magazines touting the domestic life. I poured myself a cup of coffee, curled up on the couch and reached for some magazines I'd placed on the seat beside me.

As I leafed through the issues from the 1960s, I realized "slimming," the term in almost all the articles, was synonymous with dieting. I was happy to see that there wasn't a single article about several 1950s slimming approaches I'd discovered in my online research: the round-the-clock tuna diet and the tapeworm diet were chief among those I hoped had lived only short lives. I'm not kidding. There was a time in the 1950s when eating a tapeworm seemed to be the thing to do. After all, the lore goes, opera singer Maria Callas did it and lost sixty-five pounds. And if you think this sounds damn stupid, remember Oprah did essentially the same thing with a liquid diet over half a century later. It seems nothing ever really changes. Moving on.

I also discovered a late 1950s book called *Pray Your Weight Away* by a reverend someone. And it was a bestseller. Evidently, the writer had these *bon mots* for all those housewives trying to be perfect: "*If our bodies really are to be temples of the Holy Spirit, we had best get them down to the size God intended.*" Can you hear modern women inhaling coffee up their noses as they try to contemplate the utter absurdity of this statement? I know I did. But I do have to admit that one seemed to resonate with the whole notion of visualizing, which seems to be more the rage these days. Think yourself slim? Well, perhaps it's not quite that simple, but still.

Then I discovered the cabbage soup diet that sounded disgusting. There was even a book called *Calories Don't Count* where the (doctor) author said you could eat five thousand calories a day, and it didn't matter. I remember also reading he'd lost his license over that one. Evidently, calories *do* count.

Later diets I found included the tantalizingly named sexy pineapple diet—created by a Danish psychologist. According to this one, you ate only pineapple two days a week and whatever you wanted the rest of the week. I made a note about that one and moved on.

In the 1970s, the popular diet was the Scarsdale diet, which was essentially a low-carb diet followed a few years later by "Dr. Solomon's 7-Day Wonder Diet." That one grabbed my attention because it was created by a Beverly Hills doctor—and who wouldn't follow a Hollywood doctor for weight loss? This diet had it all— something for everyone. Unsurprisingly, it was targeted at women in particular (thus, it garnered quite a bit of coverage in women's magazines), promised significant weight loss in a week and was very low calorie, low carb, low protein, low fat and very liquid—lots of water. So, essentially, it was a diet where you could drink lots of water, avoid dehydration and generally eat nothing. If eating nothing doesn't cause you to lose weight, I don't know what will. By the time I turned to the modern magazines, I was beginning to think I might actually be ready for a doughnut.

I paged through articles on intermittent fasting, keto diets, the Mediterranean diet, Paleo eating, veganism, the raw food diet (kill me now), macrobiotic diets, DASH (no idea at all) and something called Sirtfood. Evidently, that one turns on your "skinny gene" (can you see me rolling my eyes?) and has a list of foods that begins with kale. That was enough for me right there.

I sighed. It seemed that we hadn't come very far at all in the dieting realm in the past few decades. There would always be something new. *I could be rich*, I thought, *if I could just come up with something catchy to include in Erica's Fast and Easy and Delicious Fourteen-Day-Diet.*

I was just about to open a copy of *Woman's World* magazine to see more wonders of the modern dieting (how could I not want to read more about a cover story that said, "She lost nineteen inches off her waist at age 59: Discover the TikTok trend that's scored 2.4 billion hits because it will whittle your middle 442% faster—lose up to 18 lbs in one week!" I kid you not) when I heard a familiar voice.

"I suppose you could afford to lose a few pounds, Erica, but eighteen pounds in one week? Isn't that a bit drastic?"

Slender Betty sat across from me with her legs prettily crossed as she played with one of the three strands of pearls around her neck. Today, the pearls were paired with a blue, polka-dotted V-necked blouse with ruffle-edged short sleeves. Her apron was pristine white with a blue, polka-dotted ruffle. She was, in a word, perfection. And she was probably right. I probably could stand to lose a few pounds, but, in my defence, since I'd started cooking, I was tasting more. How was that going to work? Oh well.

"Just doing some research," I said as she got up and came to sit beside me. We had never sat this close before. I thought I could smell Chanel Number Five.

Betty leaned in to see what I was reading. "Oh, my word," she said. "They're talking about hula-hoops. Now, that's an exercise program I've been using. It's very popular, you know."

I looked at the article again. Indeed, it was part of an article about dieting, but the TikTok promise on the magazine's cover related to the return of the hula-hoop. Who knew? I certainly didn't realize hula-hoops were a TikTok craze. I told Betty I was researching diets for the ideal housewife.

Betty snickered and returned to her seat across the coffee table from me.

"You know, Betty, I thought cooking, and recipes, and possibly housecleaning were the threads that connected the domestic drudge from one era into the next, but it seems that diet and exercise are just as strong a thread. I was wondering if I should try a few old diets to try to be that ideal, slim housewife."

"Homemaker," she said, correcting me once again. "And you might want to lose that domestic drudge parlance." My eyebrows raised at her use of such a modern phrase. She continued. "You know, Erica, I think you're going about this all wrong. Dieting is so bone-headed. Calories *are* important, and being a homemaker means you have a leg up—if you'll pardon the expression—on the exercise situation. It's just not that big a deal. But hula-hooping *is* fun."

"But isn't there an expectation to look flawless? Isn't that the main motivation for the obsession with thinness? I mean, look at all these magazines I've been reading. Even the advertisements seem to say you have to look a certain way." I had also noticed that the modern housewife—homemaker—focused books and blogs also suggested there was an acceptable (and by definition also an unacceptable) way to look. *"Don't forget you were a person before you were a mom."* Yes, that's exactly what one of the modern writers said. Maybe I was right. Maybe feminism was dying on the vine of domestic drudgery in the twenty-first century.

Betty picked up one of the old magazines from the coffee table. "Tsk, tsk, tsk." She turned the page toward me so that I could see the ad. It was a picture of a pear with the slogan, "This is no shape for a girl." It was an ad for a girdle, but it did make one thing clear: women shouldn't be pear-shaped.

"Yes," Betty said after placing the magazine back on the table, "I suppose we are encouraged to look a particular way, but you do have to admit that you have more energy when you're slimmer, don't you?"

I knew I did, but I couldn't speak for all women and wouldn't. "Betty, what kind of exercise do you do other than hula-hooping? Do you go to a gym?"

Betty snorted derisively. "A gym? Dear heavens, Erica. No one I know would be caught dead in a gym. Gyms are for sweaty athletes and vain men. No, we never need a gym." Then she looked at me with a mischievous twinkle in her eye. "You know your contention that we're engaged in domestic drudgery?" I nodded. "Well, since everything you're experimenting with is domestic and presumably domesticity is based in your domicile—your home—shouldn't your exercise routine also be based here?"

She did have a point.

"I believe you need to step away from the dieting issue, Erica, unless," Betty said, opening another issue of a recent issue of *Woman's World* to a diet called "Secret to Extreme Weight Loss—Drop Thirty Pounds in Three Weeks" and said, "you want to start eating coconut oil. Coconut oil?" She stopped for a moment, clearly confused by what she was reading. "Who in the world eats coconut oil?"

I couldn't answer that question since I'd never understood the hype. I'd heard it was good for everything from bad hair to brain fog, a claim that was particularly suspect since it was unlikely any single food item could improve both problems and everything in between. In fact, only recently, I'd read an article where a well-qualified epidemiologist had called coconut oil "pure poison." Yet, aficionados continued to bombard us with messages telling us it was the answer for everything. Who were they trying to convince? The rest of us—or themselves? I sighed.

Betty raised her eyebrows, no doubt wondering what was causing me to sigh. She continued. "As I was saying, you probably should move away from the idea of dieting as the way to reduce overall calories. And as for gyms," her nose twitched ever so slightly at that word, "remember, they are not in the homemaker's vocabulary. Might I suggest a bit of domicile-centred exercise?"

I knew what she meant. I hadn't discovered a way to make dieting a project for my blog, at least in the short term, mainly because it would have had to involve Andrew and Maddie if I didn't want our kitchen to turn into a short-order diner where everyone ate something different. And there was no way I could see either of them agreeing to the pineapple diet—as appealing as it might sound. However, exercising was something I thought might work. Betty's idea was a good one.

"Erica," Betty began, "you might not know this, but I've discovered that homemakers in my day—the domestic lifestyle if you will—burn one thousand calories every day compared to only five hundred and fifty-six in this twenty-first century of yours." (I wondered how she could possibly know this without a deep dive into Google—but I wasn't prepared to go there.) "We also consume almost four hundred fewer calories daily. Add that up, and you can see why I'm slimmer than you are. And one more thing. The average woman in the twenty-first century weighs what the average man did six decades ago."

I was slightly mortified, but I knew she was right. "So, what exercise program do you recommend?"

Betty smiled. "I thought you'd never ask."

~

Two days later, I had a plan. I'd spent some time researching connections between being a "slim" housewife—homemaker—in the 1950s and 1960s and being one in the twenty-first century. What was startling to me was, barring the modern notion that everything today is so much better than it used to be, was how many parallels I could draw between the generations. One of the most surprising things I stumbled upon was that an exercise program that was developed in the late 1950s and early 1960s was the same one septuagenarian actor Helen Mirren used today. If it was good enough for Helen, it was good enough for me—and I'd demonstrate, beyond a shadow of a doubt, that—well, precisely what *was* I trying to demonstrate? Let's just say I wanted to show my readers that I could get down in the dirt with the best of them. (Of course, there was really no dirt involved.) That's when Sam called and asked me what I was doing, and I thought it might be a good idea to engage another person in this part of my project. Well, perhaps engage wasn't the word. Perhaps conscript might be a better turn of phrase.

"Why don't you come over on Saturday afternoon?" I said. "You can help me with this next part of the project."

"What's it all about? Should I bring wine?"

I told her with the greatest of enthusiasm that, yes, she should bring wine. I thought it better, though, not to tell her what she was going to be required to help me with. I'd let that be a surprise. I knew I didn't need to tell Sam what to wear. On a Saturday afternoon, I'd never seen her in anything but Lululemon yoga pants and a sweatshirt. It would be perfect.

When Sam arrived—dressed as I had predicted in appropriate exercise clothing—I was in the basement in our makeshift exercise room. From time to time, over the years, Andrew and I, together or individually, had gone on a fitness binge—as one does in the twenty-first century. Every one of them had been short-lived, I'm sorry to say. I'd pushed the treadmill, the stationary bike (do not get me going on how we could have been sucked into buying one of those over-priced things that the likes of Kim Kardashian shilled for), the weights, and the exercise ball to the side. Just doing that was a workout in itself. Why, you might ask, did we have all that equipment? The question makes me a bit huffy because I don't know a single person who hasn't bought a piece of exercise equipment and ended up using it as a clothes horse. We just happen to have tried it all. (I also had a thigh master once, but that didn't even warrant a place in the exercise room. I pitched that sucker right in the garbage.)

With the space in the centre of the room cleared and my iPad on the small table along the wall, I was getting the instructional video (an original one in black and white) I'd discovered online cued up so we could do the XBX exercise program—ten basic exercises for women for twelve minutes a day was all you needed to keep fit according to the Royal Canadian Airforce. And Helen Mirren.

The program had started life as the 5BX program for men in the Air Force in response to a 1959 rant from none other than His Royal Highness Prince Phillip, he of the occasional gaffe. He'd been in Canada giving a speech, affording him a public platform on which to pontificate about the average Canadian's state of fitness. He didn't think Canadians were as fit as they should be (had he looked at his fellow Brits? But I digress.). I didn't think he was as *smart* as he should be, but why split hairs? Anyway, the Air Force took him seriously and developed five basic exercises, which morphed into ten for women when they rolled it out to them a couple of years later. I guess women were in twice as much need of fitness as men, or perhaps to be the "ideal" woman and wife, she needed ten. Whatever the reasoning, here I was, with a video at the ready so that Sam could play along with me.

When I informed Sam what I needed her for, she was not entirely on board with it. In fact, she objected strongly, telling me she would sit in the wings, drinking wine while watching me perform. I showed her the video first to see if that could persuade her. It just made her laugh so hard that she snorted wine out of her nose.

"Dear god, Erica. You can't do that in public." By public, I supposed she was referring to my own personal videographer, Maddie, who seemed to be among the missing despite me telling her I'd be "performing." We watched a few more minutes of leg raises and running on the spot to familiarize ourselves with the sequence, and then Sam said, "You know, Ricky, this reminds me of that television show *The Marvelous Mrs. Maisel*. Remember those calisthenics classes Midge attended with her friend whose name escapes me?"

I did remember. Midge Maisel, a fictional 1950s and 1960s housewife turned stand-up comic, was the perfect (ideal) woman who tried to break into a man's world. Along the way, she never lost sight of who she was supposed to be—the perfect wife (although that didn't work out) and mother. And all along the way, she looked slim and, yes, perfect.

"Do you remember that scene?" Sam said, leaning against the wall where she was sitting on the floor sipping wine. "Midge's friend said, 'We do this so we can eat cheesecake.' Then she nodded toward the group of divorcees in the back of the room and said, 'They do it so they can find new husbands.' Now I'm beginning to think there was a lot of truth to it."

Now Sam was getting it. But I still hadn't convinced her she needed to be part of my experiment. So, I turned on the video and started. Toe touches, knee raises, side bends, (partial) sit-ups, leg raises and on and on until the final exercise—running in place.

And doing this for twelve minutes every day was supposed to keep you slim. When I'd finished, all I wanted was a glass of wine and a slice of cheesecake. I'd hardly noticed Maddie when she stealthily arrived, phone in hand. And I didn't care.

~

I had no idea how Maddie managed it. She had been sneaking around taking video from as many angles as possible during my little XBX demonstration in the basement, managing to catch just the right bit, like the one when I lost my balance in a leg lift, sending myself crashing into the wall. It wasn't my finest moment.

Maddie and I had agreed that I would review the footage before she did the final edits and posted it online. Although I was beginning to be more comfortable with not always looking professional and polished (I had lost my makeup guru, after all), I still wanted to "approve" the product. She added extra commentary and those little thingies that TikTok offers to jazz up what's on the screen (emojis, gifs and other things I didn't understand) before she posted, so I always had something new to see when I checked into her channel. This time, she had added footage that I hadn't seen.

It looked as if she had, unbeknownst to me, videoed a bit of the afternoon I had spent with my magazine stash. She seemed to have come in near the end—presumably when she got home from school, and I hadn't noticed. I was in the living room surrounded by magazines.

"Here's the mad homemaker getting ready for her new challenge," Maddie said on the video in hushed tones. "She is discussing her latest project—with herself. It's adorable." Then she turned the camera toward her face, looked into it earnestly, and whispered, "Or is she losing it?" Then the camera turned back to me and slowly zoomed into my face and back out.

My eyes nearly popped out of my head. There I was, sitting on the sofa, my legs curled up under me, clearly talking to someone on the chair across from me—someone just out of camera range. *Dear god, I thought, Maddie has found me talking to my hallucination. I'll never live this down.* Then, just before I switched it off, I noticed something. It was tiny, minuscule even, so small that no one but me would probably notice it. But it was there. It was the tiniest peak of blue—almost microscopic. I could feel shivers up my spine. The cornflower blue of Betty's apron ruffle.

~

# *ERICA DOES DOMESTICITY*

*What is the ideal woman—physically, at least? I'm sure I don't know. So, I did a little exercise. I plugged the question into ChatGPT, and this is what they said:*

*"The ideal woman isn't a one-size-fits-all concept. People have diverse preferences and values, so there isn't a single definition. The ideal woman for one person might be someone who is compassionate, ambitious, and funny, while for another, it might be someone who is kind-hearted, adventurous, and intelligent. It's important to recognize that each person is unique and has their own set of qualities that make them special and ideal in their own right."*

*Blah-blah-blah with all that political correctness stuff. The ideal woman—and, by extension, the ideal wife—is slim and fit. It has been ever thus if you read the women's magazines from the last six decades. So, I began to wonder when the first diet book in history was written.*

*Several sources told me it was a book called Letter on Corpulence, published in 1865 and written by an undertaker called William Banting, not to be confused with Frederick Banting, who was the co-discoverer of insulin. The first line in this diet book is as follows: "Of all the parasites that affect humanity, I do not know of nor can I imagine any more distressing than that of obesity." Makes you consider that obesity might not be such a modern thing after all. But wait. This was not, in fact, the first diet book ever published.*

*That honour goes to an Italian named Luigi Cornaro, whose book The Art of Living Long was published centuries earlier in 1558. Worth noting is that he included fourteen ounces of wine a day as part of how you could live long. Thank you, Luigi!*

*All of this tells me that we've been following diet and fitness gurus for centuries, and we seem no closer to finding the magic bullet than we ever were.*

*Mark Twain is quoted as once saying, "Be careful about reading health books. You may die of a misprint."*

# 12

# The Ideal Wife's Guide to Staying Beautiful for Him (Try Saying that With a Straight Face)

*Prepare yourself. Take 15 minutes to rest so you'll be refreshed when he arrives. Touch up your makeup, put a ribbon in your hair and be fresh-looking. He has just been with a lot of work-weary people.* ~ From *The Good Wife's Guide, Housekeeping Monthly*, May 13, 1955

COCO CHANEL ONCE SAID, *"If you're sad, add more lipstick and attack."* I've always said, just get me into that makeup chair. And now my makeup chair and its operator, Angela, were gone. But for how long?

I was considering this one morning in early June when I realized it had been almost six months since the start of my six-month sabbatical. Trevor had called me the month before, wondering how I was doing but not providing any details about how or when I might return to the fray. I had planned to ask him directly about those rumours of cancelling *The Exchange*, but he didn't let me get a word in edgewise and hung up in a hurry before I could get there. I was left still wondering. What surprised me the most was that I was also beginning to wonder if I even wanted to return. That thought shocked me.

I liked the relaxed feeling of arising each day, taking a shower and slipping into my outfit of the day—yoga pants or old jeans and a comfy sweater or T-shirt as the weather warmed up. Over the past decade-plus, I could have slipped into much the same outfit because I was picked at the same time every weekday by a driver who whisked me to the station where my power suit of the day (chosen carefully by our wardrobe supervisor) hung in my dressing room. I could have worn anything to and from the station, but I was Erica Flanagan, and one never knows who one might run into en route. Then, there was that daily production meeting.

Although the dress code for most others in that production meeting was much like the yoga pants and sweater ensemble I favoured, the old Erica Flanagan had sartorial standards. But I wore little makeup when I was off camera, so the whole make-up thing was something that baffled me.

I'm not sure when makeup became a thing for housewives—homemakers. Still, it was abundantly clear to me that being slim wasn't the only aesthetic aspect of ideal womanhood that ideal housewives needed to consider. On the covers of every homemaker-focused magazine was a well-coiffed woman with impeccable makeup, causing me to wonder if they really did do that just to vacuum behind the clothes dryer. Then I remembered all those old television shows and movies my mother had loved when I was a kid. I was born in 1970, but my parents' taste in movies leaned to the vintage, so I grew up on movies from the 1950s and 1960s. I distinctly remember scenes where the wife goes to bed after the husband (in his separate twin bed) so that he would not see her without makeup and in rollers and gets up before him so that when he arises, she's there to greet him, looking impeccable. It had always seemed funny to me, but now I wondered if there might not be some truth to it.

As I researched today's housewives, I realized that being as beautiful as possible did, indeed, involve makeup and hair. Was I going to have to improve my aesthetic routine for the sake of my blog readers? It seemed I might.

I started my research. I discovered that magazines like *Good Housekeeping* and others devoted to domestic drudgery, almost without exception, carried articles focused on how women could be beautiful—or at least move in that direction. So, you can understand my conclusion that beauty and domesticity went hand in hand—at least with homemakers of a certain economic status. What puzzled me, though, was the main focus of many of the articles. "28 Great Hairdos." "21 Hairdos as Young as Spring." "Easy and Romantic Hairstyles." "Life and Colour for Your Hair." "21 Dazzling Hairdos Plus the Latest Makeup." Then there was, "How to Cultivate a Glowing Complexion."

So many articles about hair. Were they obsessed with hair back then? Maybe, but probably no more than they are these days. As I perused the current issues, I found equally as many articles on similar topics for today's homemakers.

"Finding Mascara for Sensitive Eyes." The Ultimate Skincare for Your Hair." "Best At-Home Hair-Colour Products." "Top Tips for Preventing Eye Wrinkles." "New Haircare Secrets." "Pro Tips to Get Glowing Skin." "Top Anti-Aging Products." "Colour-Correcting Makeup and Beauty Closet-Approved Products." Wrinkles, skin, anti-aging—and hair.

I don't know about you, but I see no monumental change in how domestically oriented women see themselves. I see a tiny ripple. The message is still the same—be beautiful. But today's message is imbued with an earnestness that still doesn't bury the demand for being the ideal woman—at least not for me. But today, the modern homemaker (as per the homemaker sites I looked at) seems to be less in your face about it. Have glowing skin! Colour correct things! Be sure to anti-age and stop those wrinkles! Given my advanced age, this was possibly the most resonant topic for me—but I wasn't going to tell anyone that.

~

My first stop on my way to beauty perfection was that behemoth of the cosmetics store—Sephora. This store was a place whose doorstep I had never darkened in my life up to now. In fact, I had been pretty proud of myself for that. As I stepped over the threshold, I was immediately overcome with the sights, sounds and smells of the world of beauty products. The displays sparkled like gemstones in the bright overhead lights, and the counters sagged with every makeup product known to women.

I'd done some research before embarking on this day's research field trip. First, I talked to Maddie. What thirteen-year-old girl doesn't know where to find beauty products? She and her friends weren't as much into makeup as many others their age seem to be (thank god), but that didn't mean she didn't have a healthy interest and understanding of where the good stuff was. She was the one who led me to Sephora.

My online research had uncovered some characteristics about these stores that I found odd. First, they refer to their sales floor as a stage. So, if all the world's a stage and this is your stage, then as a salesclerk—a cast member according to the online scuttlebutt—you'd be expected to perform. I don't think I can be faulted for expecting a performance, can I? As it turned out, my definition of performance didn't exactly dovetail with theirs, but I'll get to that. Second, Sephora was also the birthplace of all those testers. Now, searching for makeup was all about touching and sampling. Whatever happened to going to the drug store, picking up whatever package looked like the correct shade and going for broke? And speaking of broke—you can drop a pile of money in these stores—makeup is pricey.

So, here I was, a fifty-something woman, publicly recognizable in some circles (but clearly not this one), entering the world of cosmetics. My first reaction was that I must have been invisible. Not a single salesclerk (cast member) so much as acknowledged my presence, if you don't count that creepy little one out front with her FBI-looking earpiece handing out baskets to fill and wishing me a happy day. As I skulked around from fragrances to hair care to makeup, I watched the salesclerks performing for their audience of young women, and I noticed that not a single one of them looked a day over thirty. Who am I kidding? They all looked twenty. In any case, in my view, ignoring customers isn't really performance.

I don't know how long I'd been in the store before a young woman finally approached me hesitantly and said, "Ma'am, may I help you find something?" Was her nose twitching?

I turned to take in the full effect of this young, black-clad makeup salesclerk (cast member) whose own *maquillage* looked, in a word, theatrical. *So,* I thought, *this is what the Sephora performance stuff is about.* She was wearing possibly more makeup than I did for my on-camera life. I hadn't thought that would be possible. I suddenly felt very self-conscious about my current makeup—a bit of lipstick and a lick of drugstore mascara. And well I might have felt self-conscious under her withering look as I said, "I understand you do colour consultations." Now, why did I say that? I didn't really want a "consultation." I wanted a few makeup items to experience the ideal housewife/woman approach to life. I wasn't acclimatized enough to makeup shopping to realize that without consultation of some sort, the salesperson would be unable to suggest anything.

The young woman peered at me critically. "Your complexion is a bit off, and I think you're using the wrong shade of eye shadow."

Oh, this was going to be fun. I wasn't wearing any eyeshadow. I peered at my eyes in the mirror at the counter where we were standing. It was surrounded by theatrical lights that you often see backstage in old movies. We didn't have them in real-life television dressing rooms because the overhead portion of them tended to give what we liked to call hag lighting, deepening shadows and making everyone look like, well, a hag. As I peered into the mirror at my eyes, I had to admit they looked a bit darkish—as if I might be wearing some objectionable eye shadow after all. I decided not to tell her.

"You can sit here," she said, pointing to the high stool directly in front of the unforgiving lighted mirror.

I did as I was told.

"My name is Ariel," she said.

I wanted to ask her if she was named after a certain mermaid but thought it might not set us off on the right foot. As I watched her, she seemed to be furtively glancing around as if looking for a better prospect than the only customer in the store over the age of thirty.

She turned back toward me, leaning in close enough that I could smell what I concluded was the odd combination of her fragrance (whose sickly sweet floral notes I didn't recognize) and what I figured were the commingling aromas of the various cosmetics layered on her face. I'd looked on Instagram before I came and had watched several "influencers" as they put on their makeup. There were all kinds of products of varying shades that they applied in lines on their faces and then blended in with vigorous swirling of what appeared to be horsehair brushes. It looked a bit torturous to me. Then, as if by magic, all those funny-looking lines melded together, forming cheekbones, narrowed faces and noses, prettily blushing cheeks and sun-kissed foreheads. I was sure I would never be able to do that, and now that I was this close to the end product on real-life Ariel's face, I wasn't sure I even wanted to.

"If you ask me, you really need a facial," she said. I hadn't asked. "You have dry wrinkles around your eyes, and those deep creases around your mouth will be hard to fix with makeup. It'll really sink in." She stood back, her hands on her hips, considering my complexion. "Have you considered cosmetic surgery? You know, people *your* age should consider starting there."

*Your* age? How old did she think I was? Is fifty-three old? I wanted to ask. But I didn't. I sat there, staring into the mirror, thinking she might have a point, and thinking about something I'd read in my initial research. Joan Rivers had once quipped, "*I've had so much plastic surgery when I die, they'll donate my body to Tupperware.*" Sure, that's what I wanted. I tried not to roll my eyes.

"I can recommend some foundations we can try," she said, reaching for bottles and brushes. "I'm sure we can find a few things that might help."

Before I could say a word, she had begun slathering my face with various shades of foundation, muttering about having to mix them together to get the right shade. Of course, I'd need to buy all of them to replicate this at home. She said as much. Then she slathered concealer under my eyes, blending it in with a stiff brush. Finally, she brought in a big fluffy brush, rolled it into what looked like powder with flecks of shiny bits, and swirled it around my cheeks and forehead. She was standing between the mirror and me now, so I couldn't see what was happening. Suddenly, she was telling me to close my eyes, open my eyes, move my head this way, and then that way, all the while taking one brush after another to my face and eyes.

When she had finished, she stood back and said, "Well, it's better. Anyway, it's the best I can do. But you'll need these eight products and these five brushes to get the look at home. I can recommend some makeup videos."

I was anxious to see what I looked like. Finally, she moved out from between me and the mirror. Who in god's name was that in the mirror? It certainly didn't look like me on my worst days at home or my best days on camera. I looked like a clown. To tell you the truth, I looked a lot like several of the older "influencers" I'd seen on Instagram—women for whom I'd felt very sorry they thought they needed so much makeup and filters. My first lesson in ideal woman beauty: never take makeup advice from someone whose makeup you find frightening.

I left the store as quickly as I could and went directly home. It took me half an hour and a half a jar of makeup remover to get it off. The drugstore would be my next stop.

~

The following afternoon, I had myself set up in our guest room since my office had turned out to be too small to store my research materials. I had gone to the drugstore after the Sephora experience, a bit more jaded about buying makeup and a bit more educated. To my great delight, I discovered that drugstores these days provide help with makeup. I was able to connect with a young man (who wasn't wearing a pound of makeup, but I believe I did discern a tiny touch of eyeliner) who helped me find some lotions, potions and makeup that I thought I might be able to use to experiment with this aspect of domesticity. To be truthful, though, I was beginning to lose the connection here between domestic drudgery and personal beauty. Nevertheless, I was hooked enough to want to see where it led.

"You're doing that wrong," came the voice from the other side of the room as I tried to apply the eye shadow that had looked so flattering the day before when the young man put it on me. "And if you think all this makeup is what will give you the homemaker experience, Erica, we need to talk."

Betty looked ravishing in her red dress with its boat neck and cap sleeves. Of course, she was wearing her pearls and a frilly white apron, but when I looked to see how many charms were on her bracelet, she wasn't wearing it today. Before I could ask her where it was, she continued.

"Erica, I suppose you've learned that being a homemaker also involves ensuring you're appealing to your husband. That is what this is all about. Am I right?" I nodded. "What you also need to understand is that it's not just for him. It's also for you. I know from personal experience that when I'm done up, I feel so much better and can accomplish so much more."

I rolled my eyes and sat back in the chair where I'd been leaning over the dresser to experiment. Maddie would be home soon, and she'd be ecstatic to do a video of her mother's attempts at ideal beauty. That thought made me think about beauty.

"Betty, I have all this makeup here that's supposed to alter my looks in a subtle way so that they resemble ideal beauty. But I have no idea what that means."

Betty sat down on the bed and twirled her pearls. "I'm not sure I do, either, Erica. But I do know that being beautiful makes one's life much easier."

I wasn't sure I agreed with her, but then I thought about how so many women, even today, seemed to be given more value because of their beauty. I still couldn't put my finger on what that meant, though.

"I suppose all this makeup is designed to make a woman feel healthy and vibrant," Betty said. "I must say, Erica, I hadn't given this much thought. Perhaps I should." She leaned over and picked up a compact that held blush. "You see this?" she said, opening the cover to reveal the little pinkish-peachish shade. "This can make your cheeks flush like you've just been kissed."

"Or had an orgasm," I said more to myself than to her.

"I heard that," Betty said, a slight smile playing at the corner of her lips. Perhaps fifties housewives weren't as buttoned up as I'd thought. She picked up the mascara. "And this might just be the most important part of the exercise. I'm sure you're aware of what Shakespeare said about eyes."

*"The eyes are the window to your soul."* It was probably one of only three Shakespearean lines I could remember from first-year English.

"Yes, quite so. And that's where it begins. Our eyes communicate things that we often cannot or will not say. What could be wrong with embellishing the windows to your soul? Your eyes are so important."

I thought about this for a moment, and suddenly, the mascara and eyeshadow were so much more than they appeared to be. Perhaps that was true of many things in my life.

*"The real voyage of discovery consists not in seeking new landscapes but in having new eyes,"* I said.

Betty smiled. "Quite so. Marcel Proust, I believe?"

Betty never ceased to amaze me.

~

I spent the following three days experimenting with the makeup—for better or for worse. Maddie, ever the creative filmmaker, always seemed to be there just at that moment when her mother was having a meltdown into her pot of face cream. I have to admit that I found all this cooking and cleaning, laundry and tidying that had to be done, along with the making of oneself ravishing for every encounter with one's husband or the general public, possibly a bridge too far. Okay, admittedly, our housekeeper (remember Alice, our part-time housekeeper) still did much of the work, but I did have a blog to keep up with. Anyway, Andrew found all of this beyond funny. It wasn't quite so funny for me, especially when he came home with news of a social event.

It was Friday afternoon, and I'd put the finishing touches on my weekly blog piece where I couldn't help but share my thoughts about my makeup-shopping experience before I got to the home-based experience. Andrew had gone into his office to divest himself of his briefcase and came out to join me in the kitchen, where I was having a cup of coffee at the breakfast counter.

"I'll have one of those," he said, taking a seat beside me.

I looked up from my iPad, where I was checking my weekly blog stats and nodded toward the coffee maker. "Help yourself." And I went back to my scrolling.

"Geesh, I thought all this domesticity might manifest in a bit of attention to your husband," he said only partially tongue in cheek as far as I could tell as he selected his coffee type and pressed the button.

"You only have to press a button," I said, not looking up.

Andrew brought his coffee over to the counter and sat down. "Erica, darling," he said, "I have a wonderful opportunity for you to strut your newly acquired talents."

I looked up. "I'm not up for giving another party if that's what you mean."

"I don't. I mean your more recent skills." He sipped his coffee. "There's a charity gala at the Carlu next Friday, and we've been summoned."

"What? Summoned by whom?" If the event was at the Carlu, one of the city's premiere event spaces, it must be something of importance to the city's philanthropic elite—the ones who live to dress up and rope their friends into giving money.

"Ted Thomas. Remember him?" Andrew's eyes were twinkling mischievously.

I hadn't even thought of Ted Thomas since that infamous day when Trevor put me on my unexpected sabbatical. I could not imagine why Ted Thomas would want to see me, *persona non grata* at his television station, at a charity gala.

"It's for his wife's pet project—the Princess Margaret Hospital. She's on the board. Anyway, Ted wants us at his table."

I may have mentioned that Andrew knew Ted a lot better than I did. They had met in journalism school eons ago and had kept in touch as Andrew's career took him to the heights of on-air journalism, and Ted had used his family connections (and money) to buy a television station—my television station, as I liked to think of it.

"I hope you didn't say yes," I said. I wasn't a big fan of those big charity events, and I didn't have a thing to wear.

"I wanted to check with you first, but I do think we should go. It's a chance for you to talk to Ted about your future."

The last thing I wanted to do at that moment was talk to Ted Thomas about my future or anything else for that matter. I was already fuming about the fact that I hadn't heard from Trevor about what my role would be after *The Exchange's* regular summer hiatus.

Andrew's smile was almost contagious. "You can also use your newly acquired wifely talents to be the belle of the ball."

I rolled my eyes. The belle of the ball I wasn't. Still, a little voice in my head (not Betty's, thank god) told me that I should probably go.

In the end, I agreed and spent the next week searching for a dress to wear like any domestic goddess from any generation. Much to my disbelief, I was beginning to look forward to it.

~

## ERICA DOES DOMESTICITY

*Have you ever looked at vintage magazine ads? Of course, as I've progressed through my domesticity adventure, I've been scrutinizing those magazines— it's research, after all—and comparing the beauty*

*aesthetic of the pre-feminist housewife to those young women in the "trad wife" movement of the twenty-first century. It's eerily similar.*

*At the risk of promoting a TikTok Channel I find obnoxious, you might surf over to one owned by a young woman named Celeste Wilson and see that I'm spot on when I say she looks like she stepped out of the 1950s. Look at her smooth complexion (although that could be a slick filter these days), her bouffant-like blonde hair and those enormous boobs often leaning into the camera like some form of disturbing pin-up bimbo. And when she posts a photo of her "date night" ensemble (I cannot tell you how much this "date-night" shit grates on me. Get real, honey; you're married, and when you go out with your husband, you're going out with your husband; you're not on a date) she pulls out all the stops. There she is in her black sheath dress with the plunging neckline and lipstick so bright red her lips come through the door before she does. And then there are the pearls. Don't forget the pearls.*

*So, now tell me I'm wrong about the new beauty aesthetic for the ideal wife not being different than the beauty ideal for the perfect wife in 1960. Tell me that young women today have come so much farther than their mothers and grandmothers. Tell me that there isn't a beauty standard for the perfect homemaker. I dare you.*

*My problem is that when I try to emulate this aspect of the ideal domestic drudge, all I can think of is the great Nora Ephron when she said, "The neck starts to go at 43, and that's that."*

# 13

# 125 Danger Signs I Might Have Cancer or Something Else (Kill Me Now)

*After obsessively Googling symptoms for four
hours, I discovered 'obsessively Googling symptoms'
is a symptom of hypochondria.*
~ Stephen Colbert

IN SPITE OF MY FEELING THAT I MIGHT be beginning to look forward to the gala, I still had mixed feelings about attending a splashy social event. Andrew and I had been keeping a pretty low profile since my involuntary sabbatical began. Neither of us had ever been much of a party animal, and we'd noticed that since we'd gotten older, we were even less interested in forced socializing. And charity events were the epitome of forced socializing. Let me explain.

These events had a playbook. First, these events have two overt purposes: presumably to raise awareness of whatever good cause the event supports and to raise money. Of course, the main objective (the one that is part of a not-so hidden agenda) is to have a social event that offers the opportunity to schmooze while wearing your most fantastic wardrobe. The chichi elite philanthropist ladies of the higher socio-economic echelons form committees in support of good causes. One of them is the chairperson, and the rest of them head up sub-committees like "silent auction," "food," and "promotion." All of them will be well-connected enough to be able to persuade (strong-arm) friends and acquaintances to donate objects and experiences for the silent auction and to buy (expensive) tickets. I had never been in these circles—although I had attended my share of such events.

I have long had a love-hate relationship with charity galas that had developed over two decades of being required to attend on behalf of one employer or another. It was rarely because I chose to attend. I wasn't much for small talk, and forced chumminess with people with whom I wouldn't choose to spend any other time was exhausting. However, for some reason, as I mentioned, I began looking forward to this one while, at the same time, loathing the very idea of this forced congeniality. But Andrew seemed to think it was a good idea.

When Maddie heard we were going, she said, "Awesome! Now you can get out of those yoga pants you've been wearing for the past six months, Mom."

I certainly did not wear the same pair every day. I'll have you know I had a wardrobe of yoga pants (and Mom jeans), but I did get Maddie's point. Seeing me dressed up might be good for my daughter—and maybe it would be good for me. Maddie also suggested I might even be able to put some of my newly acquired makeup talents to work. If I remember correctly, she may have mentioned something about walking the talk—or something like that.

By the time the evening of the event arrived, I'd found a dress, gotten a haircut (something else I'd been putting off) and determined which of my friends would be attending. Sam was a big no. "Wouldn't be caught dead there, Ricky," was her answer to my question.

My friend Evelyn, the lawyer, and Michael, her husband, the stockbroker, did plan to attend. Michael was an inveterate "networker" and couldn't miss this opportunity. His family was also old money here in the city and was well-known for its support of several high-profile causes. And besides, since Evelyn had inherited a shitload of money for her great-grandmother's estate, they had money to burn—or at least donate to good causes. So, Evelyn was a yes.

I was also happy when I called Matt, and his answer was, "You know Marcus and I would go to the opening of an envelope." It was an inside joke. Yes, they would be there, and would no doubt put the rest of the men in attendance to shame with whatever sartorial choices they made.

Now that I knew I'd have reinforcements at the event if required and they would be seated at a nearby table, I was content. I would have preferred to be able to sit beside Evelyn and gossip about everyone all evening. However, Andrew and I would be in the company of Ted Thomas, his wife Annabelle, the event chairperson, and several other of his nearest and dearest business acquaintances. There was no way around that.

We arrived at the event by Uber just after eight on the evening in question. It wasn't a long drive, but our driver had managed to fill us in on every fare he'd had for the past six hours. He deposited us as close to the door as he could get behind huge black Suburbans and a stretch limo. We thanked him and got out.

As we walked toward the door, I managed to catch sight of several to-die-for dresses that surely cost more than I had made last year—and I did pretty well until six months ago. It was a warm evening, so no one wore a wrap unless it was part of the ensemble. I was wearing a one-shoulder black sheath that fell to my ankles. It had subtle sparkles on it and a thigh-high slit, of which Andrew had greatly approved. "If you've got great legs," he had said when I modelled it for him the day before, "you should flaunt them." Then he had smiled the smile that had captivated me twenty years earlier when I'd first laid eyes on him across that crowded pub in London. We were both in the city covering the same news story for different networks. We married three months later, and after all these years of marriage, his approval still meant something to me.

The room where the gala was taking place was on the seventh floor of this historic Art Moderne building. It started life in 1930 as the flagship of the now-defunct Canadian department store Eaton's, the icon that was owned by one of the residents who had lived in my neighbourhood back in the 1960s, as I'd discovered on the same research trip to the archives where I'd first encountered

Elizabeth and Edward Crocket's names. As far as I could tell, this space had always been for events, but it was now owned and operated by two of the city's most fashionable restauranteurs.

The atmosphere was one of anticipated excitement. You could almost smell the money. The guests seemed to be of one of two types. Either they were the old money, sophisticated and subdued in their conservative—but expensively cut—black tuxedos and designer gowns or the *nouveau riche*, social-climbing fashionistas. The latter were like peacocks in their myriad colours and textures—including the men. Andrew and I fit into neither category as far as I could see.

We wandered past the silent auction items: gaudy but expensive jewellery, baskets of high-end snacks (I saw a few cans of caviar), silk scarves, experiences like skydiving and chef's tasting menus, a weekend at a chalet, numerous pieces of artwork mostly of a modern and odd nature, a private boat cruise including cocktails. One item that especially caught my eye was the hot-air balloon ride, but I could see several women festooned in glittering jewellery skulking around that one, upping the ante every time someone dared to lift a pen to make a bid.

Andrew and I found our table. Ted and Annabelle, whom I had met once before but she didn't remember, were already there. They introduced us to the other two couples at the table, and I promptly forgot their names. That was so not like me. In my career as a television personality, I had always found it useful to remember people's names. There had been a time when I'd even practiced techniques for doing so. You know, things like focusing on their faces when being introduced, repeating their names once or twice in conversation—the usual. These two couples looked interchangeable with any other couple among the old-money sophisticates. I fit right in with my black dress, although I knew beyond a shadow of a doubt that mine had cost considerably less than theirs. You can just tell. It had been an inspired choice, though. I was, however, still wondering why Ted had invited us.

As the evening progressed, Evelyn stopped by, and we had a too brief chat.

"How are things going over here?" she said, sitting in Andrew's chair while he was at the bar. "Have you figured out why Ted wanted you here tonight?"

"Not a clue. I'll let you know if anything transpires."

After she left, Marcus and Matt stopped by to say hi. They were among the *nouveau riche* with their creative approach to formal dressing.

Matt, the more subdued of the two, wore a traditionally cut tuxedo jacket made from black brocade shot through with silver threads. He was wearing a black velvet bowtie and black tuxedo trousers, seamlessly stitching together the *nouveau* with the old money. Marcus, the artistic one of the two, wore a maroon-coloured silk tuxedo with a black velvet shawl collar. I looked down at his shoes and wondered where in the world one found maroon patent-leather court shoes to match what I would bet was a designer tux. They looked magnificent. After a very brief chat, they went off in search of champagne while I was left alone at the table with Ted.

Andrew had asked Annabelle to dance, and they had disappeared into the crowd. Everyone else at our table was also either up dancing or schmoozing, so that left me with the boss of bosses.

"Finally, alone at last," he said, pouring more champagne into his flute and mine. "Erica, do tell me how you are."

I mumbled something about being fine—as one does—and sipped my champagne.

"We haven't had a chance to chat since your on-air rout of that young woman." Was he smiling? He took a sip of champagne before continuing. "Of course, it was the wrong way to go about it, but I do have to admit it made for great television. And you did have a few valid points to make. Too bad about the political correctness police."

I decided the less said about that event, the better. I must admit that I was surprised by his perspective on the matter of my little meltdown. I wanted to ask Ted about the station's plans for my future return to *The Exchange*, but before I had a chance to get to that, he asked me about my current project.

"Annabelle tells me you've embarked on a little venture while you're off chilling out and taking a breather, so to speak."

I was astonished that Annabelle knew anything about my project at all, and when I mentioned my surprise to Ted, he said, "You underestimate your influence, Erica. And that TikTok channel. It's pure genius. I have to admit that I was more than a bit surprised that you'd let your hair down, so to speak, but I must say it's entertaining."

I told Ted I was enjoying my project but that I was looking forward to the next phase of my career.

"You know, Erica, I've always wondered why you left the news world to entertain homebound women and senior citizens on afternoon television. Don't get me wrong. I've always been impressed by your work on *The Exchange*, but you were a good newsman, if you'll pardon the sexist language."

"I made some difficult decisions, Ted—decisions that men don't usually have to make, so it might not have occurred to you."

"How so?"

"Andrew and I chose to be parents, so I chose to take a job that didn't require me to travel so much. And I've never regretted it." I was being entirely truthful, notwithstanding my recent discontent with my job.

Ted looked thoughtful, and I wondered what was going through his head. Before he could say anything, Andrew and Annabelle returned to the table, breathless from their turn around the dance floor.

"Andrew, man," Ted said, getting up from his seat and clapping Andrew on the back, "let's take a trip to the bar."

That left me alone at the table with Annabelle since everyone else was dancing to the strains of the Big Band and its 1940s and '50s music. Did I mention the theme was "Swing the Night Away?"

"Erica Flanagan, I have very much been looking forward to chatting," Annabelle said, sliding into the chair Ted had just vacated. She lifted his champagne glass and drained it before pouring more, emptying another bottle. I supposed Ted and Andrew would return with another one. "I insisted that we have you and Andrew here this evening." *So, that's how it happened*, I thought. She continued. "Everyone's talking about your domesticity project. It's *so* interesting. We're all a bit perturbed with these young women who seem to think that returning to domestic drudgery is the way of the future."

By "all," I presumed she meant the women in her social circle, all well north of fifty or sixty years old, and not a single one among them who hadn't been born with a silver spoon in her mouth. And, of course, none of them would know a domestic chore if it came up and bit them in the ass. As a former journalist, it was my job to keep up with these things. Anyway, I didn't mention any of these thoughts to Annabelle.

"You know, Erica, your little undertaking has hit close to home for several of my friends—and me, if I'm being totally honest."

Oh, there was nothing I wanted more than to hear total honesty from Annabelle Thomas. There was a time, back when I was a real journalist when sitting as quietly as a church mouse and listening to slightly drunken, well-connected people running off at the mouth was a gold mine of information worth following up on. I had no idea where she was going with this, but I was sure I could tuck it away for future reference. Once a journalist, always a journalist, I suppose.

"Erica—and you must keep this a little secret between the two of us—even my own daughter seems to think it's just fine to sit at home and bake bread." She lifted her champagne flute by the stem and daintily sipped. "You cannot even imagine how much we spent on her education." Oh, but I could. "You know, she graduated summa cum laude from the Harvard business school and had such a bright future with the firm who took her on. Ted even hoped she might move up in the station and take over from him someday. But no. She's been listening to her girlfriends whose approval seems to matter more than her parents. To tell you the truth, I was watching your show that day you lambasted that delightfully fatuous young woman. You should never have been taken off the air, but what can you do? You know the advertisers are touchy about that kind of thing."

That kind of thing. Yes, I suppose candour and honesty weren't quite their thing. Then, before I could continue this unexpected conversation with Annabelle, she was off in a different direction as if we hadn't just been talking about her over-educated, bread-baking daughter. She began waxing poetic about her pet cause—and the real reason anyone was here this evening. Cancer.

Yes, she was obsessed with cancer. Her work with the Princess Margaret Hospital, a cancer hospital, had a long history, dating back to her father's death from pancreatic cancer fifteen years earlier. I hadn't been aware of that until this moment.

"Did you know," she was saying, "that there are dozens of signs you might have cancer? I mean, I just wish everyone knew that things like bloating, coughing, headaches, bruising, fatigue, and so many more things we experience every day might mean you have cancer. We need to pay attention to the little things. We cannot ignore them. People should know this."

I wasn't at all sure people should know this and start believing that everything they experience in the run of a typical day might be cancer. I shuddered at the thought of people running to their doctor with every headache—just in case. I was so shocked thinking about this possibility that I almost missed it when Annabelle swooped in with her pitch.

"You have those all-important communication skills that we need," she was saying. Was she suggesting I do volunteer work to help her spread the word that everyone needs to be concerned every moment of every day that they might have cancer?

As I listened to her, I felt I was in the presence of a rabid health fanatic. She seemed to have drunk the Kool-Aid, as the expression goes, and there was no getting away from her. Finally, I told her I'd get back to her and escaped to the ladies' room. By the time I returned to our table, everyone else was back, and she seemed to have moved on to her next potential acolyte.

Finally, the evening wound down. As Andrew and I waited on the corner for our Uber, all I could think about was the article I'd seen recently in one of those women's magazines I'd been using for research. No kidding, the article was titled "125 Signs I Might Have Cancer." I shivered.

~

We hadn't been away for such a long time. So, when Andrew said we should take a weekend in Niagara-on-the-Lake, Maddie and I jumped at the chance. We spent two days attending summer theatre, eating beautiful food and touring wineries, all less than a two-hour drive from home. It was magical. By Monday, I'd decided the next phase of my project was to look at women, domesticity, and health stuff.

There was no doubt in my mind that personal and family health were the purview of the homemaker—both today and in the past. Even the young woman I'd so infamously skewered had a chapter in her book on staying healthy. Evidently, it was a requirement of being a good wife. One had to not only be beautiful (as I've already discussed), but one had to be healthy. I suppose it might be safe to say health ought to come first, but that's not how it happened for my project.

It hadn't been lost on me, either, that I'd seen so many articles and advertisements for women and their health in both the magazines of the past and the present. Then, after Annabelle's uplifting (not) exhortation on how many everyday aches, pains, and hiccups might actually be harbingers of cancer and imminent death to hear her talk, I thought it only right to pursue this for my faithful blog readers.

As I began rereading some of the articles I'd put aside, I wondered if my reaction to Annabelle's fanaticism about cancer might not be related to my age—and hers. After all, I was already over fifty and staring down the barrel of my own mortality. So, it seemed appropriate for me to be interested in how women deal with being the keepers of domestic health. I just wondered what was in the minds of those younger women bent on domesticity and what all this health stuff meant to them. I wondered if it had anything to do with the fact that when we're younger, we think we're never going to die.

I had recently read Erica Jong's book *Fear of Dying* (as opposed to her novel *Fear of Flying,* a favourite book of my mother's back in the 1970s. I never did figure out why she was interested in the zipless fuck, but that's a story for another day.). Among other things, Erica Jong says, "*Death is fearless. It's our anticipation of dying that's the problem.*"

Oh, so true. And it seemed that older women were the only ones who really got that. I loved Nora Ephron's book *I Feel Bad About My Neck, And Other Thoughts on Being a Woman* and had highlighted the following passage: "*Death doesn't really feel eventual or inevitable. It still feels... avoidable somehow. But it's not. We know in one part of our brains that we are all going to die, but on some level, we don't quite believe it.*"

These were the thoughts on my mind as I opened a couple of new magazines for domestic women. Alongside the recipes and instructions for starting your Christmas DIY projects in August were the health articles. Many of them seemed to have checklists for how to be healthy. *Great! Just what a busy wife needs*, I thought. *Another checklist.*

There were things like "MD's Miracle GI Rescue." Did enough women need to have their bowels rescued that it warranted a magazine article? Then there was "The Cayenne Cure: Bye, Bye Chronic Pain." Well, it might remove the pain in your wrist, but I'm not sure about your tongue. Moving on. There were articles about "herbal cures" and magnets. Yes, apparently, magnets can make you look ten years younger. I stopped reading and flung that last one across the living room, watching it land on the chair opposite me.

"My, my, my, Erica. Testy today?"

I looked up and, yes, it was Betty. She was standing by the fireplace, stroking her pearls as usual. And, as usual, she was meticulously dressed—this time in a black sheath dress, black heels and a black and white apron. She looked like she was going to a party and had forgotten to remove her apron.

"You're looking like you might be ready for a party," I said.

Betty looked down. "Yes. We're off to a cocktail party. I just needed a few moments before facing another social event."

So, Betty and I had that sentiment in common.

Betty looked at the open magazine on the sofa beside me and then glanced at my notes on the coffee table. "So, you're reading about homemakers and health, are you?" I nodded. She picked up one of Mom's old magazines and read from the titles on the cover. "'Cures for Those Vague Aches and Pains.'" She put it down. "Ah, yes. Women's health issues are really just vague aches and pains, you know. Nothing to be concerned about." Was that sarcasm I heard coming from the perfect Betty, the homemaker? She picked up another one and flipped through. "Oh, yes. See these advertisements?" I looked over. "Make no mistake. A healthy wife also douches regularly." She noticed me wincing. "I suppose that's no longer something important?"

I then launched into the modern rant against such a mind-boggling imbecilic activity for women (that men had thought so necessary). Bacterial overgrowth, pelvic inflammatory disease, and even cervical cancer—all identified as side effects of said barbarism. What I also knew, however, was that up to 40% of women still engaged in this absurd activity. Then I remembered Gwyneth Paltrow and her "Goop" store online. As much as I thought some of what women did in the past was beyond senseless, really, today's women were equally gullible.

Remember the whole vaginal steaming thing? Gwyneth was seemingly devoted to the notion that women would benefit from sitting their delicate parts over a steaming bowl of water and that this misguided activity would do wonders for—wait for it— clearing their fallopian tubes, among other things. Does she even know where our fallopian tubes are? And if that one doesn't leave you scratching your head, there were GP's jade eggs. The instructions were that you were supposed to put these expensive things (that she sold, of course) into your vagina, purportedly to prevent a sagging uterus and balance your hormones. Of course, that one resulted in lawsuits for false claims, yet women continued to listen to her. And let us all take a moment to appreciate the utter lunacy of her "This smells like my vagina" candles that flew off the shelves. Were women really so starstruck that they took total leave of their senses? When I read the book *Is Gwyneth Paltrow Wrong About Everything?* that had been written by a well-qualified, quackery-debunking academic expert, I was delighted to learn the answer was a resounding yes. But now I also realized that, perhaps, we hadn't come as far as I thought.

"What's all this about?" Betty said, pointing to an article in a recent magazine about keeping healthy by going gluten-free. "What the heck is gluten? Do homemakers now have to put their children on special diets?"

I wasn't sure how to explain to Betty how fads like this one — and others like the raw milk movement and all that kale — came to represent how homemakers could and should live to be healthy. But I had to try. She listened as I talked. But as I spoke, I realized I was trying to make the case to myself. I was trying to understand my own peers. Were we really trying to cheat death? Were we really trying out all these outlandish approaches to health in a vain attempt to trick the Grim Reaper into thinking he should pass us by? Everyone was going to die. Life is, after all, terminal. No one gets out alive. I now had a topic for my blog, but I wasn't sure Maddie and her trusty iPhone camera could work with this one.

~

## *ERICA DOES DOMESTICITY*

*Let me begin this week's blog by stating the obvious. Life is terminal. No one gets out of this life alive. Healthy, however, is another story, and it seems that today's (and yesterday's) domestic drudges are not only responsible for the perfection of home, hearth, children and their own faces, but they are also*

*responsible for maintaining the family's perfect health. And if you're twenty-five years old, like so many of the perfect trad wives on TikTok and Instagram, it's not that difficult. Let's take a moment to consider what might happen to the ideal wife as she ages out of her natural beauty and health into something less than perfect.*

*First, consider that the queen of the absurd when it comes to trying to stave off the ravages of aging and environmental health hazards, Gwyneth Paltrow, is now over fifty. Yes, that's right. She is my contemporary. She is not a contemporary of the new trad wives. But they do have something in common: a fixation on wellness trends.*

*It seems her latest weird wellness foray is into what she calls ozone therapy, which is administered—wait for it—rectally. You can't make this stuff up.*

*There are lengths each of us would go to for our family's health. I cannot deny that. But sometimes you just have to take a step back and say, "This is just weird. No."*

*But consider, too, that each of these twenty-something trad wives who are now influencing hordes of young, unsuspecting women will someday be fifty. And we all know that life happens. People age and develop illnesses and lose their natural beauty. Where will they be then?*

~

As I put the finishing touches on my blog piece about homemakers and health, I sat back wondering about myself. I was continuing to have conversations with my hallucination. Of course, I realized I was probably having these conversations with myself, but they seemed so real. Betty seemed so real. I didn't talk about her to anyone. After I first mentioned my hallucination to Andrew and he suggested I chat with Peter, we hadn't really talked about it again, although he occasionally asked how it was going. I always smiled and said I was happy with our sessions, and

Andrew left it at that. He knew if and when I wanted to talk about it again, I would bring it up. Our relationship had always been like that. But now, I was wondering about rationality. Could someone be mentally stable and continue to talk to an apparition? Or had I gone bonkers?

I wanted to discuss this with Sam, who knew me almost as well as Andrew did, but in a different way. Yet I couldn't bring myself to let her know about Betty—at least not yet.

# 14

# The Art of Being a Well-Dressed Wife

*If you adore her, you must adorn her. There lies*
*the essence of a happy marriage.*
~ Anne Fogarty, *Wife Dressing: The Art of*
*Being a Well-Dressed Wife*

I THINK I'VE ALWAYS BELIEVED IN THE POWER of an image. That image might be as compelling and meaningful as a picture of a young naked woman fleeing the Viet Cong's napalm attack or as trivial as a power-suited woman chairing a Fortune-500 company's annual investor meeting. But is the power suit on the woman as trivial as it seems at first glance? The nakedness or the power suit—both make a statement. And for a woman, that statement about her image always begins with wardrobe.

Although my family might have been starting to disagree, I'd always believed in dressing appropriately for the occasion. Lately, I'd slid down the slippery slope of comfort dressing, as one does when working from home. (If the pandemic did nothing else, it taught us that everyone is capable of slovenliness.) Who can argue with the position that the appropriate dress code for the home office is yoga pants and a sweatshirt? I must admit, though, that I'd occasionally thought about what someone had once told me about Mary Kay cosmetics salespersons.

Cosmetics mogul Mary Kay believed in the power of image. It was part of her business philosophy that in addition to the inevitable makeup—which was her bread and butter—clothes, as part of that image, had an essential impact on self-confidence. Consequently, as the story goes, part of the training for her sales force involved the admonishment to be well-dressed and fully made up whenever conducting business. Evidently, Mary Kay even instructed her sales force women to stare into a mirror when making phone calls from a home office. Perhaps this is business folklore, but it does have a ring of truth to it.

In the years before I became an afternoon television personality, I was a real reporter who covered stories in disparate parts of the world. You've seen reporters who've made safari jackets their go-to uniform of choice, possibly conveying the image of the rough-and-ready, on-the-ground personality. These are usually men. But, as I said, I've always believed there was something to be said for dressing for the occasion. This philosophy meant different outfits for interviewing troops in Afghanistan and covering an American election from Washington. In those days, I chose my own wardrobe, which often consisted of jeans and a buttoned-up shirt. All that changed when I left hard news reporting.

As a television personality, someone else dictated what I would wear. Like an actor on a stage (or a salesclerk in Sephora, for that matter), I was playing a role. There was a specific wardrobe style that helped to magnify my particular role—the erudite, professional, older woman bitch. So, suits were my everyday garb on air. My producer, via his wardrobe staff, dictated my clothing to portray a specific image. Half a century ago, for a housewife, that dictator might well have been a husband. After all, wasn't a housewife simply playing a role?

These were the things on my mind as I moved into the next phase of my project. All along, even when studying the recipes and makeup ads, I had been mesmerized by the wardrobe choices of the housewives portrayed in the old magazines. In the 1950s and 1960s (and less so in the 1970s), homemakers seemed to take the view that dressing for the occasion meant dresses or skirts, low-heeled pumps, pearls and the ubiquitous apron. They looked so happy staring at the camera while washing dishes, perfectly coiffed and made up. Even Betty, a figment of my imagination, had the uniform. If I were going to explore this idea, I'd have to get into it. That would mean a bit of vintage shopping and doing the vacuuming in heels. But I was going to need some help. I'd need to do some research.

I scoured the online sources and found, much to my abject horror, that the new "traditional wife movement" members—the trad wives—espoused a similar view of homemaker dressing. One such blogger even said that putting this kind of attention on her appearance—and dressing up to clean the toilets—had improved her homemaking. Seriously? Well, we'd see about that.

Then, I found the gem I'd been searching for. It was a book by a lesser-known 1960s fashion designer named Anne Fogarty. The book was called *Wife Dressing: The Fine Art of Being a Well-Dressed Wife*, and it was a treasure trove of perspective and ideas.

The newly available edition was a plain pink hardcover adorned with only the title and sub-title. When I found an original 1959 edition, I jumped at it, ordering it immediately.

On the front of this first edition dust jacket is a beautifully dressed wife wearing a charming bateau neckline top and a wide full skirt. Her hair is gathered into a beautiful knot at the back of her head, and she has her hands clasped on her lap as she gazes to the left—what is she gazing at? Oh, I know. I looked down to see the sub-sub-title at the bottom of the cover. It said, *"With provocative notes for the patient husband who pays the bills."* There was now little doubt in my mind who she was looking at so imploringly. But the wisdom inside was the real jackpot.

*"When your husband's eyes light up as he comes in at night, you're in sad shape if it's only because he smells dinner cooking."* When I read that, I thought she might be onto something. I wondered if I should ask Andrew his opinion on the subject, but perhaps I didn't want to know the answer!

Anne also said, *"Courage and discretion go hand in hand: the courage to dare to be yourself, the discretion not to overdo; the courage to do something unusual, the discretion to temper it."* This seemed like a fine philosophy for dressing in general, but it didn't help me to figure out what I would have to wear to complete this next phase of my project. My next stop was a vintage shop only a few blocks from where I lived, where I'd made an appointment to chat with the proprietor.

~

I'd read an article about this shop in the local news media sometime in the previous year. Nestled between a coffee shop to the north and a pet grooming facility to the south, Cool Cat Couture was a treasure trove of all things vintage—at least in the fashion sense. I had discovered they were not a consignment store. The local fashion doyennes couldn't drop off their worn-only-once items in an attempt to recoup a bit of the eye-watering price they'd paid. This place was a curated shop and was the real deal when it came to fashion history.

The proprietor was named Bethany Anderson, but as she told me, everyone called her Bitsy. Bitsy had a fine arts degree from the College of Art and Design and focused her work on authentic mid-century (twentieth century, to be clear) clothing and accessories. Hers was the place to go if you were going to a *Mad Men* party. I only wish I'd thought of her when I did that a few months earlier!

I'm not sure what I expected, but I wasn't expecting a thirty-something Marilyn Monroe look-alike, authentic right down to the Chanel Number Five I could smell as I leaned in to shake her hand.

"Ms. Flanagan, I'm delighted to meet you," she said, leading me into her office at the back of the shop. "I must say I was surprised when you called. I mean, after your last appearance on *The Exchange*."

I tried to focus on her words, but I was distracted by rack after rack of colourful vintage housedresses, sweaters and cocktail dresses and cabinets filled with strands of pearls, brooches and charm bracelets—lots of charm bracelets.

Her office looked like the set for a 1960s family sitcom. When I was surfing the web a few months earlier, I'd fallen down a rabbit hole of 1960s television shows featuring housewives. This room reminded me so strongly of the living room on the *Dick Van Dyke Show* that I expected Mary Tyler Moore to appear at any moment wearing her ankle-length cigarette pants, sweater and ballet flats. She was a trendy, modern housewife of the mid-60s—no wide skirts for her!

I sat beside Bitsy on the gold brocade sofa, wondering where she had managed to acquire the enormous gold-embossed table lamps at each end. I told her to call me Erica.

"Erica, would you like some tea?"

Bitsy had set out tea and tiny sandwiches that looked like ones we had the day Sam and I had gone to high tea at the Windsor Arms Hotel a year or so ago. Once she poured, I told her about my current project, but I needn't have. She told me she was an avid reader of my blog and watched Maddie's TikTok reels religiously.

"You know, Erica," Bitsy said, "I understand the Gen-Z and Baby Boomer angst about this return-to-homemaking movement, but I wonder if you quite understand where it's all coming from."

I asked her about her perspective.

"I'm an artist at heart," Bitsy said. "That means I'm not really a part of this movement, but many of my customers are, and I've talked to them about their motivations. These women want a simpler life. They've been unhappy with the lack of work-life balance."

I had to bite my tongue to keep from reacting. I'd long believed that since work *is* a real part of real life—and a huge one at that—this nattering about work-life balance was a waste of the energy that could otherwise be put into understanding that simple fact. But I held my tongue admirably, I thought.

Bitsy continued. "I think most of them are reclaiming domesticity."

Reclaiming domesticity? What kind of utter drivel was that? Still, I kept quiet. I wasn't here to argue the finer points of feminism and whether the "new domesticity" was a legitimate part of it. I was here to find clothes that spoke of homemaking in the most traditional (anachronistic) sense.

"So, Bitsy, why do you think these young domestics are choosing the kinds of clothing you sell here?" I really wanted to ask her about the Marilyn vibe she had going, but that would just be a distraction.

Bitsy finished her tea and put her fine China cup back onto its saucer with a tiny clatter. "Come with me, Erica. Let's have a look at some of the choices they make."

As we walked along the racks, Bitsy said, "I think most of the women who've moved back into the home by choice are trying to inject a bit more glamour into a role that hasn't been seen as very glamorous."

That struck me as a bit of an understatement. What was glamorous about taking an old toothbrush to the toilet flange? It also puzzled me. If a young woman wanted glamour, surely she could find a more compatible calling than domestic drudgery. But then, I remembered all those new homemaker blogs penned so prettily by young women who revelled in baking banana bread and scrubbing the kitchen floor. But I could be wrong.

Bitsy pulled three dresses from the rack. These dresses were ones my mother might have called housedresses. She would never have worn one, but her mother, my grandmother, Nora, probably did. They all had narrow tops with buttons down the front, short sleeves and full skirts that would fall to about mid-calf. Each one was in a different print in fabric that appeared to be cotton. I would have called them dignified and slightly prim—they certainly weren't Marilyn Monroe! The similarities in their design suggested to me that conformity was also important.

"A housedress was the uniform, as I'm sure you've figured out," Bitsy said, hanging them on a hook by the dressing room so we could take a better look. "It had to be comfortable, roomy enough to bend and stoop to do housework and be washable. But it also had to have a certain feminine quality about it. As a homemaker of the day, you could never look frazzled. There had to be a perpetual elegance. No one wanted to be caught out looking like a fright if someone came to the door. Sweats and T-shirts would never have cut it." I shook off the feeling that she had somehow peeked into my recent life. Bitsy stood back to take a better look at the dresses. "Erica, don't you think there's something to be said about how you feel when you know you look well-dressed?"

I knew she had a point, but I was thinking about some of the pictures I'd seen in the magazines. "What about all those pencil skirts? It must have been difficult to do housework in those," I said, also thinking about one or two of Betty's recent outfits.

"My research tells me only homemakers who were really interested in fashion would give up the comfort of a wider skirt and looser top for the confinement of a pencil skirt and closely fitted sweater. It's not so different from today, though, is it? Look around at all the young women today in stilettos and skirts so short they have to continually try to hold them down. They've given up comfort for what they believe to be fashion."

Bitsy was so right. I can't tell you how often I've walked down a sidewalk behind a young woman who is continually pulling at her too-short skirt to keep it from riding up any further. I'm always tempted to tap her on the shoulder and tell her that she wouldn't have to do that if her skirt were a few inches longer.

"Did housewives ever wear pants in the 1950s?"

"Some did, but it wasn't until later in the decade that pants were advertised to women. Then, there were ankle pants, capris and shorts in the 1960s, along with the dresses. Again, mostly fashion-forward women moved from housedresses to pants."

I was remembering Mary Tyler Moore again. And, yes, that was a few years later. "Who's your main customer these days, Bitsy?"

"You'd be surprised, Erica. Most of them are in their twenties and thirties. Many are stay-at-home wives, just like back in the 1950s and '60s. It's quite a phenomenon."

It was, indeed, a phenomenon—one I thought I might never understand, no matter how hard I tried. But I was here to immerse myself in the experience, so with Bitsy's help, we selected half a dozen dresses for me to try on. When I left the store an hour later, I had a carrier bag containing two housedresses, a string of faux pearls, and a pair of (slightly worn) pumps with modestly high heels. The adventure was about to begin.

~

The following day, I donned one of the dresses and descended to the kitchen to make breakfast. Luckily, I made it before either Andrew or Maddie got there. I intended to be the picture of the perfect homemaker with breakfast just ready to be served when they appeared.

Half an hour later, Andrew finally made his way into the kitchen in search of his first cup of coffee. Before he had a chance to touch the on switch of the coffee machine, I handed him a steaming mug of coffee I'd just poured from our cafetière—the French press I'd unearthed from the back of a cupboard. Andrew and I had gone through a phase where only French press coffee passed our lips. That idea soon wore off as we discovered pressing a button was so much more efficient. He turned to take the mug from me.

Andrew's eyes widened. I wasn't sure what made them widen—the fact that he was now taking in the aroma of fresh coffee or that his wife was smiling prettily in her housedress adorned with tiny yellow flowers as she twirled her pearls. And let us not forget I was also wearing an apron with yellow embroidery that said, "You don't like me? That's a shame. It'll take me a few minutes to recover from the tragedy." Okay, so it wasn't an authentic apron, but when I saw it, I realized it was too "me" to pass up. I could see Andrew's lips beginning to formulate something when Maddie came into the kitchen.

"OMG, Mom! What the actual fuck are you wearing?"

"Maddie! Language!"

"I'm sorry, Mom, but this might be too much." She quickly whipped out her phone and started taking videos and snapping photos. She was laughing uproariously as she did so.

Andrew had closed his mouth and continued to stare. Finally, he found his tongue. "Dear god, Erica, I think Maddie is right. This," he said, waving his hand over me, "might be too much. Wherever did you get that outfit? And what are you planning to do today while wearing it?"

I had the distinct impression he was terrified I might be going out, and I might be seen in public. Judging from Maddie's current behaviour, I figured that was a given if you consider social media to be public—which I do.

I explained to my dear family what my objective was in selecting my wardrobe. I explained that I intended to spend my housewifely day doing housewifely activities in a housewifely dress and heels.

Andrew looked down at my feet. "I'll make a bet with you, Erica. I'll bet you that you can't spend more than three hours in those things, and you'll be wearing sneakers when I come home this afternoon."

"You're on," I said optimistically. I wouldn't tell him, but I would have bet me the same thing. Damn. Now I had to try to make it to dinner in these things.

After my little family left me alone, I sat down to contemplate my day. I was sipping my second cup of coffee and paging through a magazine at the kitchen counter when I heard Betty's voice in my ear.

"Erica Flanagan! You must stand up. You must show me that outfit!"

I turned to see her standing in the doorway as usual in an impeccable homemaking ensemble of crisp white shirt, full red skirt and the inevitable pearls.

I got up and stood there under the intense scrutiny of someone who was an expert in what I was trying to pull off.

Betty clapped her hand over her mouth. "Where did you get that dress?" she said, looking slightly alarmed.

"At a shop not far from here."

Betty came closer and looked at it, tipping her head from one side to another as if trying to figure something out. "Where did the shop get the dress?"

"Where did the shop get the dress? I don't know what you mean."

"I can't be any clearer, Erica. Do you happen to know where the owner of the shop acquires his merchandise?"

"It's *her* merchandise. A young woman owns the store, and she told me she has several places where she picks up her merchandise. She gets a lot of it from estate sales or donations. It seems many women keep their clothes for decades. I didn't ask her specifically about this dress."

Betty sat heavily on one of the stools at the kitchen counter and clasped her hands in front of her. "This is so strange, Erica. So very strange."

I had no idea what she was on about.

"Erica, do you mind if I look at the label in the neckline of the dress?"

I shrugged, opened the top button of the shirt-style bodice and reached around behind me to turn the label toward her. As I came closer to her, once again, I could smell the faint scent of Chanel Number Five. I heard a sharp intake of breath as she moved in to look.

"Erica, did you look closely at the label?"

I hadn't looked at it at all. "What's wrong with the label?"

Betty sat down once again at the counter and spoke softly now. "I used to have a dress exactly like that one. It was one of my favourites in my first years of marriage. I bought it at Eaton's. You know Eaton's?"

I did know Eaton's. It was the department store that once occupied the space where Andrew and I had attended the gala a week ago. I started to get an odd feeling of déjà vu. "What does the label say, Betty?"

"Just as I suspected, it says Eaton's. It was one of their house brand dresses a few years ago."

"Define a few years ago."

Betty took a deep breath. "Oh, 1952, I think."

"What happened to it?" I said, intrigued by the fact that Betty had the exact dress I was wearing.

"It's in my closet."

I shook my head. Of course, that was impossible.

"But that's not the whole story, Erica," she said. I asked her to elaborate, and she did. "I have a funny habit. I suppose it's a bit of a quirk or idiosyncrasy. I put my initials on the labels of all my clothes."

"And?"

"And that dress has my very tiny initials in indelible ink on the corner of the label."

I almost jumped out of my skin. "Are you trying to tell me that I'm wearing your dress?"

"I know this is impossible," she said. "But there it is."

I was going to have to consider another appointment with Peter Sparrow. Things were getting weird. Of course, I knew that when I took the dress off later, there would be no such initials, so I closed my eyes for a moment and shook off the feeling before moving on to a new topic.

"One thing I don't understand about these outfits, Betty, is why the pearls? Why do you always wear pearls?"

"It's like Lady Sarah Churchill once said: I feel undressed if I don't have my pearls on. My pearls are my security blanket."

I thought about that for a moment and suddenly realized that the clothing—and those pearls—was like a security blanket. It was true of housewives in the 1950s and 1960s, and it is true today for many, if not most, women—and perhaps men, for that matter. Before I had a chance to say anything about my sudden brain wave, Betty pulled my copy of Anne Fogarty's book from the pile on the counter.

"Oh, I know this one. It's a bit like a bible, isn't it?" she said. "*The Art of Being a Well-dressed Wife.* I'm not a big fan of much of what she espouses, though, you know."

I didn't know, and I was surprised to hear that—perhaps even intrigued.

She flipped open a page and started reading. "Look at this one. She says here, *A wife's regard for her husband's preferences and judgment on how she looks add up to a happy marriage.* Can you imagine the situation if that's what formed the foundation for a happy marriage?"

I couldn't, but I had no idea what did. I only knew I had one— a happy marriage, that is. I also knew that one of the rules in the housewife's playbook was keeping her husband happy. That particular task might be worth examining further.

Marilyn Monroe once said, *"Give a girl the right shoes, and she can conquer the world."* Maybe she had a point. But could she make a husband happy?

~

## *ERICA DOES DOMESTICITY*

*Housewife fashion. Domestic drudge attire. Homemaker clothing. Yes, it's a thing. Over the past week, I've donned my housedress, pearls and pumps and flitted about doing my domestic duties. Why, you ask, wouldn't I just wear yoga pants and a T-shirt? Why, indeed. Well, it's all part of the project.*

*Let's take a step back into history for a moment, shall we? Let's step back into the late 1950s and early 1960s when being polished was the general approach to dressing for any occasion. Those were the days long before ripped jeans became a symbol of trendiness instead of a sign you found your clothes during a dumpster dive. It was also before it became acceptable to wear your pyjamas on the street, and it was okay to wear a cropped top so short the lower part of the boobs shows. It's hard to look away, isn't it? It was a different era, and I know times have to change, but there was something to be said about the self-respect that a more elevated approach to dressing demonstrated. Just saying…*

*But what about the housewife uniform? And, yes, there was one.*

*In the late 1950s and early '60s, men had their jobs, and their wives had their homes. And it was oh so important that the little wife present herself in a very specific, feminine, conservative way—important more to the husband than the wife, it has to be said. Seriously, though, wouldn't they have jumped at the chance to clean the toilets in yoga pants instead of a voluminous skirt, collared blouse and pearls? Can you even imagine what a 1960s homemaker would have made of ripped jeans? There would have been a lot of smelling salts required. (Did they use smelling salts in the 1960s? No idea, but you get the picture.)*

*Fast forward to the trad wives of today in their little housedresses and pearls. I suppose I could get it if these girls (their ages still qualify them as girls) could come clean and say, "I just like how I look in these, even if my husband prefers me in jeans." But that's not how it goes for them. If they were the "vintage style, not vintage values" aficionados swanning down the street in the vintage clothes they'd wear even to a club, I might even get it. But doing it because it's expected of you? Feminism might well be dying. Kill me now.*

~

By the way, Andrew won the bet. By the time he and Maddie arrived home at the end of the day, I was still wearing the dress, but my feet were now adorned with sneakers.

As I carefully took the dress off later, I laid it on the bed and remembered my conversation with Betty about the label. Yes, it was from Eaton's, so it must have been a popular model that year. Then, I peered more closely at the label. I reached for my reading glasses on my bedside table and examined the label. In tiny black letters (so minuscule you could have easily missed them) were the letters "EC," Elizabeth Crocket. I stifled a scream.

# 15

# Happy Husband, Happy Life? Or The Myth of the Perfect Marriage

*In my sex fantasy, nobody ever loves me for my mind.* ~ Nora Ephron

HERE'S SOMETHING I HADN'T THOUGHT ABOUT at the outset of my project, and perhaps it's fundamental to the whole thing. In the world of domestic drudgery, as I've defined it, without a husband, there is no wife. It's impossible, isn't it? (Unless you're a same-sex couple, and that's a discussion for a different day!). And since I've been confining my project to my own situation—I'm a straight woman—being a wife involves having a husband. So, as I moved toward the natural end point of my homemaking project (or was it dying a natural death?), it occurred to me that I might have started in the wrong place. And since you can't go back for a do-over, at least I needed to rectify the problem by ending with it. Husbands. Sex. Marriage. Love. Isn't it all part of being the ideal wife? Well, it depends on who's doing the asking.

There is an old saying that I'm sure you've heard. *Happy wife, happy life.* As annoying as it is, there is probably some truth to it. How, then, did the happy homemaker seem to devolve to be the servant of the master? Happy husband, happy life? Let me back up.

This whole project began as what I now see as a bit of a knee-jerk response to the new movement of young women back into domestic drudgery, purportedly by choice and being put on involuntary leave—my sabbatical, to frame it differently—to

216

contemplate my on-air behaviour. As a fifty-something woman who had worked long and hard for women not to be tied to the home and kitchen, it seemed like an abomination. It seemed like a step backward. It seemed like a cop-out. Perhaps this last description is the one that bothered me the most. It smelled to me like young women blowing off the years of progress we'd made as women, moving from the kitchen to the boardroom. And yet, those fully invested in this move back to traditional roles have the audacity to say it's their choice. They say it's a feminist thing to do. Well, ladies, I've got news for you. All you're doing is sliding back into servitude, doing things that men (who want wives like you) aren't willing to do themselves. (PS There are, thank god, oodles of men who really don't want you, by the way.) And as the mother of a teenage daughter, I was shaking in my boots at the thought she might make this "choice" and join the #tradwife movement. You know, there's actually an Instagram account called "The Tradwives Club," and at last count, it had more than twenty-five thousand followers.

These were the things I was contemplating and trying to write a blog piece about on a sunny July morning when I really wanted to get out in the garden. I could feel the end of this project getting closer. After all, how many topics could you cover in the domestic drudgery world? This final foray into the world of the homemaker was going to be especially challenging because I had no idea what I could "do" that would be the slightest bit interesting to Maddie's TikTok audience. I tapped my pen on the desk, where I gazed at a blank document on the computer screen in front of me. Perhaps I could return to my original research to see what ideas might arise.

I shuffled through some notes I'd made longhand and noticed that I'd highlighted one.

*"I put my husband's wants ahead of my own, and it has done nothing but benefit me and my marriage."* These *bon mots* were expressed that influencer Celeste Wilson, doyenne of the twenty-first-century traditional wife movement. Being all twenty-five years old, she could be counted on for advice and inspiration to quit one's career and spend life doting on a husband who doles

out the money like candy to children on Halloween. Gag me now. I'd forgotten about this one.

I clicked over to YouTube to review this research. Yes, there she was again in all her bouffant blonde hair glory, her ample bustline enhanced by the camera angle that always seemed to put those girls front and centre while she baked bread and "spoke her truth" about how wonderful being a domestic drudge was. The question highest on my mind was this: in the twenty-first century, what kind of man wants this traditional wife whose life is about nothing more than him—whose most riveting conversations revolve around nothing more interesting than cooking, cleaning, chauffeuring children and finding the perfect lipstick shade so he'll find her more alluring? And let's take a moment to remember that this man—this husband—makes and controls all the money and gives permission for the wife to do just about anything. And this is supposed to be what feminism looks like? I suppose we should "literally celebrate" other women's choices, as one online dimwit said.

I was listening to Celeste babble on the screen about what she was doing that morning, occasionally preaching about her choice in life. One of the lines I had found particularly obnoxious as I'd listened to her and others like her was the belief that "women were built for this" and "housework is women's work." Where did they get that idea? As long as there was women's work and men's work, there would never be equality. It was galling to see this archaic and frankly chauvinistic attitude in a twenty-something. Then it occurred to me that so many of them were mommy bloggers and housewife TikTokkers because they needed others around them—their tribe—to support their choice. Perhaps they weren't as sold on it as they let on. As for me, I had begun to enjoy some of my newfound skills.

No one was more surprised than I was to discover I enjoyed a bit of cooking and had actually learned to make a pie. I also loved doing the laundry. Who knew? I loved the smell of the fresh sheets as I pulled them from the dryer and then held them against me to feel that dryer warmth. Why was that dryer warmth so different and so much better than warmth from a radiator? I had no idea. I only knew it made me feel safe. Whenever I thought about returning to the daily television grind, I felt a bit uneasy. I wondered if I would still have time to pursue my new domestic skills—in a very limited way, mind you.

I started mindlessly flipping through a few vintage magazines on my desk as I considered my future. I was looking for articles about husbands and marriage when I felt like I wasn't alone in the room.

I looked up and over by the window in my little office where Betty leaned against the sill, backlit by the sun that streamed in. She looked a bit like a goddess. Her usual bouffant hair, which young Celeste's resembled, was swept back, revealing small diamond stud earrings. But that wasn't the only thing that was different about her.

"Betty, you look so different today," I said, staring. "No pearls."

Betty glanced down at herself. "No. No pearls today," she said, smiling. "No apron, either, in case you hadn't noticed."

I had noticed, but those weren't the only things that looked different. She was wearing pants! Her light pink capris and short-sleeved white shirt with a small bandana tied around her bare throat reminded me of a photo of Jackie Kennedy from around 1960. And the bracelet hadn't reappeared. I was still curious.

"Wow, Betty. What's up? And where's your bracelet?"

She looked down at her wrist. "I lost it when I was trying to fix something under the sink in the kitchen. Edward says he'll find it for me," she said, wrinkling her nose and coming over toward the desk. She looked down at the magazine stories I was perusing. Then she looked at the screen where Celeste's TikTok channel continually looped her perfect smile as she leaned down into the camera to proselytize about something wife related.

"You're asking me what's up with *me*?" she said. "What in the world is up with *you*? Who is that young woman, and what is she saying?"

I turned it up for a moment while Betty listened closely, making faces like she was sucking on a lemon. Then, as best I could, I told her about the "trad wife" movement and all it entails.

"So that's *her* choice, is it?" Betty said, sitting in the small chair across from the desk.

"So she says. And she isn't the only one."

"I suppose the man she married has nothing to say on the matter? In my experience, the choice isn't entirely free." Betty then sat silently for a moment as if considering the situation. "You did mention this to me some time ago, Erica. I suppose I simply didn't believe you. Or at least, I didn't want to believe you. Being the real-life equivalent of June Cleaver is hardly something to aspire to, but for me and my peers, there are few options."

Betty was referring to the one character on television that has often been described as the quintessential wife and mother, the gold standard—June Cleaver, the mom on the 1950s television show *Leave it to Beaver*. Early on in my research, I looked at a few clips to get a sense of what was revered back then.

"Are you telling me you aren't living your ideal life?" I was still perplexed by Betty's current appearance and was beginning to detect an attitude that I hadn't noticed before.

She shrugged. "I suppose I've been spending too much time here with you." She leaned over the desk again and lifted one of the magazines. She flipped through and stopped at an ad. She turned it toward me.

It was a half-page advertisement for Budweiser beer. The husband (presumably he was the husband, anyway) is holding a can of Budweiser while he watches his wife (I presume it was his wife) with a prim ribbon holding back her blonde hair as she leans prettily over a frothy beer stein filled to the brim with beer. Her lips are pursed, ready to take that first sip. The caption reads, "When you need to get her drunk."

I rolled my eyes.

"You know, Erica, I've seen this advertisement a few times, and every time I see it, I wonder what kind of man he is to need a woman to be drunk to..." She trailed off. She looked at me. "I suppose you wonder what kind of man wants a woman like this—like me—anyway."

Had she learned to read minds? Oops. I almost forgot. If Betty was a figment of my imagination, she could, of course. She was me. Or was she?

"Look at this one," she said. "This is more like it."

It was an ad for Smirnoff vodka this time. The frazzled woman sits at the kitchen table wearing a tatty bathrobe, cigarette between the fingers of her right hand, and a half-empty bottle of Smirnoff to her left. This caption reads, "Every morning's a Smirnoff morning."

"This one's probably more honest, if I may be blunt," Betty said. "I often wonder why more women don't take to drinking just to get through their day." Then she giggled. "I suppose many do."

Was this disdain about the housewifely role she seemed to have been defending to me for months? Where was this discontent coming from, I wondered. She wasn't smiling as much as usual today, and she seemed a bit agitated.

"Betty, is everything okay with you?"

"I suppose as fine as it ever is. I think I'm going to miss you."

"Miss me? Where are you going?"

She smiled oddly. It didn't look like a happy smile as much as a knowing one. "I'm not going anywhere, Erica. But you are. Your project is coming to an end, and I'm just a little sad about that."

"How can you be so sure it's about to end?"

"Trust me about this, Erica. You've come as far as you can on this one."

I wasn't sure I liked the sound of that. I was sure I should be the one to come to that conclusion on my own. Then I thought about Betty and who she was. I realized that I needed a serious talk with someone about Betty. My mind was so jumbled on that topic that I could not figure her out for myself. I remembered something Peter and I had discussed the first time I went to see him—something I'd completely forgotten.

In all his psychobabble glory, he asked me if I thought Betty was my shadow. He suggested that I had a deep-seated domestic drudge somewhere burning in my psyche, and Betty might be the manifestation of how I was learning to see her as an essential part of my personality. I hadn't bought it then, but perhaps he wasn't so off base after all.

Maybe it was time I talked to Sam or even Mom about it. I'd see if one of them was available for coffee (or something stronger), then I had to write this blog piece and talk to Maddie about how we'd handle the video on this topic. I looked up from the note I'd made to ask Betty if she had ever considered leaving her husband and children. I was too late. She was already gone.

~

It had been more than six months now since I'd been on the air, and although I'd tried to get an audience with Trevor, it seemed he'd gone off on a six-week vacation and wouldn't be back until sometime in August when I should be rejoining the team to get the fall season off to a sparkling start. What bothered me the most was that I wasn't feeling the love when I considered returning to that studio with my co-hosts, chatting about recipes and décor and the latest books for women. I felt more excited about working with Maddie to get something on her TikTok channel this week. What does that say about this fifty-something woman? Anyway, Maddie and I had work to do.

When I told Maddie the gist of this week's topic, she sat on the sofa for a while, pondering the dilemma of not having anything for her mother to screw up this week. Finally, she said, "What's going to happen to these girls—women—when they're left on their own after a divorce?"

I was more than a little surprised by Maddie's grown-up take on the topic.

"What makes you think they'll be divorced?"

Maddie rolled her eyes. "Geesh, Mom. How could they not be? Even the boys I know would be bored by them after a while. What do they even talk about? I mean, this is so bogus. I'm disgusted by what they're doing, and so are my friends."

I was imagining Maddie and her posse of almost fourteen-year-old girls watching the "trad wives" on TikTok, mimicking them and generally making fun of them. It suddenly occurred to me that everything in life is like a swinging pendulum. Just wait a generation, and things will swing back. I was part of the workaholic generation that eventually had to make some hard choices in life to accommodate career and family. You'd think Maddie would be part of the generation that swung in the opposite direction, but since I'd been an older mom, it seemed like she was in the next generation after the girls of the trad wife movement. I was elated.

"Well, Mom, what are we going to do to entertain my followers this week?"

I had an idea I hoped she'd be on board with. "Maddie, do you know what a rant is?"

She rolled her eyes again. "Dear god, Mom. Of course. I mean, every one of your blog posts is a rant. And people have them on TikTok every day. I mean, just look at this." She clicked a few things on her phone. "I mean, look."

She had keyed in the hashtag #rant, and I found myself looking at angry faces—mostly under age thirty, mind you—ranting about any number of things. Racism, stupid students (this from a teacher), problems of a woman getting her car serviced (she thinks we need all-female shops where we can get our cars serviced—that one didn't seem too out there), Taylor Swift (not everyone loves her evidently) and the problems of having to write an English essay. By the time we got to the pissed-off parent rant about an unauthorized teen party, I knew we were onto something.  My topic might find an audience. I wanted to talk about men who want traditional wives and what that looks like from the outside looking in.

Maddie pointed out that people will just say they're doing what they want, and I should mind my own business. I considered that perspective and decided there was no place for being reasonable on TikTok anyway. So, I'd take the view, "My rant, my opinion." We'd let the chips fall where they may. End of story.

Maddie and I decided to do one of those urban rants that had made television funnyman Rick Mercer so popular ten or more years earlier. Since Maddie was a baby in those years when I'd been watching Rick rant about the weather, Tim Horton's, snow days, modern technology and daylight savings time, we reviewed a few of his rants that were filmed with his cameraman walking backwards in graffiti-lined alleys in downtown Toronto. Maddie loved the urban grit and was keen to try that approach. I wanted her to see how they had been done, but I had not necessarily figured we'd go to a back alley and film there. She wanted to try. We compromised.

We asked Andrew if he'd come along and help. We found a quiet place behind our local elementary school where there wasn't any graffiti, but there were plenty of chipped bricks and dust. I'd do a bit of walking as I talked, but I was no Rick Mercer. I wasn't sure I could actually walk and talk at the same time.

Two days later, I'd finished writing my rant and figured I had it down. We knew we'd probably have to do multiple takes, and Maddie assured me she didn't mind editing—she considered this a step forward in her film career.

It was hot that Saturday afternoon as we set up in the deserted parking lot. By the time we got started, I was sweating like a glass of ice water on a sizzling day. I was concerned about sweat marks. Maddie thought they were authentic. At least something about me was authentic these days. Andrew just laughed.

Andrew would do some backward walking with his phone camera while I held Maddie's selfie stick out in front of me and started talking. Maddie stopped me after only a line or two to remind me that I wasn't just supposed to stand there staring at the phone on the end of the stick. I was supposed to walk. I started again.

"You know who you are, boys. You're the ones egging on those young women who seem to think they've made a choice to be a stay-at-home girlfriend or a homemaker, or a good old-fashioned housewife. Yes, I hear all you girls when you tell me the rat race is too fast, the work too unfulfilling, too much stress and not enough work-life balance. WTF? Stop right there, girls. Like it or not, work is part of life. Suck it up. Just think about that. I have no issue with stay-at-home mothers unless they're also submitting to their husbands, who dole out the money and insist they get permission for every little thing they do. Sure, you think it's just respecting your husband. What about him respecting you and your autonomy? What kind of man are you if you expect your little woman to be waiting for you at the door with your slippers in hand and a nice home-cooked dinner? I hope you're planning on giving her a great big fat alimony cheque when she leaves you so she can go back to school and try to pick up the pieces of a lost career and lost self-esteem in the big bad world. Every one of you seems to think it was a happier time back in the 1950s when women stayed home, and men went out to work. You seem to think that everything was happy when you could come home at the end of the day to find a perfect martini and an even more perfect wife ready and waiting. Then life happens. Are you going to be ready when it does?"

When we finished it, I remembered something Gloria Steinem once said. *"Men should think twice before making widowhood women's only path to power."* I thought we'd left that far behind, but perhaps not. Give them ten years, and all those trad wives out there were going to have to learn to hold themselves back from the knife block.

~

It was now August, and I still didn't know when I'd be returning to work. Sam and I had coffee a few times in July, but every time I broached the subject, she was vague about the details of what was in the planning stages for the fall season. This response was making me crazy since I knew only too well that the team would be in full-on planning mode, setting out the stories and guests for the first quarter of the season. Sam should be knee-deep into a spreadsheet at this point. All her vagueness did was make me think there were changes in the air, that I was one of them, and Sam didn't want to be the one to get into it with me. To be fair, though, it wasn't really her job. I just thought I could use our friendship to find out a bit more. In any case, she wasn't the only one being careful. As much as I wanted to share my story about Betty and get Sam's take on the state of my sanity, I felt oddly guarded. I wasn't sure how my pragmatic, no-nonsense working-mother friend would react. She didn't have a lot of time for mumbo-jumbo, which is what she would likely think of my conversations with a hallucination. She might even think I'd gone off the deep end. So, I kept that to myself with much difficulty.

After my third *tête-a-tête* with Sam, where I still didn't tell her about Betty, I felt I had to talk to someone. Andrew was too close to it. I could count on one hand the number of times he'd broached the subject, always happy with a one or two-word response from me when he asked how it was going with my phantasm, as he liked to call it. If I said, "Fine," he was fine with that. Andrew was like Sam — and, to tell you the truth, like I'd always been. He was hard-nosed, sensible and very practical. Those had been the characteristics that had drawn me to him. I used to be all those things, but now I wasn't so sure. I called Peter.

"Of course, Erica. I'd be delighted to see you," he said when I asked if we could get together. "Before you come, though, I wonder if I might ask you to do a bit of homework." I was all ears. "You may remember a brief discussion we had about Carl Jung. Well, I think we need to explore that a bit more. I'd like you to read a book called *Introducing Jung: A Graphic Guide*. It's a slightly flippant introduction to Jungian psychology and an easy read, but I think it might engender some internal dialogue you might enjoy before we discuss it."

Peter texted me the details about the book, which I dutifully ordered online and started reading it immediately. A few days later, I sat with Peter in his breakfast room.

"Well, Erica, what stood out for you in the book?"

I took my phone from my purse and opened my e-reader, where I'd made some notes and highlighted some passages. I started reading my highlights. "*Jung had a strong suspicion there was…some 'Other" in him…"* I looked up at Peter, who didn't react to my selection. I continued reading. *"He believed he had two different personalities…"* I looked at Peter again. Still, he sat there, an enigmatic half-smile on his face. "Well, what do you think?" I said.

"What do *you* think, Erica?"

Like many other people—patients, I suppose, although I didn't like to think of myself as a patient of a psychiatrist, retired or not—throughout history, I found it infuriating when people reflected my questions back to me. But I did understand why he was doing it.

"I think Jung's personal experiences informed his eventual theories about our psyches."

"Very erudite. Did you note the part about how he came to understand his own two sides?"

I scrolled through my notes and highlights. "He called them number one and number two." I read a bit of the highlighted notes. "Number one was his usual, everyday personality that got him through the things we all have to deal with in our lives."

"What about number two?" Peter said, sipping his tea.

"Well, it seemed that number two was his more troublesome side. It was the side he tried not to expose to the world."

"Yes, and it seems to me he also suggested his second side was more mysterious, perhaps even connected to something deeper, perhaps hidden for some reason, and yet something he needed to introduce himself—and possibly the world—to."

I had noticed that and, being an intelligent woman, I realized this was what Peter likely thought was happening to me. He thought I was connecting with some part of me that was deeply buried. Perhaps it was even deeper than the shadow that we'd discussed at an earlier session. I sighed.

"I suppose you think Betty is the part of me I've buried."

"Is she?"

I shrugged, not wanting to go there. "If that were the case, then I'd have to admit I have a part of me that sees herself as a kept woman."

"Don't be so hard on the idea yet, Erica—or yourself. Why would you describe it as a kept woman? Maybe it's simply a part of you that wants to be both nurtured and nurturing. Would that be so hard to accept?"

Yes. I wanted to scream, yes, it would be hard to accept—except for one thing. I think I'd already wondered about that. After all, how in the world did Erica Flanagan ever admit that she liked making pies?

When I asked Peter when Betty would go away, he told me it was up to me. "When you don't need her any longer."

When would that be?

~

With Peter's perspective under my belt, I decided to accept Mom's invitation to lunch at her new condo. It wasn't really new at this point, but I hadn't been inside it since the day she moved in. I'd helped her, and then every time we got together, it was either for a family dinner at my home or a restaurant. She had asked me to lunch a couple of times. I finally said yes.

"Mom, this is beautiful," I said, genuinely impressed by what she'd done to the small space. She had told me about the designer she'd hired. The work had been completed only recently.

The apartment was less than a thousand square feet but had high ceilings and wall-to-wall windows overlooking a vast, urban cemetery. That meant the view was quiet all year round and very green at this time of year. The walls were dove-grey with dark trim and pops of red in the form of toss cushions on the curved sofa. It felt both sophisticated and homey, a combination not easy to pull off from what I'd learned in recent months.

Mom had set her round dining table with white linen and crystal wine glasses. She had ordered lunch from a chichi, high-end grocery store that delivered. I remembered a time when Mom would come home from work and turn on the oven for dinner even before she had her coat off. I think she deserved a bit of a break now. I loved that she had ordered take-out.

Of course, she first wanted to know everything about her granddaughter, who was preparing for junior high school, which she would begin in a few weeks. Although, truthfully, since Maddie and her friends attended an all-girls school that had grades from pre-kindergarten to high school graduation, she would be on the same campus. Still, for her, it was the beginning of something new. I was then surprised to hear that Mom religiously followed Maddie's TikTok channel.

"I didn't think you'd be interested, Mom," I said as I bit into a divine cheddar and caramelized onion biscuit.

"What you mean to say, my darling daughter, is that you didn't think your older mother would be *au fait* with the new technology," she said without a shred of irony.

I should have known better. My mother was always *au fait* with anything she wanted to be *au fait* with. It had been that way my entire life.

Then I asked Mom about Anthony, with whom she'd gone on the cruise before last Christmas.

"Anthony? He was a bit of fun, but in the end, more annoying than amusing. He always wanted to be around, and you know me. I need my freedom and privacy."

"So, you dumped him?" I was astonished.

"Oh, don't be so judgemental. You've always been too judgemental, Erica. Perhaps that's why you don't have a job right now." Ouch. Mothers like mine always knew just how to drive it in and twist it. "Oh, Erica, forgive me. I realize you did what you had to do. I've never mentioned this, but I probably would have done exactly the same thing if faced with that misguided airhead. So, we're more alike than you think."

I wasn't sure, but at least it gave me an opening. "Mom, there is something I'd like to run by you."

"It's about time you got to it, Erica. You've been vibrating since you walked in the door. Let's hear it." She wiped her lips on the linen napkin and sat back.

I started. I told Mom about the first time Betty had appeared and about how she continued to reappear. Mom mostly listened, asking only for the odd detail. I told her about Betty's hair, clothes, and jewellery. I told her about how Betty and I discussed issues of domestic drudgery then and now. When I finished, Mom continued to sit there, not saying a word.

"Mom, she seemed so real. I think I might be losing it. What kind of woman talks to hallucinations?"

"*The world of reality has its limits; the world of imagination is boundless.*"

"Rousseau?" I said. Mom nodded. It was an easy guess since Mom's work at the university had often focused on Rousseau, an eighteenth-century Swiss philosopher whose work I knew had influenced Western culture to a degree most people will never understand—me included.

"You know, Erica," Mom began, "despite your insistence on being so logical and concrete as an adult, you were a very imaginative child. I've often grieved the loss of that whimsical child." I started to interrupt, but Mom held up her hand and continued. "Please don't misinterpret. You have always had a logical side, but you let your adventurous child explore your world more when you were very young."

I felt my back starting to go up. "How can you say I haven't been adventurous as an adult, Mom? Remember all those war zones and interesting places I visited to do on-air reporting?"

Mom shook her head. "That's not the kind of adventure I'm talking about, Erica. Those were of the real world to which Rousseau refers. Those events were all limited. But imagination? There are no limits."

I thought about that for a moment. "Then you think Betty, as a figment of my imagination, is simply me being that inventive child again?"

"Not at all, Erica. I'm saying quite the opposite. I think that you need to open your mind—open your imagination. You need to be willing to look at all possibilities. What if Betty isn't a hallucination?"

"What else could she be?"

"Again, open your mind, Erica, and consider the imaginative possibilities. I know what you're feeling right now. It's called cognitive dissonance. You're torn between your rational, skeptical side and your desire to believe or understand this far-fetched concept. It's the clash between these conflicting thoughts that's emotionally uncomfortable. But stay with it a moment. Where did Betty tell you she was from?"

I thought back to my first encounter with Betty Crocket. "She told me she was escaping from the past temporarily, as I recall. The past, Mom. Are you hearing this? She was from the past."

Mom nodded knowingly. "Open your mind a bit wider, darling."

I sniffed. "Sure, but if I do that, I have to believe she really did come from the past like some bizarre time traveller in those science fiction books. That's impossible."

"Try to entertain the bigger ideas, Erica. Try to believe the impossible."

As I sat there trying to fathom how my mother, the brilliant philosophical scholar, could be telling me to entertain the possibility that Betty was from 1960, Mom got up. I watched her walk to the bookshelves on the far side of her living room, where she pulled out a volume and brought it back to the table. It was *Alice's Adventure in Wonderland* by Lewis Carroll, of course. She opened a page and started reading.

*"Alice laughed: "There's no use trying," she said; "one can't believe impossible things." "I daresay you haven't had much practice," said the Queen. "When I was younger, I always did it for half an hour a day. Why, sometimes I've believed as many as six impossible things before breakfast."*

~

I was trying to digest Mom's bizarre take on a very personal figment of my imagination as I walked back into the house later. The idea that Betty was somehow real was too absurd even to contemplate. As I put my purse on the kitchen counter, I noticed Andrew's legs sticking out from under the cupboard beneath the sink.

"What are you doing?" I said, rounding the end of the breakfast bar to stand over him. He started to slide out. "Careful of your head."

"Erica. You're home," Andrew said as he pulled himself out and sat on the floor, wiping his hands on a towel. "I'm trying to fix that leak we've been having from time to time. I had to cut a hole in the plasterboard in the back."

He turned back to the cupboard and started to remove his tools as I walked to the coffee maker to turn it on. When I turned around, he was standing up with an odd look on his face.

"What's wrong, Andrew?"

"Nothing's wrong. Just something strange." He extended his arm and opened his hand.

There, in the palm of his hand, was a puddle of gold. I walked over and lifted it from his hand. "What's this?"

"Not sure. I found it behind the plasterboard."

I lifted it up and started to feel dizzy. I'd seen this before. I was holding a charm bracelet. I was puzzled as I examined the charms. I saw a tiny gold spatula and a feather duster before my eyes started to mist. I could hardly see the book, the martini glass, or anything else. Suddenly, I felt so light-headed that I had to put it down. I thought I was going to faint.

# 16

# Resurrection or You Can't Keep a Good Woman Down

*Women may be the one group that grows more radical with age.*
~ Gloria Steinem

"WHAT'S WRONG, ERICA?" Andrew said as he helped me to the table, where I practically fell into a chair.

I could see bursts of light pinging across my field of vision and then a moment of blackness. When I looked up, Andrew stood over me, holding a glass of water.

"You gave me a scare there for a moment, honey. I never thought you'd swoon like that at the sight of a gold bracelet. What gives?"

I took the water from him and gulped down a mouthful. This couldn't be happening. First, there was Mom's bizarre suggestion that I should somehow get my head around the idea that Betty had mysteriously weathered the space-time continuum to visit me not once but on several occasions. Now this. And this was impossible to explain.

When I finally got my bearings, I looked around, hoping the bracelet had been a figment of my over-active imagination and that it would be gone. But there it was. On the table. In front of me.

"Andrew," I said, "would you pour me a drink?"

He looked puzzled at this turn of events but said, "Sure. What can I get you?"

"How about a big glass of that scotch you like, and then maybe we can sit in the living room. I have to talk to you about something."

Fifteen minutes later, after splashing water on my face and changing into a pair of old black yoga pants, I sat with my legs tucked under me in one of the big chairs beside the fireplace. Andrew did as I'd asked and poured the drinks. Then he sat down in the matching chair opposite me and said, "Okay, Erica. Time to tell me what's been going on."

It turned out that Andrew had sensed there was more to the story of my hallucinations than I'd mentioned. In his view, the problem wasn't that he didn't want to hear more about Betty but that I seemed unwilling to say more, so he'd left me alone and hoped I could work it out with Peter as the professional ear. I started at the beginning and tried to include as much detail as possible.

Just as Mom had done, Andrew said little, mostly letting me tell the story my way. He interjected only a few times, asking for more detail about what I'd been doing when Betty appeared. Unlike Mom, Andrew, ever the keen-eyed journalist, wasn't interested in how she dressed or whether she was wearing pearls. But he was very interested in what I'd found in the city archives about the name of the former owners of our house.

Andrew sipped his scotch and sat back, pondering this information. "Wow, Erica, this is fascinating."

"That's one word for it," I said wryly as I thought about the entirety of the situation.

"Do you remember when this Edward and Elizabeth Crocket bought the house?"

I reached for my iPad on the table in front of me and clicked on my notes. "They bought it on June 7, 1939, and the records suggest they owned it for fifty years. It was next sold in October 1989. But the odd thing was that both names were on the original deed, but only one on the bill of sale in 1989. Sometime during those fifty-three years, Betty seemed to have fallen off the radar."

"There must have been some kind of official registration if the name on the deed was changed."

"I suppose there is, but it didn't seem that important at the time. I didn't look for that information. And really, Andrew, how would that help us?"

He shrugged. "Not sure, but it's fascinating. Are you absolutely certain you didn't know anything about this person, Elizabeth Crocket, before Betty first appeared in your imagination?"

I was almost insulted but calmly assured him that her name was news to me. Then, I lightly broached the subject of Mom's input that I was still trying to process myself. Andrew was amused—very amused. He laughed so hard he almost spilled his expensive scotch.

"So, your mother, the esteemed Dr. Maureen Flanagan, professor emeritus of philosophy and all-around competent woman, thinks Betty might have travelled through time to visit you here in her old house? Do I have that right?" He was barely keeping it together.

I sighed. "So it seems."

Andrew got a hold of himself and refocused. "So, what happened this afternoon when I showed you the bracelet?"

I took a deep breath. "Andrew, that is the bracelet Betty was wearing the first few times I found myself talking to her. Each time, another charm would appear." I told him the story of how charms would appear and how, after Betty had disappeared, I would find the bracelet, and then it would disappear. "But on the last several visits, I noticed Betty wasn't wearing the bracelet. The last time I saw her, I finally had a chance to ask her where the bracelet was. I'd noticed it because it was so beautiful, and it seemed to have another charm every time." I stopped for a moment and took a sip of scotch to fortify myself. I could hardly believe what I had to tell him. Then, I took a deep breath. "You are not going to believe this, but she said she lost it when she was trying to fix something under the sink in the kitchen—our kitchen, if the story is to be believed. She said Edward told her he'd find it for her." I stopped, thinking

that what I was about to say might make me sound demented—
even more demented, perhaps. "I guess he never had a chance."

That sobered Andrew up quickly. His eyes widened. "Are you
trying to tell me…"

"You know what it looks like, Andrew. And you know what
they say about something when it walks like a duck and quacks
like a duck."

"It must be a duck," he said. "Even if it's impossible."

I nodded, and we sat there, each lost in our thoughts. I was
thinking about my conversation with Mom earlier in the day. It
had done nothing to make me feel more grounded about this. As
Mom had said, I was feeling cognitive dissonance—that
discomfort that arises when you try to hold two contradictory
ideas in your head. It seemed to me I was feeling the typical
anxiety and strong desire to resolve the inconsistency. But how
could I do that?

I supposed I could change what I believed about this silly
notion of time travel, but that seemed unlikely. I could ignore it
and move on with my life, but that made me feel even more
anxious, and I had no idea if "Betty" would reappear. Maybe Mom
did have a point, after all. Maybe I just needed to open my mind
to possibilities, and perhaps another new and more plausible
possibility would arise. We would see.

~

I let it go for a few days. Andrew and I spent the weekend
listening to Maddie as she told us, in every way she could, how
successful the rant had been. It seemed that seeing Erica Flanagan
in a dusty schoolyard ranting about her pet subject was something
of a hit. She wanted to do more. I told her I'd think about it.

The following Monday morning, I received a text from Ted
Thomas. Receiving a text from Ted—or any personal
communication from him, for that matter—was something that
had never happened before. He wanted to see me in his office the

following afternoon at one pm. I was sure I was finally going to be terminated.

"Why are you so sure he doesn't want to offer you a new contract?" Andrew said when I told him about it later.

"Oh, Andrew. You know how it goes. It's so late in the game for me to be rejoining them for the fall."

"Has Sam said anything?"

"You know, it's weird. She's been very vague about it all, which is one of the reasons I think I'm about to get the axe."

"How do you feel about that possibility?" Andrew said. "I've known you a long time, Erica, and I get the feeling you're not as bent out of shape about it as I might have expected."

Andrew was right. I wasn't as peeved about the possibility as I thought I should have been. I had always maintained I was the aggrieved party in all this, despite a niggling feeling that I might have gone a bit overboard. I still figured it was my job to skewer the philosophies represented by the likes of Laura-Lee Cox and her "trad wife" ideas, although perhaps less so as an afternoon television personality than if I'd been an interviewer on a news show. I realized that now. Anyway, Ted Thomas said it had made for good television, so there was that.

The following afternoon, precisely at one pm and not a moment earlier (would I never get over myself?), I stepped off the elevator on the twenty-second floor and felt a shiver up my spine. The last time I'd been here, Trevor had kept me waiting in the lobby before unceremoniously putting me on leave to slap me for not behaving. I'm not sure what I expected to see when I stepped off the elevator, but it wasn't this.

When the doors opened, Sam and Ted were both standing in front of the reception desk, hands clasped behind their backs, smiling broadly. Was this an ambush? If it was, it seemed it was to be an amiable one.

Sam hugged me, and Ted held out his hand for me to shake, then pulled me in for a hug.

"Welcome back, Erica," he said as he led the way to his corner office. Welcome back?

I had never been in this office. It was, indeed, in the corner with south and west-facing views of the lake and the lakeshore leading west. And since the building was so close to the lakefront, no sixty-story buildings blocked the view. It was breathtaking.

Once we were settled in—Ted behind his massive desk with Sam and I in the white leather chairs facing him (we had the better view)—he began immediately. Ted Thomas hadn't made it to the top of the television food chain by beating around the bush.

"We have an offer for you, Erica. It's an offer I hope you won't be able to refuse."

I was seriously puzzled. An offer for me? Where was Trevor? Why was Sam here? Not that I was complaining, but it seemed odd.

"Well, Erica, as I think I may have mentioned to you the last time we chatted at that tedious social event, I've always admired your journalistic capabilities. And I've enjoyed your on-air persona—notwithstanding your last appearance. Well, Samantha, why don't you tell Erica what we have in mind?"

Sam smiled. "I'd be delighted." She turned to me. "Erica, Ted and I have come up with a concept for a new show, and we'd like you to anchor it for us."

"You and Ted?"

"Well, I might have pitched it to him initially," Sam said, looking at Ted, who was smiling on the other side of the desk. "In any case, we've been working on it for months, and now we're ready to pitch it to you."

I was intrigued. "So, I suppose this is why you've been so vague every time I've mentioned returning to *The Exchange*." Sam shrugged. I continued. "The truth is that I'm not sure I really want to return to a weekday afternoon show. Over the past months— my sabbatical—I've begun to realize I might have moved past this."

Sam's smile was even wider. "Then welcome to *The Pulse*."

I was confused. "*The Pulse*? What would that be?"

Then, Ted took over and explained their concept. I would anchor a weekly semi-news show focused on taking the pulse of women and feminism. And the icing on the cake was that it was to be a prime time show.

"We'll have correspondents scattered across geography and issues, including teen girl issues. Erica, we want Maddie to do a segment from time to time," Sam said.

"Do you think your daughter would be willing to take the pulse of teenage girls?" Ted said.

I was sure Maddie would want to do it. I wasn't sure her mother would want her to. Anyway, it was a lot to take in.

"And how would you feel about a traditional wife's view from time to time?"

As weird as this sounded, it wasn't completely obnoxious. "I suppose in the interests of balance, it could work. But isn't there still some unfinished business? What about the threat of those lawsuits? Surely, that must affect the wisdom of hiring me into this new role."

Ted waved his hand as if to brush away the idea. "It seems that the old saying is accurate. Any publicity is good publicity, or at least, that's what we've been led to believe happened. Apparently, your tirade resulted in our young author becoming even more of a social media sensation than she had been, and her book sales soared." I wasn't so sure that was entirely good news for feminism, but it seemed to be good news for me. Ted continued. "They've dropped all movement in the direction of a lawsuit. Probably wouldn't be good for her image at this point. And she might lose!" He almost winked at me.

I still wasn't sure what Sam's role was other than the person who evidently came up with the idea. I asked.

Ted looked like a proud father. "Samantha will be the producer." He turned to Sam. "A promotion that's long overdue."

So, Sam would be my boss. This was going to be interesting. And yes, I thought I might consider taking the pulse of women's issues on prime-time television. I only hoped the audience would consider watching.

~

It was decided. Sam and I would have a celebratory lunch meeting the next day at the restaurant at the Four Seasons. As I went down in the elevator, I was thinking about the definition of resurrection.

*Resurrection (noun): the act of bringing something that had disappeared or ended back into use or existence.* ~ Cambridge Dictionary

I suppose, in a way, I'd been resurrected. Why was I still feeling uneasy? Perhaps it was because I had expected resurrection to take me back to feeling like I had before the fall, as it were. I realized I wasn't the same person I was all those months ago when I dressed down that misguided young woman. Or perhaps that uneasy feeling was because Sam and I had been close friends for so many years, and I hadn't even mentioned my hallucinatory experiences to her. I planned to rectify that omission at lunch.

~

I went in the Bay Street door of the Four Seasons, Toronto's home-away-from-home for the rich and famous and walked up the stairs that led to the maitre d' desk for Café Boulud at noon. As the young, black-clad woman led me to a table, I could see Sam across the restaurant, the sun streaming in on her. She was already seated on the banquette side of a table for two, watching the door.

She got up when she saw me. As I neared the table, Sam threw her arms around me in a bear hug, saying, "I'm so happy to be able to boss you around now! Kidding! Can't wait to work together on this new project!"

Once I was settled in the chair across from her, Sam ordered two glasses of Perrier-Joüet champagne—only the best would do, evidently. We got caught up on our kids' and husbands' activities, and when the champagne arrived, Sam raised her glass. "To a new level of partnership," she said. "And to our new star!"

I was more than willing to drink to that. Then Sam brought out her laptop, and we began reviewing her notes and ideas. Judging from the number of ideas she began sharing, it was clear she'd been working on this project for some time. The plan was for the show to launch its first episode in the middle of October. That gave us only six weeks to get it all together. Sam had already started interviewing staff and told me she had hired me the best floor director. "You'll meet him next week," she said. "And I have your favourite makeup pro lined up. In fact, Angela said she wouldn't miss the chance to work with you again since you're such a makeup luddite." I winced good-naturedly, and then Sam began the run-down of topics we'd tackle first and correspondents we'd need. I was happy to let her talk because my mind was wandering to other places.

"Did you hear me?" Sam waved her hand in my face. "Earth to Erica. Are you still with me? We were talking about ideas for other correspondents."

Were we? I had drifted off.

"What's wrong, Ricky? I thought you were excited about this."

"Sam, I'm very excited. It's just that…" Why was I having so much trouble broaching the subject of my hallucination with my best friend? Was it because I thought she might think I'd gone off the deep end and couldn't be counted on to anchor the new show? No, that wasn't it.

Sam closed her laptop and placed her folded hands on top of it. "Okay, Erica. It's not at all like you to nurse a glass of champagne for this long—especially not such a good one. You should be ordering a second glass by now. What's going on? You've been acting weird ever since you sat down." She sipped the last of her champagne. "And, to tell you the truth, I've been wondering about you for months. You don't seem yourself, and don't tell me it's because you've turned into one of those domestic drudges you've spent months vilifying."

I took a deep breath. "You're right. There has been something on my mind for a while. There's something I want to talk to you about," I said. "And it's going to sound like I've lost my mind."

Sam rolled her eyes. "It wouldn't be the first time, Ricky."

She was right about that. I took a deep breath and started at the beginning. "I've been having hallucinations, Sam." Her eyes widened. "Or, more to the point, I've been having the same one appear to me over and over." I hesitated before continuing. "Her name is Betty."

Sam's eyes widened even further, if possible, but, like Mom and Andrew, she stayed silent while I spoke. By this point, I was getting good at telling the story and figured I had all the bases covered. Except Sam's interest was piqued by something entirely different than either Mom's or Andrew's had been.

"Wait a minute," she said. "Are you telling me your apparition has a first and last name?" I nodded. "It's Betty Crocket?"

"I know, I know, Sam. It's just like Betty Crocker. But it's not."

Sam was shaking her head. "No, that's not it. There's something about that name." She furrowed her brow as if trying to conjure up a distant memory. "Wait. I think I know where I've heard that name before."

"What? How is that possible?" This was bizarre even for Sam, who loved bizarre things; the more outlandish, the better. I should have filled her in months ago.

Sam opened her laptop while waving off the server, who had appeared to take our orders. She clicked a few times, then said, "Yes. I should have remembered." She looked up at me. "Her full name was Elizabeth Crocket, right?" I nodded. "And she supposedly lived in Toronto back in the 1960s?" I nodded again, not believing we were talking about my mirage as if she had really been a woman who had lived in Toronto in the 1960s. Then Sam turned her laptop around.

I was looking at a grainy black-and-white photo of a group of women surrounding a man who was seated on the edge of a desk smoking a cigarette. He was wearing a suit and tie, and he seemed to be having a conversation with a woman who was sitting in the desk chair. Around him were more than a dozen women sitting in chairs and on the floor, drinking coffee and chatting by the look of it.

"What am I looking at?" I said, trying to examine each aspect of the photo as I used to do when I was a journalist.

"What you're looking at is a sit-in at the offices of the *Ladies Home Journal* in New York City back in 1970 when they had a male editor-in-chief, published stories on housework and beauty and told women how to be ladies. You must have reviewed some issues for your project."

I certainly had. "Yeah. I was particularly nauseated by that monthly column they ran called 'Can this marriage be saved?' where women wrote in for advice. They gave her advice like, 'You're probably not making your husband happy enough,' even if the problem was that he smacked her regularly."

"That's the one," Sam said. "The feminists were protesting. Now, I want you to look more closely at the woman in the back, second from the right." Sam nudged the laptop closer to me. "Now, I'm going out on a limb here, but does anyone look familiar?"

I scrutinized the photo and then gasped. She looked a few years older, but it was Betty. My Betty. I pushed it away. "That's impossible, Sam."

"So this woman does resemble your Betty. Have I got that right?"

Just then, the server arrived to take our order, so I had a moment to catch my breath. When he had gone, I said, "Who is that woman?" I pointed to the grainy image of someone who looked like Betty had looked to me.

Sam explained. "It took me a moment, but I finally remembered where I'd heard the name before. It was in one of those feminism courses I've been taking in grad school. That woman is Elizabeth Crocket, late of Toronto."

Sam went on to tell me that Elizabeth Crocket had been a Canadian contemporary of American feminist Betty Friedan and the author of a book Sam had been required to read for one of her courses.

"The author of a book? When was the book published?" I said, disoriented beyond belief.

Sam clicked a few more keys. "It was published in 1968. It's called *Because You Told Me Not To*."

"What?" I was having difficulty processing this. "When did Elizabeth Crocket die, Sam?" I was thinking about the deed to our house that her name had been on originally but had disappeared by the time Edward Crocket sold it in 1989.

"Well, her Wikipedia entry says she was born in 1920 and died in 1970." She scrolled down the page. "Wow. I didn't realize she'd died so young. I wonder what caused her death." She continued scrolling. "It looks like she may have died in a car accident."

I don't know why, but that news made my heart jump into my throat, and I had to swallow hard to avoid crying.

The server placed our lunches in front of us and asked us that obnoxious question. "Would you like any freshly ground pepper?" and, as usual, I had to hold myself back from saying if the chef had meant it to have pepper, he or she would have put it in. So, no, we didn't want pepper. The server fled.

Sam had pushed the laptop to the side to make space for her plate but continued to scroll while lifting a forkful of omelette Florentine. I picked at my chicken salad.

"Are there any better photos of her?" I said, hoping the server would be back soon to top up our wine. I needed another glass.

Sam clicked and then turned the screen so I could see it. There on the screen was Betty. My Betty. There was no mistaking it. My Betty *was* feminist author Elizabeth Crocket. None of this made sense, though. My Betty was a housewife. Elizabeth Crocket was a woman who travelled from Toronto to New York City to participate in a protest against that very thing.

"And you're sure you knew nothing about her?" Sam said. I was sure. "Okay, as Alice in Wonderland would have said, curiouser and curiouser."

Sam started reading me pieces of a *New York Times* article published a month after Elizabeth Crocket died. There were more details about her death. Elizabeth—Betty?—had been killed in a car accident on October 11, 1970, eleven months after the sit-in that had taken place at the *Ladies Home Journal* offices in March. By all accounts, the accident happened on the 401, the major highway through Toronto, and the car had become an incendiary. There had been nothing left of her and the passenger in the car. The passenger seemed to have been something of a mystery, although there was speculation at the time that it had been her lover. She was survived by a daughter and a son, as well as her former husband, Edward Crocket. So, they had been divorced by that time.

All of this was fascinating, but I was stuck on one single fact. Elizabeth Crocket—Betty—had died on October 11, 1970. The day I was born.

# 17

# Déjà Vu or I Think I've Heard This Before

*What if déjà vu just means you lost a life and you are starting off back at your last checkpoint? ~*
Anonymous

AFTER LUNCH, SAM AND I RETREATED to my kitchen to do some more research on Elizabeth Crocket. The first thing I did when I got home was track down a copy of her book. I finally found one on a used book site. It would arrive in a few days. Then Sam and I went over every single piece of material we could find about Betty on the internet.

According to the articles and one dissertation about her, she had, indeed, been a stay-at-home, albeit well-educated housewife until around 1960. According to an interview she gave to a PBS reporter when her book was published eight years later, in 1960, she had experienced a personal epiphany.

"I could suddenly see clearly what was happening around me," she told the reporter. "I could see women trying to claw their way out of the avalanche of household responsibilities that was killing their independence and their creativity—including mine. I suppose I had a kind of come-to-Jesus moment when I realized that we were making progress. Still, there was every possibility that someday in the future, another generation of young women would take this all for granted and begin the parade back into the home, back under the protection of the men in their lives. I could see it clearly. And I had to address that."

When she was quoted as saying she had written her book as a parable set in the future, my heart started racing. I was practically vibrating. When her book was released, many critics panned it for its image of the future, where people talked to one another through screens and information was at their fingertips on computers twenty-four hours a day, seven days a week. They were especially derisive about her ideas that women would be media and political leaders and that gay couples could marry.

That's when Sam dropped her preposterous explanation.

"You know what I think, Ricky? I think you either you were Elizabeth Crocket in a past life or maybe your mother has a point. Maybe timelines do cross once in a while."

I nearly swallowed my tongue.

~

Over the next few weeks, between meetings and media interviews that Sam's assistant had set up to introduce me as the "star" of the new show, I read everything available on Elizabeth Crocket. Of course, the more I knew about her, the closer I felt to her. I cannot tell you how many times I hoped I'd turn around and see her lounging against a windowsill or sitting in the chair across from me. I had so many things I'd talk to her about now—so many questions. Then, I'd shake myself and tell myself that Betty wasn't real and Sam was as crazy as I was. Still...

And then there was the matter of the charm bracelet. I finally had the presence of mind to take a closer look at it. Of course, I remembered the spatula, the feather duster, the book, the martini glass and the baby's pacifier. There were also charms I hadn't seen before. There was a spool of thread, a tiny lipstick tube, a caduceus and a pair of stilettos. These represented almost all the topics I'd covered over the past months in my project. And I could not deny that it was real. So, what about Betty? How would I come to terms with my experience?

I tracked down a copy of *Because You Told Me Not To*, Elizabeth Crocket's feminist manifesto, and the moment it arrived I started reading. I read it from cover to cover in one sitting. It took me all day, but I couldn't put it down. Her parable had nailed what seemed to be her conversations with me. It was impossible. I was still thinking about this the day I walked into the new studio to meet the production staff.

The truth is that I was walking into the same studio that I'd been in for over a decade. *The Exchange* had been cancelled, and the studio was being transformed into the new home of *The Pulse*. It was beginning to glitter as the workers scurried around, hanging more and more lights and perfecting the backdrops covered in reflective surfaces of myriad colours.

"How do you like it?" Sam said, hurrying over when she saw me. Sam's new uniform was head-to-toe black, a sophisticated far cry from the jeans and shirts she favoured when she had been my floor director. Producing a show meant upping one's wardrobe quotient.

I looked around in amazement at how much the crew had accomplished in such a short time. "It's wonderful, Sam. It's going to be mesmerizing."

"That's the spirit," she said, looking around. "I want to introduce you to Karam." Her head swivelled toward where I could see a tall man with jet-black hair listening intently to a young woman who I knew to be an assistant director. "There he is. Karam!" She waved him over.

As he approached, I could see his face with a smile as broad as possible, his dark eyes sparkling. I felt a jolt of electricity pass through me as I realized I'd seen those eyes before, but they had been ringed with exhaustion and worry then. Now they glowed.

"Karam," Sam said, "I want to introduce you to our star."

"There's no need," Karam said as he reached for my hand.

"You two know each other?" Sam looked confused.

"In a manner of speaking," Karam said in perfect, lightly accented, British-tinged English. "This beautiful person is the reason I am here in this studio today."

Now, it was my turn to be confused. I knew I'd met him before, but I had nothing to do with him being here. He continued.

"Samantha, if it had not been for this wonderful woman, I would not have been able to be in contact with Mr. Thomas, he would never have received my CV, and I would never have met you." He turned to me, still holding my hand, smiling into my eyes. "Ms. Flanagan, it is such a pleasure to be formally introduced. Last winter, when you turned to my family, I felt from you a human warmth that perhaps had been buried. When you gave to my family that gift of money, it might have been a small thing to you, but I assure you it was as if we had won the lottery. And not only because of the money but also for the lesson that my children learned that day about how to treat people. They learned what it is to receive a gift, and I hope one day they will be able to bestow a gift of such importance."

I then remembered the details of encountering Karam and his family at that coffee shop that wintry day. I'd been struck by their lack of winter clothing and did nothing more than anyone might have done.

"It was nothing, Karam."

He shook his head. "It was something, Ms. Flanagan. It was more than something. And there is no way to thank you except to be the best at my job for you."

Karam Ahmad had been an Afghan translator for the military during their operations in Afghanistan. After several years in a refugee camp, he and his family finally got that golden ticket: admission to Canada as permanent residents. Karam told me that he had taken that money to the store I'd suggested, and each of them had been fitted with a parka. But the most important thing of all was that he had found a small shop selling refurbished cell phones and had been able to pursue finding a job. As it happened, he had been a translator during the war, but before that, Karam had worked as a producer at a television station. His goal was to produce television shows again, but he was more than content to be the floor director of this new show in his adopted country.

"You can thank me by calling me Erica, Karam," I said as the tears began spilling from my eyes.

What in the world had become of the old Erica, I wondered? As I sat in my newly refurbished dressing room later, I hoped I could live up to myself. I had discovered that I was more than one thing—and I was enough. I looked at the copy of Betty's book that had been the first thing I'd brought to my new dressing room. *Because You Told Me Not To. Hmm*, I thought. *I wonder what you did and who told you not to do it.* Perhaps I'd never know, but I could imagine.

# Meanwhile, In 1960

JOHN FITZGERALD KENNEDY won the American presidential election that year. Harper Lee's book *To Kill a Mockingbird* was published. The Americans sent their first thirty-five hundred soldiers into Viet Nam. *Psycho* premiered. All of these would make history, but there was one event that slid under the radar that year. Sri Lanka elected the world's first female prime minister. I could hardly pinpoint Sri Lanka on the globe, but I thought that was the most important thing that happened all year. Oh, and I told Edward I wanted a divorce.

It was 1960, and, as one might expect, my husband was nonplussed. Of course, I couldn't have a divorce. How would I support myself? What could I do? What would become of the children? And, of the highest importance, what would people think? Quite. What *would* they think?

They would be horrified, possibly even outraged, although it was really none of their business. But they would think it was.

I was unsure who would be the most horrified. Would it be the men who thought Edward Crocket could not control his wife? Or would it be the wives who would be worried about a newly single woman in their circle on the prowl? Would they have to hide their husbands from me? They needn't have worried, though. I had no intention of staying in that circle. And I knew at least two women who would be envious. I knew this because each of them had, on separate occasions, confided in me that they were this close to committing murder. Or suicide. And they could think of no other way out. I had more imagination.

I was tired of being an appendage. I was tired of being told what to wear, what to do and how to act. I was tired of being what everyone else wanted me to be. I was tired of always needing approval. It would be some years before Gloria Steinem would say, *"Once we give up searching for approval, we often find it easier to earn respect."* I had long craved approval, but what I now knew I needed was respect. But that year, I also learned that going too far in the other direction could happen. It was possible to have all the respect in the world and to squander it. That was the year that, entirely by chance (at least, I thought it was by chance), I met Erica Flanagan, and my life was never the same.

# Erica's Bookshelf

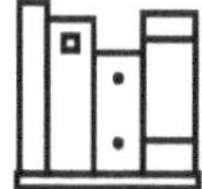

*12 Rules for Life* by Jordan Peterson
*The Feminine Mystique* by Betty Friedan
*Women in Magazines: Research, Reputation, Production and Consumption* by Rachel Ritchie, Sue Hawkins, Nicola Phillips and S. Jay Kleinberg
*The I Hate to Cook Book* by Peg Bracken
*Our Lady of the Lost and Found* by Diane Schoemperlen
*The Life-Changing Magic of Tidying Up* by Marie Kondo
*The Common Sense Book of Baby and Child Care* by Dr. Benjamin Spock
*Fear of Dying* by Erica Jong
*I Feel Bad About My Neck* by Nora Ephron
*Is Gwenyth Paltrow Wrong About Everything?* by Timothy Caulfield
*The Art of Being a Well-Dressed Wife* by Anne Fogarty
*Introducing Jung: A Graphic Guide* by Maggie Hyde and Michael McGuiness

# About the Author

PATRICIA J. PARSONS has written over twenty books, including health and business books, a memoir, two historical novels, and women's fiction, including the "almost-but-not-quite-true" series. After a decades-long career as a university professor in communication studies, she now pursues her other passions: fashion design and sewing, which she writes about online at *The GG Files* at gloriaglamont.com, and writing about strong, funny women. She lives in Toronto with her husband—her alpha reader.

Connect with her on Instagram @patriciajparsons
Join her on Facebook @patriciaparsonswriter and at
facebook.com/groups/12dresses
Visit her website at www.patriciajparsons.com

www.ingramcontent.com/pod-product-compliance
Lightning Source LLC
Chambersburg PA
CBHW061804190726
48289CB00007B/2070